GW01158271

AR' BACK YARD

AR' BACK YARD

Enjoy the ride —

Anwar Dharma

ATHENA PRESS
LONDON

ISBN 10-digit: 1 84748 158 2
ISBN 13-digit: 978 1 84748 158 0

First Published 2008 by
ATHENA PRESS
Queen's House, 2 Holly Road
Twickenham TW1 4EG
United Kingdom

For more information regarding the author and *Ar' Back Yard*,
go to http://arbackyard.com

Printed for Athena Press

For Hannah, Ar'kid and Mamo
(basically the three women in my life I couldn't stand to be without)

In memory of a true Manchester legend, Tony H Wilson (1950–2007), who was without doubt a true visionary. We all owe a great debt to him for all the good times he instigated through his pure genius.

ONE

I honestly couldn't feel my legs. Where the fuck had they gone? That was them right there in front of me, wasn't it? Yeah – they were still there… I could see them after all. So that was OK. At least I thought it was anyway. Shit! I think the question I should have been asking myself was where the hell my *head* was – not my bloody legs.

The bag was filled with a powerful aroma that I'd always loved for some bizarre reason, despite what its actual contents did to me. The potent fumes were making their way through my mouth and nose like a hungry pack of wolves. As I opened my red-raw eyes and tried to focus, everything around me was a haze of colours that blurred into one.

I pulled away the clear plastic bag that had covered the lower half of my face for the past five minu—Hell, what was I saying – I had no idea how long the bag had been there. As I stared vacantly into the bag, its sides dripped with condensation as on a steamed window. I watched the spittle that had come from my gaping mouth spin and twist towards the yellow, rubbery substance that was to be found at the base of the bag.

I could hear the voice; at least I think I could. It was becoming louder and more urgent; at least I think it was.

'C'mon, Billlllllyyyy. Aren't you done with that bag of Evo yet, ar'kid?' It was Scotty's voice that I could make out. And even in my current state of mind, as the fumes from the glue continued to do their trick, I knew for certain that he was blatantly taking the piss out of me.

Yes, it was true that my name was Billy. However – and he knew this better than anybody – I was never referred to by that name except by maybe my parents (or the police). Scotty, like everyone else, had always referred to me as Chopper. The name referred to an old bike that I was never without back in the seventies. The name just seemed to have stuck as the years passed us by.

"'Ere 'are, Billy,' laughed Scotty as my head rolled in slow motion towards what appeared to be his direction, "ave some of this, Chopper.'

He held in his hand – which protruded comically like Mr Stretch's from *The Fantastic Four* – what appeared to be a gigantic spliff, although I realise now that it was probably no bigger than any normal-sized joint we'd been slouched there smoking all afternoon.

I mumbled something that was obviously so incoherent that my best friend creased up in hysterics. His manic laughter gave him the appearance of a psychotic clown on mind-bending drugs. I took hold of the smouldering joint and pressed it tightly between my lips, inhaling even more crap that was only going to screw things up more than they already were.

But hey, what the hell? The two of us were only a couple of kids without pretty much a care in the world. All any of this was merely escapism from what surrounded us on a day-to-day basis in 1983. Or else we did it because we enjoyed it: sniffing glue and smoking some freshly imported Skunk weed from Amsterdam. We were only thirteen years old, after all: enough time to grow out of such shit. At least that's what I kept telling myself anyway.

'What you laughing at, Chopper?' asked Scotty, a little too intensely. He was paranoid.

I didn't even reply. I merely stared at Scotty O'Conner as he twitched nervously, sprawled on the floor against the wall where our latest piece of work was clearly on display. Graffiti, or bombin' as we preferred to call it, was part of our lives back then.

We had just completed a new design featuring a couple of cat burglars we'd named Sneaker and Peaker. The empty spray cans were all around us, scattered between the empty beer crates and old decrepit barrels that looked as though they had been left there to rot back in the sixties. We were behind this filthy establishment known as The Greyhound. There was the stench of old beer and even older piss. And there was another unpleasant aroma that I couldn't quite put my finger on. Or maybe that was merely the state we'd gotten ourselves into.

As I looked up to the dismal, yet very familiar, sky that hung heavily over the Salford skyline, I found myself smiling. It seemed to be a permanent fixture over Manchester and its surrounding boroughs, threatening a downpour at any given moment. Unlike anywhere else in the country, rain always materialised at a moment's notice.

As I glanced back down from the darkening clouds, an intense array of colours protruded almost violently at me from all directions. The graffiti – the intense colours, the design itself – was dancing my way and then the next as my hallucinations became overwhelming.

The clash of what hung so dauntingly above me and what encircled me was like a scene I had seen only days before when Scotty and I had sneaked into the cinema on Oxford Road and watched a movie called *Rumble Fish*, starring Mickey Rourke and Matt Dillon. I didn't actually remember much about the movie itself as I was pretty stoned at the time and we merely ducked in there to escape the rain – other than it was filmed entirely in black and white, apart from this scene with the fish that kept appearing – very bizarrely – in colour.

I glanced round at Scotty, who was staring intently at his hands with the stupidest of smirks upon his long, drawn face that always appeared to be smiling at you in any given situation. His appearance had always reminded me of that crazy mechanic character from the television show *Taxi*. I think it was Christopher Lloyd, but I wasn't certain.

There was no doubt in my mind that Scotty was my closest friend back then. His family had all emigrated from Northern Ireland to the streets of Manchester before Scotty had been born, though I didn't think of them as emigrants, given the short distance.

We both lived in a part of Manchester known as Hulme. It was a large, underdeveloped estate that had once been seen as a way forward, a solution around the inner-city housing problems that were so prevalent back then.

However, by then it was a sorry sight to look at: high rises with an endless amount of balconies upon balconies. Decrepit flats that snaked their way around, making up the estate.

The city council had commissioned for the estate to be built as quickly as possible. A local company won the contract to build the flats and had put together what can only be described as concrete jigsaw pieces, in order to speed up the building process.

But, as time passed, damage and decay began to take hold of it. And as we grew up, we observed that, in effect, over time the estate ceased to belong to the city council. Instead, Hulme became the residents' estate, thus ensuring its rapid demise. The place was built up of mainly a mass of squats. A large percentage of people residing there never paid rent and never intended to. The way they saw it, Hulme belonged to them anyway. The way the two of us perceived it was quite simply this: Hulme was one giant playground for all ages, all sizes and all races. It was ours. Or so we liked to believe at that age, anyway.

The two of us had been the best of friends for well over a decade already, doing just about everything together. We never went to school any more, finding it much more educational to bunk off, dossing around both the estate and town. We were both always in and out of trouble with the law, and had been since being little kids.

Scotty had always been like a brother to me, and with neither of us having any siblings of our own, the same could be said for Scotty's feeling towards me. That's the way it had always been. I imagined that it would never change.

The two of us did whatever we could to get by, moneywise. Generally, we went into town on a daily basis, shoplifting anything we could possibly get away with. We'd then blow the money made from our hauls on newly imported records or top-of-the-range sports clothing such as Adidas, Nike and Kappa, to name but a few.

With the rise of the hip hop and the Breakin' craze that had arrived in the early eighties, we were always decked out in the expensive sports gear that was the staple of that sub-culture back then. Basically, we dressed just to get wasted from smoking weed and sniffing glue.

So Scotty and I were just a couple of young scallies enjoying ourselves during a time of change. We did what we did and didn't care about anything or anybody else. I mean, we were only a couple of kids, right? So what did it matter anyway, right?

'Fuck me!' Scotty laughed, breaking my train of thought as my head began to clear. 'We're taking pure liberties 'ere, Chopper. If that landlord comes out the back door we'll be fucked for sure.'

Suddenly remembering where we were, I shook my head. We'd just sprayed our latest piece of graffiti against The Grey-hound's back wall, but we were actually here for more than that.

The early evening had brought us round from our drug-addled state of consciousness. I said to Scotty, 'We'll be all right, mate.' I was smirking away like some complete idiot in my heightened state. 'Don't worry about it… 'Ere, have some more of this,' I added, handing him back the bag filled with the potent Evo Stick Adhesive and watching intensely as he buried his comical face into it without a second thought.

Leaning back against the cold wall behind me and relighting the heavily loaded spliff, I began to inhale the pungent smoke. My head began to spin again as its density filled my lungs. I admired the piece that we had been working on, and full as I was with a mixture of glue, paint and weed fumes, the design suddenly became even more animated than before. The colours became so much more enhanced that they were almost dazzling to my eyes, usually only accustomed to dismal Manchester sky.

I swear that the two characters I'd designed – Sneaker and Peaker – were dancing all over the wall to an imaginary beat that was now pounding its way through into my mind. I even began to rock back and forth to the non-existent track.

Scotty was still smiling as he removed the bag from his face. He suddenly sat up straight, looking all serious. 'You hear that, Chopper?'

'Hear what? What you on about, Scotty,' I sniggered, stoned out of my mind, still hallucinating intensely from the colourful artwork moving before me. 'I can't hear shit.' I shook my head frantically, my eyes rolling around and the colours still blinding my perception of anything.

'Shush… listen. Can't you hear that?' His face appeared to be actually strained with concentration. I'm sure that he even had his hand to his ear to enhance the audible noises that were buzzing about his head. The sight of this seemed really humorous to me and I began laughing feverishly.

Suddenly, the sound of shattering glass and screams and loud shouting brought the two of us round as we jumped to our feet without thinking. We both stared at each other for what seemed like an eternity, frozen to the spot.

'Fuck me!' I gasped out loud, realising how shocked I must look as Scotty grinned at my expression. 'This has gotta be it, Scotty.' As I said the words, we both began laughing for no apparent reason. Fuck – we were in a worst state than I had realised.

The next thing I was fully aware of was that the two of us were charging on unsteady legs in the direction of the commotion. We were completely wasted from the weed, glue and fumes from the spray cans. I don't think either of us was at all sure exactly where the hell we were – or exactly what we were doing there.

But just as we emerged into the car park situated at the front of The Greyhound, reality kicked in.

Clear as day, we saw Paddy's right arm slicing through the warm summer air with deadly accuracy, and in his right hand he was holding one ugly-looking machete.

Fact was, it almost looked to be an extension of his arm. Paddy's face was screwed up in sheer rage, giving him the appearance of a deranged psychotic inmate from the local psychiatric hospital. But then, Paddy always looked that way – whether he was enraged or not. He had the appearance of someone who had never had anything to smile about in life, forcing his features into a permanent scowl that was set in stone upon his face.

As the blade swished through the air I witnessed Paddy's victim's head swerve around violently towards us as we stood rooted to the spot, unable to move as the violence unfolded before our very eyes.

The sharpened steel split open the left side of his face with no effort whatsoever. He made no sound as the flesh tore open, gaping. The dark crimson blood sprayed wildly from the wound, which ran the entire length of his face, winding up in his short, dreadlocked hairline.

With no warning Scotty suddenly threw up the Jamaican jerk-fried chicken and dumplings that we had eaten earlier in the day from Sampson's.

Totally ignoring this, I glanced rapidly from Scotty back to Prey, the victim, who merely grimaced at what must have been an agonising injury, just as the razor-sharp blade struck down again with vicious, deadly accuracy…

What we were now witnessing was precisely the reason that the two of us had made the journey across Manchester to Salford in the first place: to see exactly what was going to happen between Kieran O'Prey and Patrick McNally.

Nobody ever recognised the former by his full name. Like most kids growing up round our way, he'd been stuck with a favoured alternative, becoming known simply as Prey. He was the one who ran the main crew of lads from our estate.

Prey was of mixed-race background, his father being from Northern Ireland and his mother being Jamaican, both of them having had, it was said, naturally explosive personalities.

Not that Prey had ever actually known his father, who had only been present for the birth. He disappeared soon after and was never to be seen again on the streets of Manchester. Then Prey's mother had died from a nasty heroin overdose whilst he was still a young child, leaving his Jamaican grandmother to raise him.

Prey was a colourful character who caught people off guard. He'd always reminded me of the boxer, Sugar Ray Leonard. With his boyish good looks he appeared to those he met as a harmless individual – I suppose in a way a little like Sugar Ray himself.

Although somewhat older than me or Scotty, he looked a lot younger than he was. But this was used to his advantage in catching and ensnaring people for whatever reason.

For Prey was one of Manchester's most ruthless characters. And those who knew him invariably obeyed him and got him whatever he set out for.

Prey's crew were the older lads on the estate, several years older than Scotty or me. I suppose in a way we both kind of looked up to them. Well, either that or we just couldn't wait to get up to all that they were notorious around town for.

Prey resided in what I suppose you'd officially have to call a squat, as he didn't pay rent, located on Bonsall Street (although perhaps 'squat' was the incorrect word for it). In fact, it was a complete understatement considering the flat's décor. I mean, thinking about it, Prey could have lived anywhere he wished as he ran Hulme and everything that made good money in it. This, what with us having Moss Side directly behind us, was no mean feat. But for whatever reason (maybe he was comfortable surrounded by his crew and the community that he felt safe within) he has always resided on one of the worst of the city's estates. And despite his being only twenty, he was already one of the main heads in town. He commanded a lot of respect from those around him, including the older heads who had witnessed his rise from nothing more than a little scally to his position running this important area of Manchester.

The thing was, he'd not had the easiest of lives and had always been in and out of trouble with the law. But what made him different was that he knew how to use his brain (or noodle, as he liked to call it). He claimed that it was not only essential to be streetwise, but to see that you always kept your mind active, which was the key to surviving our world. Thus, using both his skills and intellect, he made his money by any means necessary.

By the tender age of thirteen he was already into mugging wealthy businessmen at knifepoint as they left work, or sometimes staking out a score and waiting for hours beneath their cars, ready to strike fear and terror into them.

The local paper, the *Manchester Evening News*, had caught on to his escapades and had published articles on a regular basis concerning them. This caused embarrassment to the authorities, as they were never successful in retaining (or, for that matter, attaining) enough evidence to discover Prey's true identity. He just quit one day, leaving them with nothing but open cases.

From there, he moved on to armed robbery. He'd been brought into these jobs by some of the older lads from surrounding areas of town. This alone had made others sit up and take notice of him. Prey did know, however, that as careful as he was in these fields, he couldn't continue in them for much longer without his eventual demise.

The way he perceived it was that it was quite literally a mug's game to get too caught up in it. He figured that it would be better to make a break from them at the earliest opportunity. So he used his proceeds to invest in the drug business that was already flourishing on Manchester's streets.

The profits appeared to be exceptional, and, despite his mother's overdose, he knew how much money was involved on the estate alone. Despite the danger and risks, he wanted in on those profit margins for both himself and his crew. So Prey began buying and selling wisely. And, slowly but surely, he began building a tight crew around himself.

Glancing back to Prey, the first thing I noticed was the machete striking him again. But then everything seemed to change suddenly, as Prey ducked swiftly with the speed of a hunting cheetah, ensuring that the machete only made contact with the harsh concrete. Sparks glittered from the sheer intensity of the blade's impact upon the floor's abrasive surface.

Suddenly and without any warning, Prey's arm struck upwards with accurate speed. He looked to be holding a small baseball or rounders bat. It was junior size, which could be easily concealed up the sleeve of a jacket. I also noticed that the bat was covered with silver duct tape around the extremity. This more than likely meant that it had been hollowed and refilled with melted down lead for extra weight.

The bat suddenly made clean contact with Paddy's face, knocking him over viciously. Then without hesitation Prey stepped forward and began repeatedly beating Paddy with the bat…

Patrick McNally, or Paddy as everybody knew him, was, at nearly twenty-seven, one of the town's older heads by quite some years. He also had a notorious reputation. Paddy ran part of the Salford area, known as Crumpsall, Salford being like a city in its own right.

Gun culture, as it would become known, hadn't yet hit town the way it would in subsequent years, although it was a well-known fact that Paddy was already playing around with guns, even shooting at a so-called mate as target practice. I think it was more than safe to say that he was not of stable mind.

More notorious tales surrounding him included ones concerning his favourite 'machete of the week', it being his weapon of choice. There were many stories of people being left near death from his crazed attacks, with none of them pressing charges through fear of retribution.

I was also aware, as was everybody else who knew of him, of this one time that he crossed the line and actually killed somebody. This young lad had been walking along Cheetham Hill High Street with his girlfriend. Paddy merely hadn't liked the way the young lad had looked in his direction, so had proceeded in no uncertain terms to hack away at him.

The case was thrown out of court, 'due to lack of evidence', as the judge had conveniently put it. Once again Paddy had beaten the system and managed have the charges against him dropped.

I remembered this so well because there was a lot of outrage at the time. A combination of the failure to convict Paddy and the fact that the victim hadn't been involved at any level on the criminal ladder, had left the public outraged that he'd walked. It turned out the lad had been a law student taking advantage of the cheaper rents in Cheetham Hill.

This reputation of Paddy's obviously drove fear into people, and he used that fear to control his crew and all of those around him. He could basically do whatever he so desired without much protest.

I could see Paddy rolling around now, squealing like a tortured pig from his beating. You could distinguish the dark bruising appearing on his enraged face, and his skin beginning to break, dark blood oozing freely. You could clearly see that Prey's physical anguish was driving this deadly assault upon his victim – and Paddy was enduring immense grief at that very moment.

The crowd that had gathered were all shouting and jeering for Paddy to fight back. But that's when I suddenly began to panic. Observing that Paddy's lads were all beginning to move in on Prey, I grabbed hold of Scotty's shoulder and tried bringing him fully to his senses; he was still doubled over, coughing the remains of his puke up.

Scrutinising the entire scene before us, I realised that nobody had even noticed that Scotty or I were stood there.

Everything was a maddening haze to me as I tried to take in as much as I possibly could. Scotty was now rolling about the wall directly behind us, completely stoned out of his mind. But wasted as I was, something was amiss… only I couldn't think what. What was it?

That's when it suddenly hit me: where was Prey's crew? Surely he wasn't fighting a one-man battle. Then I had an even worse thought. What if they'd already fought and only Prey remained standing?

The problem that had arisen between Prey and Paddy's crews in the first place was that one of Paddy's crew, Chris Walker, had screwed over Sean Macreedy in a heroin deal. Now, Sean was what Prey liked to refer to as his Chief Lieutenant. Everyone knew this. The two of them, pretty much like Scotty and me, had grown up in Hulme together.

The sample of heroin provided hadn't turned out to be the real product. Now Prey was considerably out of pocket from the deal. And whether Paddy knew about Chris's intentions or not, that wasn't really the issue here. It had been down to his crew member and he was blatantly refusing to address the matter. He'd kept mouthing off around town about not caring what Prey thought or didn't think in regard to his involvement, dismissing it by saying it wasn't down to him personally. Prey, like most of town, had never liked Paddy. He had always considered him to be unpredictable and very rarely used his resources, but there had been a bad drug drought at the time. Paddy's crew seemed to be the only ones holding any heroin, or smack as it was more commonly known on the street. Money was being lost. So business had been set up through Chris, with Sean handling the final deal.

Everybody round town had heard of the sour deal one way or the other. And without trying to show it too much, they were all more than a little anxious to find out what Prey was going to do about the situation. Obviously Paddy was a complete psychopath and had a number of years over Prey and his crew. But Prey was most definitely not somebody to go messing with.

Prey respected the simple fact that Paddy had been around town for a lot more years, but Chris should have shown more respect towards both him and his crew. Chris should have known that Prey would have to keep face and deal with the situation. Maybe that's the way they'd planned it all along. Maybe Paddy wanted this confrontation…

'Scotty, Scotty, for fuck's sake!' I screamed at him, trying my best to bring him round as the reality of everything had begun to bring my own head round somewhat.

We had to do something. We had to help in some way. Saying that, though, I honestly didn't have a fucking clue what that something actually was.

Scotty had now slumped to the floor and was laughing uncontrollably at nothing. He was obviously hallucinating from the delirious look upon his face. I desperately wanted to help Prey – had to help him in some way – but I knew that my mind was merely racing alongside my adrenaline.

As Paddy's lads were only moments away from their onslaught against Prey, a movement abruptly caught my eye at the edge of the car park. It was Sean, who'd casually walked straight into the car park totally unnoticed.

And not only that, but there also were Knieldy, Parksey, Diamond and Johnny, all in tow behind him, each of them fully armed with full-sized baseball bats. I suddenly realised that the other 'lieutenants', as Prey referred to them, had finally arrived at the scene. In fact, even in my drug-induced state I realised that they must have planned it this way from the very beginning.

Glancing quickly back at the fracas, I noticed that still none of the crowd had noticed they were being advanced upon.

Sean casually sauntered through the crowd to where Prey was still kicking and punching Paddy. Sensing the additional presence, Chris began to raise his head – and I honestly believe that must have been the last thing he saw that day as the baseball bat came violently crashing down into his bewildered face…

By the age of sixteen, Prey had managed to cleverly and meticulously take complete control of Hulme's drug trade for himself and his own crew of lads – the lads who had just arrived on the scene.

He formed what can only be described as a military-style operation, putting together one of the town's most organised crews. Despite their tender teenage years, he set up one of the tightest crews the town had ever seen. And they were not a crew that could be easily dismissed or ignored.

So he surrounded himself with men he trusted his life with and who he designated to became his so-called 'lieutenants'. Each of the lads held down a different area of the estate, and they all had their own tasks to keep control of. Below the lieutenants were 'foot soldiers', as Prey referred to them. They were the ones who handled all of the street trade.

Surrounding the entire estate were lookouts, whose job entailed what their title suggested. Although they never possessed any gear themselves, they could easily set up deals with foot soldiers if required. But their main job was to keep an eye out for the police, who continued their uphill struggle in the battle against drugs and with finding a way into what appeared to be an impregnable crew.

For Prey to take control of Hulme hadn't been at all easy to say the least, although he had sent his predecessors through hell before taking it from them. The two main families from the estate back then had been the Jacksons and the Wests. They had controlled Hulme for years in their own way, without any real organisation. They battled continuously with each other for complete control of the estate.

Prey had eventually used this to his advantage, using it against them to gain control. They'd been so busy fighting each other that neither family had noticed that Prey was playing them off one another like puppets.

He had continued to let them put opposing family members into the critical unit at Saint Mary's Hospital, all the while waiting patiently, biding his time.

Before long, Pete West had taken a Smith & Wesson revolver around to Alan Jackson's front door. As Alan began to open the door, baseball bat at the ready, Pete's gun exploded. Shots echoed throughout Hulme's endless balconies, again and again, until all six bullets had been emptied into Alan Jackson at close range.

Not being the sharpest tool in the shed, Pete shot Alan in the middle of the day when there were more than enough innocent witnesses around to confirm that it had been him. So, along with a string of various other charges, Pete West was convicted and sent to H M Strangeways to serve two life sentences running consecutively.

Not that any of this had mattered to Prey. His plan had worked and he had quickly resolved business in the area by taking complete control of it.

Once again he'd used his noodle in achieving what he desired.

The violence in The Greyhound erupted all at once as the rest of Prey's crew along the perimeter of the crowd began swinging wildly at Paddy's lads.

Sean was swinging his baseball bat against Chris's already split skull. I'd have sworn I saw brain matter. In fact I was almost sure of it. But I was hallucinating so much that I wasn't entirely sure what was what in terms of reality.

Although Prey's crew were outnumbered by at least two to one, they were causing serious damage. They were viciously attacking everybody and everything in sight. Bats were swinging, skulls were breaking, and bones were being crushed. The car park was beginning to change colour with the crimson tide of the blood being spilled.

Just then, and without any warning, Scotty rushed straight past me into the crowd, kicking and punching wildly as he did so. He must have been completely out of his mind. A minute earlier he couldn't even stand up, and now he was in the middle of the brawl. Then, without even giving it a second thought, I found myself also running forward and leaping straight onto the back of some lad who had hold of Sean.

But just as quickly as Scotty jumped in, I witnessed him being thrown back from the centre of the ruckus, his limp body hitting the wall. I was still grasping onto my guy, hitting and kicking with all the force I could muster. Sean rose from the ground with the bat, just as my guy pulled me over his head with ease. My body was thrust hard onto the harsh abrasive concrete.

Dazed and confused, I saw Sean glance at me before beginning to strike blows upon my assailant. Prey was still kicking Paddy as hard as he could. Surely he was unconscious by now. Chris lay motionless beside me, bleeding badly.

I felt my body rising from the ground, almost like I was flying, so I began grinning like an idiot – until I looked down and realised that I *was* flying. One of Paddy's crew had launched me through the air into the same wall Scotty had hit.

I lay half-slumped next to Scotty, who didn't appear to be with it at all.

'You all right, mate?' I asked Scotty urgently as I crawled over to him.

'What… where… what… who are you?' He laughed hysterically; he was really out of it this time.

I mean, in all honesty, I still have absolutely no idea what we were thinking. We were only a couple of kids at the time. Both of us jumping in there like we were ten men rolled into one – although we were so wasted we probably did feel like ten men rolled into one.

As we continued to watch the glorified mayhem before us, I remember thinking that it was one of the craziest things that I had ever seen. But reality wasn't quite hitting home, as I never even heard the sirens wailing away, getting closer and closer, louder and louder, until…

'Fuck!' I yelled, scrambling to my feet and pulling Scotty up from his slumber.

Scotty began to duck imaginary punches. We were both well out of the way since being thrown there, yet Scotty obviously thought he was still in the thick of it.

The reality of it all completely kicked in as the police vans screeched into the car park and everybody began to scatter.

I pulled Scotty frantically with me, and the two of us leapt at the wall behind us. But as I pulled my body up, I could already see that Scotty was falling back down the wall, flat onto his arse. He was still laughing, oblivious to the situation at hand.

The police were running in all directions. The place was a complete mass of unrestrained mayhem. Just then, an officer who seemed to have appeared from nowhere, began striking Scotty's defenceless body with his truncheon.

I screamed out at him, the anger streaming through my voice as I did so. 'Oi! Don't fuckin' do that!'

But it didn't made the least bit of difference as Scotty's blood sprayed so freely against the wall. I couldn't believe how hard the officer had struck him.

That's when everything around me appeared to fall deadly silent. I knew it wasn't really the case, as I could see people screaming at one another; but they were mute, as if someone had pressed the button on the television. Only one thing was for certain – this was no dumb-as-fuck scene from the *The A-Team*.

'You fuckin' bastard!' I yelled, only hearing the words inside of my head as I leapt off the wall at the officer.

As my new Nike Cortez struck him directly in his solar plexus, I sent him crashing to the ground, totally knocking the wind from him. Grabbing Scotty from the floor, I began dragging his dead weight as the blood poured freely from his open wound. I was scrambling like mad to escape, pulling Scotty's limp, heavy, anaesthetised body away from the hub.

But as I turned to check Scotty, I noticed that the winded officer was already climbing to his feet. That's when I really began to panic, as he ran directly towards me with what can only be described as pure rage. To make matters worse, I then felt Scotty being dragged from my grip; there was another officer dragging him in the direction of the of the police vans.

Without warning, an immense sharp pain drove its way through my body. I screamed out in agony; my body dropped in what seemed like slow motion towards the concrete. Through blurred vision, I could make out the officer I'd winded, withdrawing his truncheon from my groin area. It suddenly hit home where the bastard had struck me.

My body felt numb throughout as I was hauled along the concrete (with no concern for my new Nikes, I hasten to add).

The officer hauled me from the floor and threw me violently into the back of the van. As I struck the cold steel floor, I made the decision right there and then – that it was in my own best interest to stay put if there was going to be any chance of making it home that evening to ar' back yard.

TWO

L ying there doubled over from the intense pain, my ears were still ringing and throbbing agonisingly. The only person I was sure of being with me was Scotty, since I had vaguely recognised his new Adidas Gazelle trainers – that and the fact that he kept giggling uncontrollably every couple of minutes for no apparent reason. I drifted off dreamily.

As I started to come round from the dream-like state which I seemed to have been in for hours (but was actually more realistically minutes), my body still felt quite numb as the rear doors of the police van were flung open. I was aching all over. I had not moved from that cold and filthy steel floor. And as they dragged me feet-first from the van and pulled me upright, my joints ached as if I had aged forty years in the last half hour.

We'd been taken to the main police station in Salford, Crumpsall. I proper hated this place, having been detained there the previous year. Both Scotty and I had been in some horrible police stations before, many times before. But this lot was the worst of the lot. They blatantly refused to take any kind of crap from anyone. If you didn't call them Boss when requesting anything from taking a leak to asking for a light, then they refused to do anything at all for you.

They dragged Scotty and me straight from the desk sergeant into separate interview rooms.

The pain had begun to wear off a little by now. Although my head was still spinning from the glue, the paint fumes and most of all the skunk, my concern was only for Scotty. God only knew where his head was at by now. I mean, we'd been wasted many times before, but I honestly didn't think that I had ever seen him this bad.

PC Newman, the same officer who I'd knocked flat on his arse (and who had almost claimed my balls), threw me roughly into a blue plastic chair that was bolted to the floor. I could easily perceive from his eyes, which glared coldly down at me, that he felt nothing but pure hatred and contempt towards me.

As he stared closely into my stoned face, I began to foolishly smirk back at him. I also couldn't help but notice that his breath stank badly, which suddenly made me very conscious of my own Evo-stick, skunk-stinking breath. But the thought only amused me. So, without thinking of any of the consequences, I made up my mind to show this copper what bad breath really was, and I exhaled all of my putrid breath into his face, grinning as he grimaced at its foul odour, a vile combination of my evening's activities. His sudden backhand caught me off guard, as I didn't see it coming, my reflexes temporarily slow. I felt the weight of my body being lifted from the hard, uncomfortable blue plastic. Still handcuffed, I was unable to break my fall and I hit the cheap-carpeted floor hard. My mouth made contact with the surface and I spat warm sticky blood. But as I looked up at Newman, I was still smirking away. I honestly didn't care. Actually, I found myself to be highly amused by my achievement.

'You fucking little prick! Just you wait… I'm goin'—'

Just then the door flew open, crashing against the wall.

'What the fuck are you doing to that kid, Newman?' bellowed a familiar voice.

Standing there, his large frame taking up much of the door-way, was Detective Inspector Walsh. He wiped sweat from his brow with a white handkerchief as he entered the room. He was a very large man of over six foot, but was heavily overweight, with signs of grey beginning to show through his walnut-coloured hair. I guessed him to be in his late thirties, possibly early forties. He looked out of shape, considering his age. *Too many pub lunches*, I thought, smiling to myself.

'I, er… we…' Newman began feebly.

'I asked you what the fuck you were doing! He's just a fucking kid, you pri—' He managed to stop himself before screaming the obscenity. 'Now get the fuck out of here! We'll speak later on, you hear me?'

Newman sheepishly left the interview room. I began pulling myself back into the chair, staring directly at Walsh.

'All right, son… let's start with the basics, shall we?' Walsh stared at me with menacing eyes that told me he was in no mood for any funny business. 'Name and address,' he said abruptly, whilst lighting a cigarette.

'Have I been charged with anything yet, Walshy?' I asked, smiling knowingly at him.

You see, I realised straight off that they hadn't even read me my rights. And, although this was my first personal encounter with him, Walsh was known around town and I'd seen and heard them before and I wanted him to know that I knew this.

A look of recognition briefly crossed his face. 'How'd you kn—whatever. Look, son, I still don't know what the fuck you were doing there. The rest we brought in are a good bit older than you or your mate Scott O'Conner, who we've got in there. Yeah, that's right: we got his name. Now what's yours?' he snapped harshly.

'What's your fuckin' problem?' I snapped right back at him. All the while I was doing my best to focus on him without making it too obvious. The substances still had something of a hold on me.

Walsh was clearly annoyed by the whole incident as he snarled at me. 'Look, son, your mate isn't making any fucking sense whatsoever back there. Just gibbering complete bollocks, for fuck's sake. That, along with his head bobbing about like one of those bloody plastic dogs that you see in the back windows of cars. Now, I want to know what you know about tonight's events, you little…' He stopped himself and took a deep breath.

I could sense that he was already becoming agitated with me, so I was chuckling away with all the over-confidence that I could muster.

I said, 'Look, I ain't your fuckin' *son*, as you keep calling me. So why don't you just back the fuck off, Walshy? You know that I ain't saying shit to you.'

'Oh! Like that is it, you little twat! Well, I got news for you, *son*. If you don't cooperate with us then… Well, I'll just have to presume you're an elder.' He sighed deeply, then stared directly at me once again. 'You know that I'll just have to presume you're somebody who doesn't need his parents here for this. You know what that means, don't you? No? Well, let me tell you, you little shit.' He let out a wicked snigger before continuing. 'It means I'll stick you in the cells with the big boys. They'll just love someone like you. You know – a sweet innocent little thing.' He sneered the words at me, winking as he did so.

He was obviously trying to scare the crap out of me. But the more I thought about what he said, the more it appealed to me. I laughed for a second or two, then smiled back at him confidently. You see, this wouldn't be my first time in a cell, and I think that Walsh was beginning to realise this.

'All right, Walshy, let's go then,' I replied, returning his wink.

'You'll be smiling from the—' He stopped once again, staring coldly at me. 'Last chance. Tell me what I need to know, son. It'll be a lot easier on you.' He inched himself closer towards me, shaking his head as he did so. 'We already got Scott's name. Come on now, son.'

I knew Walsh's game, though. Damn coppers were all the same.

'Fuck you and your fuckin' questions, Walshy. I ain't answering shit for you about anything, you out-of-shape old prick.'

Maybe it was still the glue that was making me act this way; I wasn't entirely sure at that precise moment. All I was certain of was that I wasn't any kind of grass. No way was I going to give up anything that I knew.

'What did you just say?' he yelled back at me. You could almost see the steam coming from his ears as his voice echoed around the bare walls of the interview room.

'Fuck you too!' I calmly replied.

You see, I knew that if I gave any answers about anything they'd twist them to their own personal advantage. Especially once they discovered that we were both from Hulme, the same as the others were. After all – they'd nicked me on the other side of town.

Walsh stared at me, then sighed as though he'd won the battle. 'So be it. Just remember though, when they're pulling at your pants, I warned you. Oh, and as for Scotty boy, well, he's completely fucked.' He shook his head in disbelief. 'We've got him sat there staring at the ceiling, his daft little head bobbing back and forth, just repeating "chop, chop, choppeeee", whatever the fuck that means. Dumb little prick. He'll soon give us everything we need, though. Don't you worry about it,' he said, grabbing my arm tightly and tearing me from my seat.

But despite all of that I couldn't help but crease up at what he'd told me about Scotty.

That was the thing with the police, though. Walsh had come in nice enough. Then, because you're not Mr I'll-do-whatever-you-ask, they revert to being themselves again. All right, so I wasn't being a good helpful citizen, but that damn Newman had left a bad taste in my mouth… or was that just the glue?

Walsh escorted me towards the cells. He was obviously expecting me to break down and start crying.

'You sure you're going to be all right, son?' Walsh smiled at me. 'All alone in those cells with just other men keeping you company?' He sneered the last words at me in that assured manner of his.

'Oh, it's all right, thank you,' I laughed out loud. 'I hear your old dear's gonna be in there to keep my cock warm, Walshy.' I knew that I was pushing it here, but I just couldn't help myself.

'You little…' He was becoming increasingly pissed off at me and his face reddened. I enjoyed the moment immensely.

'Let's go then, Walsh,' I responded buoyantly, looking at him with mock excitement.

He grabbed my arm, twisting me towards him. He screwed up his face at me, sighing deeply, and then threw me through the open door into the cell.

'Don't do anything I wouldn't, you little prick!' he shouted after me.

I was already screaming at the now closing cell door. 'Fuck you, Walshy!' I ran foolishly at the cell door as it slammed shut. I kicked out hard against the steel, then fell helplessly to the floor.

As I was helped to my feet, I soon realised that it was Sean aiding me. 'All right, Sean. How's it goin', mate?' I asked, dusting myself off and feeling really proud of myself for some stupid reason. I mean, what the hell did I have to be proud of, spending my evening banged up in a cell in Salford?

Looking around, I saw Parksey lying on the plastic mattress. He merely nodded at me.

'What the fuck you doin' 'ere, Chopper?' asked Sean, looking at me with utter disbelief. 'I thought that was you back at the boozer; I just couldn't be sure.' He grinned at me. 'Looks like you pissed old Walshy off.'

Awaiting the long night ahead of us, the three of us settled into the cramped damp-smelling cell the best we could. I then relayed the entire story to Sean about what had happened. He loved the story, especially the part about my being so reluctant to give my name and address, hence my being thrown into the cells. Walsh had told me that not giving my address didn't mean my parents wouldn't find out. Not that they'd care anyway. Well, having to travel to the other side of town to collect me might bother them.

Sean told me they'd be itching to find out what they could about the night's events, and said I'd better stick with my original methods.

We must have been sat in there for well over three hours before the cell door banged open abruptly. It was Walsh with the detention officer.

'All right there, Billy Chorlton?' he smiled triumphantly at me. 'Come on, then. Your old man's here for you.'

I wasn't able to work out how he'd got my name. Maybe Scotty had given it to them. But I knew he would never do that (would he?). Although, the fact of the matter was that he was so wasted from all the gear we had caned that he could very well have told them the size of his cock if they'd asked for it and not even known he'd done so.

As it turned out though, they'd phoned Scotty's old man, and he'd called mine for a lift to Crumpsall. Once they both arrived at the station, my old man had also enquired about me.

The fact is, Scotty and I rarely did anything separately. And we'd been arrested together more than several times whilst still growing up. Both sets of parents had become used to this. In their own way they'd quietly given up on the two of us. It was better for them to hold on to their own beliefs as to just what it was that we got up to, rather than deal with the reality.

So, in effect, it was my old man who had given me up to the police. I have to admit that I found this thought amusing.

My old man had to sit in on the interview because of my young age. DI Walsh and PC Newman were both already seated and waiting for us as we entered the interview room. I observed Walsh loading the blank cassette into the machine, and, in all honesty, I intended on keeping it as blank as possible. And it wasn't just to piss them off some more, I swear. Well, OK, maybe just a little, I suppose.

They started with the usual: your name, date of birth, address and so forth. So I obliged and gave them all of the information that they required. But after this, it was purely 'no comment' all the way.

The problem with the police is that they have a way of twisting your statements into further charges against you. The more that you try to blag your way out of it, the deeper you dig yourself in. I'd discovered that the best policy is the one they inform you of when they arrest you – that you have the right to remain silent. It was always the best advice to take. And it also wound them completely the wrong way. They hated it when you refused to make a full statement.

You might not think a thirteen-year-old lad could be so streetwise and cynical. But as I've already said, we never really went to school, so life on the street to us was by far the best education we'd get.

'Will you stop saying that, Chorlton!' Walsh yelled out loud, after almost an hour's questioning.

I was smiling as I could clearly see that I was getting to him by now. 'Sorry, Walshy… No comment.'

'Just tell us what you know, for fu—' Newman stopped himself. 'Look, Billy, listen to me. I know you were involved. I was there, remember.' He stared coldly at me. But Newman didn't quite have that cold, intimidating stare down just yet.

'Oh, so I do, officer, you're quite right. Didn't you smack my mate in the head and me in the bleedin' balls with your fuckin' truncheon?'

Newman shifted uneasily in his chair. 'We're asking the questions, Chorlton, not you.'

'I'll take that as a "no comment" then, Newman,' I laughed.

Walsh was shaking his head as he stared around at my old

man, who was positioned behind him. I don't think he was too impressed. The thing was that he'd been through this too many times to mention. He knew what my approach was to these matters.

So he always took the next step: made himself as comfortable as possible, then took a little nap. Basically he didn't care about me as I was nothing but trouble to him. And as long as I was out of his way and out of the flat so that he could flick frantically like a man obsessed between the four different television channels, then he was more than happy enough. God knows what he'd be like if we lived in America and he had a thousand channels to choose from.

Walsh was still shaking his head as he turned back to me. Newman was still going for the long, hard glare (and failing miserably, I might add). So I merely began yawning my response back to him, stretching my arms.

'What a fucking pair you two make, eh,' Walsh exclaimed, as he glanced back towards my old man, whose breathing had now passed into snoring.

I began rubbing my bloodshot eyes. 'Will there be anything else, gentleman? Y'know I'm a busy lad,' I asked, as if bored by the entire matter.

'Get him the fuck out here… both of them,' Walsh snapped at Newman.

'But, sir, we…' He trailed off, knowing it was useless to argue the point.

'I'll be seeing you around, Billy,' Walsh said, glaring hatred at me.

'Not if I see you first eh, Walshy,' I winked, with all the conceited arrogance only a dumb thirteen-year-old could muster. Staring straight back at him and rising from my seat gleefully, I nudged the old man, who awoke with a start.

'Eh! Billy!' he said, giving a little jump as he sat upright. 'Whoa, where the hell am I?' He looked around the room dazed and confused as I laughed, and Walsh merely shook his head.

Scotty and his old man were both waiting outside when they finally released me. The two of them were sat on the station wall. My old man trailed behind me, yawning sleepily, simply glad that we were finally leaving. He was just as bored of the whole matter as I now was.

I stared at Scotty and grinned. He still appeared well and truly stoned out his mind. His eyes were completely wasted. His forehead bore a small lump on it, which had been covered crudely by the police doctor to stop the bleeding.

I smiled warmly at him. 'You all right, ar'kid? How's that head of yours?'

'What... I... well,' he replied, rubbing the lump.

'What you tell them, Scotty?' I asked, looking into those stoned eyes. I didn't suppose the smack to his head had helped any.

'Well... I just... kinda... er... What was the question, Chopper?' he slurred sluggishly.

'Tell 'em. Feckin' tell 'em, Chopper,' Scotty's old man, Kevin, blurted out at me in that strong Irish accent of his. 'He couldn't tell 'em feck all, son. Just look at him will yer, for feck's sake.' He shook his head. 'He's off his feckin' head. Just look at his feckin' eyes, son, will yer. What the feck have yer two been up to this time?'

I just glared back at him. 'I don't know what you're on about, Kevin,' I replied with all the innocence I could gather, looking from Scotty to his old man. 'Who says we've been up to anything?'.

He was really enraged this time; you could read it in his eyes.

'Look at his feckin' head, Chopper, will yer! I tell yer... Yer two will be the death of me.'

'Oh, just leave them to it, Kev,' my old man added, stretching and yawning lazily.

'What did Newman say about his head?'

'They said it happened as he fell from the wall,' he sighed deeply. 'They said that he just knocked his head against it.'

'Lying fuckers! Bunch of lying twats!' I screamed back towards the station doors.

'I told you before, Kev. We just can't stop them any more,' my old man tried again.

Kev's anger merely rose to another level. 'What? What was that yer say, Jack?' he scolded my old man. 'Yer feckin' know what the copper's told me, for Christ sake! They said that my Scotty was too fecked up and too feckin' t'ick to tell 'em anything,' he yelled at both of us.

For despite the fact that they never gave us the time of day and probably called us all the names under the sun when we weren't around, your father insulting you was one thing – but it was another for somebody else to insult us, namely the police.

But all the same I couldn't help it any longer, and I doubled over in hysterics. Too thick! The glue really had taken it out of Scotty this time. My old man swiped half-heartedly for the back of my head.

'Stop laughing, you little twat,' he half smiled. 'Can't you see Kev's upset?'

As he said this, I could clearly see that he was also trying to keep a straight face.

THREE

'E re'are, Chopper. Keep an eye out, will ya?' Scotty said in hushed tones.

The two of us were behind Ladywell flats in Salford, trying to find a suitable vehicle for our latest job. I was keeping a lookout whilst Scotty scoured the car park.

Scotty and I had grown up considerably in the last couple of years, both physically and mentally. Plus our crimes had evolved from petty shoplifting to pulling down some major scores, breaking and entering and robbing some of the town's more prestigious retail establishments. We'd never hit anybody's homes though. It wasn't so much that we'd suddenly got morals; it's just they really weren't worth the hassle for the return that you received.

Between the two of us we'd been hitting some of the major retail units in town for the past eighteen months, stealing anything that would pull in a good mark-up back on the street. We even stole to order at times. I'd begun to master security systems more and more with each job we pulled. Scotty was always in charge of handling the transport, hot-wiring the vehicles we required for each job dependent upon the size of it. He really seemed to enjoy that side of things.

But for me it was the security of the buildings that fascinated me. From the time we'd pulled down our first job together, I'd worked on the alarm systems. As time and scores had passed, I had become more and more aware of just how similar all the systems actually were. The money we were making from these alone was superb.

An added bonus was the quantities of weed we'd also been knocking out to the younger kids on the estate. Prey had favoured this immensely as it kept them away from his crew members. He'd constantly tried to put us on his payroll as foot soldiers, but we just weren't interested. It wasn't that we didn't appreciate the offer: we did. We just had our own game plan in life, that's all.

'Chop… Chopper, c'mon man… quickly, mate,' Scotty suddenly called out.

I leapt straight into the passenger side of the dirty white Bedford transit van he'd just acquired for us. I also briefly noticed some logo painted down the side of the van. The transit vans were always the easiest to steal. We were already pulling out into Eccles New Road within a minute of Scotty jumping in.

'Like the transport I picked? Well top ain't it, mate?' He was grinning away, obviously pleased with himself.

'What's it say down the side of it?'

'Carpenter and Sons, Painters and Decorators,' he laughed.

Totally confused, I stared at him. 'What's so fuckin' great about that, eh?'

He still hadn't taken that daft look off his face. 'Look, if the coppers clock the van they'll just presume we're on a job. And we are. Just not a painting and decorating job.' He roared with laughter at his plan.

I began laughing along with him. Scotty still cracked me up with his ways of thinking. And I had to admit that it did make sense.

Just as we eased the van over to the lights by the huge roundabout that took forever to get round, I noticed a dark-coloured Mercedes Benz pull alongside of the van on Scotty's side. I could just about make out the guy sat there, staring directly ahead whilst screaming at God knows what. His features were twisted and he looked deranged. And even though it had been quite some time since I'd last seen him, there was no doubting who the character was.

I nodded my head at Scotty, who saw what I had also seen. Just then, the lights changed to green and the Mercedes sped away, leaving us in its trail.

'That was Paddy, wasn't it, Chopper?' Scotty said, more of a statement than a question. He glanced over at me as I nodded. 'Y'know, that's pretty fuckin' mad seeing him. Considering that only earlier today I was thinking about that fight over at The Greyhound with Prey and Paddy. Do you realise that that was over two years ago now, mate?'

'No shit,' I exclaimed. 'That doesn't seem like all that long ago, does it? Y'know, I still remember it like it was yesterday,' I added, smiling to myself.

'Not really. It's still just a lot of blurred images to me, y'know?' Scotty laughed.

''Ere'are, mate,' I said, turning towards him. I passed him the smouldering spliff. 'What you looking so content for?'

'This sure is the life, in't it, Chopper?' He drew deeply on the spliff and let the smoke drift aimlessly back through his nostrils and open mouth.

The two of us had been lying around the park all that afternoon enjoying ourselves and deciding just what we were going to do that night. It had been an unusually hot afternoon for April. We should both have been at school. Apparently it was our final year.

The thing was, neither of us could remember the last time we'd actually been to school. If we had turned up now, the teachers would probably assume we were a couple of new pupils. Attending school just wasn't part of our schedule. We had more important things in our lives to be getting on with. Things like this that we were doing tonight.

'So anyway, Chopper,' sighed Scotty. 'Are you actually going to tell us what this job is tonight or are you going to just keep me in the dark until we get there?'

I smiled at him in the dark interior of the van. He was right: I still hadn't told him exactly just where it was we were going or just what we'd be doing. It wasn't that I didn't trust Scotty: I trusted him more than anybody else. It's just I knew that he would not have been at all keen on the score that I had lined up.

'I've been thinking, you know. Between the two of us we've got ourselves a proper nice record collection,' I said, apparently changing the subject as I glanced over at him. He continued to drive through the quiet streets. 'I mean for some time now, we've been collecting imports and other quality tunes—'

'Yeah, so what, Chopper?' he responded nonchalantly, sniffing as he did so.

'Well, what the fuck do we play all that shit on, eh? That crappy old Hitachi record player of ar's. Or that really shitty Sharp job of yours, mate.'

'So,' he shrugged. 'What's your point – apart from slating my record player, that is.' He grinned at me to let me know that he really wasn't offended.

'Well, how about getting ourselves a decent set-up?'

He looked at me. 'You mean like a DJ set-up? Technics and shit like that? Is that what you're on about, mate?'

'Yeah, so what if we know fuck all about mixing. We can learn.'

'Sound, Chopper. That sounds all right, y'know.' Now he looked a little concerned. 'Are we going to buy the shit though? I hear it ain't cheap, you know.' He sighed.

'So… that's why were gonna hit that electrical gaff in St Ann's Square tonight.'

'You mean that Bose or Boss Sound and Vision gaff? What's it called again? Whatever! Are you trippin' or what, Chopper?' he laughed at me. 'They make you ring the bell before they'll even let you in the gaff. You not remember that armed blag against them a few years back? Ever since then they don't let no fucker in there if they don't like the look of them. It's got to have security coming out of its arse, for fuck's sake.' He stared at me, all serious.

'I know that, you daft twat.' I was laughing along with him now. 'What did you think I meant? That we hit it with our cocks in our hands tomorrow? No, I mean we pull it down *tonight*.'

'What about the security system though, Chopper? Hey, I know you're good, ar'kid, no disrespect meant, but…' He trailed off, unenthusiastically staring at the road before him.

'But fuck all, mate. I already checked it out early hours of this morning. It'll take a little time to bypass. But you know me, mate.'

'What d'ya mean this morning? What the fuck was you doing up this morning?' he enquired suspiciously.

'All right, mate,' I grinned back at him. 'More like the middle of last night then. What can I say, eh? I'm like a night owl.'

'You're more like a fuckin' bat than an owl, mate,' Scotty chuckled at me.

'I just couldn't get me head down, that's all, mate.' I returned his smile. 'Anyway, you in or what? We're almost here, Scotty.

Y'know, I don't want to make you do something that you don't want to.' I was only winding him up and he immediately started to protest.

'Eh… c'mon, I never said…' He just smirked back at me. 'C'mon, Chop… you know I'm always in, ar'kid.'

'You keep an eye out down that end, Scotty,' I nodded in the direction. 'Are you sure the van's out of sight?'

'Sound, mate, on both scores.' He smiled and winked at me. 'I stuck the van behind the church, mate. You all clear that end?'

'Yes, mate. I'm going to sort that alarm out. Just make sure you keep your eyes open.' I checked my tools once again. 'It may take a little longer than usual.'

The alarm system looked to be top of the line. And the story I'd told Scotty about checking it the night before had been the truth. Only it had not been a thorough inspection. It was a Sabre System, as the outer box said. And I had to admit it looked fancy enough. Well, at least that was until you removed said box and discovered a run-of-the-mill system. Shaking my head, I then went straight to work on it.

Bypassing the alarm, I then filled the outer box, which contained the actual bell, with insulation foam. It was the type that hardened immediately. It was merely a back-up, as the sound of the bell would cause us no end of problems if I made a mistake with the bypass.

Whistling softly for Scotty's attention, I then signalled for him to join me. He arrived at the rear fire exit doors, just as I was popping the lock open with a crowbar. The tension against the outer door put pressure on the fire door handles and eventually the pressure gave way. The large, heavy wooden doors creaked loudly as we eased them open.

As the two of us crept silently into the back area of the store, it felt both cold and damp despite the warm summer night. I immediately made my way through to the front of the store where I could make out the yellow and bright white lights – street lamps blazing out in St Ann's Square. Their glare shone through the windows and doorway and bounced from wall to wall, blazing upon rows and rows of what could only be described as some of the best electrical systems that I'd ever laid my eyes upon.

Despite the light provided from outside, I found my eyes were still having to adjust to the darkness as I began scanning the shop floor. As I stood in the centre of the floor, I was overcome with a very strange sensation that I couldn't quite figure out. Maybe it was because before now we'd only ever seen the shop floor from the exterior. Although, saying that, it had never occurred to us to just ring the bell. But then, they'd never have let a couple of scallies like us in… would they?

''Ere'are, Chopper. Come 'ere, mate. Check this out,' Scotty called from the back of the store.

Only then did I realise that he hadn't followed me through to the front of the shop. 'Where the fuck are you?'

'In 'ere,' he whispered quietly.

I could see his ray of light shining from what appeared to be a small stock room. Shining my own small Maglite into the room where I presumed him to be, I was momentarily taken aback by the size of the room. It was huge. I couldn't believe just how spacious it was; it was twice the size of the shop floor. I continued to shine my light around the room in awe at the amount of boxes containing an untold amount of stock, stacked from the floor to ceiling. Contained within the four walls was what would be our biggest score to date by far. Eventually my light landed on Scotty, who was sitting, smiling triumphantly, on a pile of Technics boxes.

'Look what I've found, Chopper.'

'Shit, Scotty.' I was amazed at the amount of gear we had stumbled on to. 'Y'know that we've hit it big 'ere, mate. I mean, have you seen all this gear, Scotty? This is so sound, y'know.'

'In't it. It's the bollocks,' he said, jumping down from the boxes.

'All right, we've got to be double quick 'ere. You go and get the van, Scotty. We ain't going to fit all of it in and it's way too risky to make two trips back 'ere, so I'll sort out what's best to take, all right.'

'Sweet, mate. Just one thing though. I want to browse the shop floor first, mate.' He smirked mischievously at me.

'Ah, fuck that, Scotty. We got more than enough shit alone in 'ere.' I stared at him, my voice taking on a much more serious tone.

'C'mon, Chopper.' He sighed, shaking his head. 'Y'know that this lot wouldn't normally let me in 'ere, would they? I just want to get a feel of the store.' He smiled at me.

I knew exactly what sensation he was feeling, as I'd just experienced similar emotions myself before I'd entered the stock room. 'C'mon then. Let's be quick though, Scotty.'

'Sound, mate.' He smiled, and then darted past me and proceeded to wander around the shop floor.

What is he like? I thought to myself as I observed him. *He's actually browsing like he really wants to buy something.* He was touching and stroking the stereos, smiling to himself. (I think that was more at the thought of all the stock that we were about to steal.)

He stopped at this particularly nice Kenwood stereo, and he was touching the knobs and really examining it when suddenly he accidentally flipped a switch. Abruptly, deafeningly, it blared loudly. 'Shit... fuck... shit!' He began flapping his arms in a right fluster, not knowing quite what to do.

I leapt forward as quickly as I possibly could, hitting the power switch. I stood there glaring at him with piercing eyes that told him that he'd pissed me off, when a bright light abruptly shone through the store's window, catching us off guard.

We both hit the carpeted floor hard. I lifted my head just enough to be able to see. *Oh fuck.* I could see a young police officer pressing his face against the window, trying to get a better view of the interior.

His light effervescently jumped from one of the displayed systems to another, reflecting and then re-reflecting off the polished and mirrored surfaces. I was certain that it was only a matter of seconds before his light settled upon us. We both stayed crouched there like a couple of stalked deer that had sensed immediate danger ahead.

I could hear the sound of our breathing: it was fast and unrestrained. I was praying – although not exactly sure who it was that I was praying to – that he wouldn't see us. Then, just as suddenly as he'd snapped the light on, he abruptly snapped it off.

Glancing up once again, I let my breath out slowly as I felt the tension ebb away. I finally smiled as I observed him walking away.

'We all right?' asked Scotty urgently, still unmoving and crouched on the floor.

'Yes, ma…' I trailed off as it suddenly hit me. 'Oh shit!'

'What? What is it, Chopper?'

'The back door… the fire exit… He'll check the back door!' I leapt from the floor and sprinted the short distance to the back area of the store.

I could still hear Scotty crouched there in the darkness. 'Oh fuck, shit… We're fucked, Chopper.'

Grabbing the cold steel bars of the fire exit, I began to slowly ease them back into position. Just then, I heard a noise from outside. Or did I? I was positive that I had. I listened intently for any movement outside, knowing if he was there and heard the doors lock we'd be in a real sticky situation for sure. It would not only give us away, but we'd be locked inside. All he'd have to do would be to wait for backup to arrive and assist him.

Suddenly his radio blared out loudly into the night: he was closing in. The radio became all the more audible as he approached. Hearing a scuffle behind me, I turned to face Scotty, who was stood there holding a fire extinguisher.

'I hope you plan on hitting him with that and not just putting him out,' I whispered to him.

This amused Scotty, who began to giggle like a frightened child that didn't realise they were actually scared. I knew that it was just as much from panic as my comment. Glaring hard at him, I whispered, 'Shush, you idiot! He'll hear you.'

Scotty was chewing frantically on his bottom lip to try and control his fit of giggles. He'd obviously got this mental image of himself spraying the officer with the contents of the extinguisher. And it was obviously tickling the hell out of him as well. Shit! I wished so much that I hadn't said anything now.

The copper was right outside the door. He was clearly within earshot, as his radio blared away in the still of night. I suddenly felt him twist the handle, and I held onto it for dear life. No way was I letting him get in here. No way in hell. I began praying again as I tightened my grip.

Sweat began to trickle down the length of my face; I could taste the salt as it trickled over my lips. Then his radio suddenly blared out loudly again, making me flinch involuntarily.

'Any officers in the region of Market Street...' blurted the radio loudly. His grip loosened. He spoke into his radio.

I didn't even hear his response. The only sound I heard was the one I wanted to hear: that of him moving quickly away from the back door. For the second time that night, I let my breath out, feeling the apprehension ebb away gleefully.

I then turned to Scotty, who was still stood there, armed with his fire extinguisher. I found myself glaring at him.

'Right, Chopper... Let's get the fuck out of 'ere,' he blurted out, frantically dropping the extinguisher and running at the door.

'You what!' I asked in utter disbelief as I placed my hand against his chest to stop him from leaving. 'Fuck that, Scotty. We've got all this gear 'ere and you want to just walk away? We're not just fuckin' it off. Just think about it. You know it's worth it, ar'kid.' I shone my light into his face.

He began to smile and then chuckled as his senses came back to him. 'Shit... I don't know what quite came over me then,' he said, shaking his head.

We loaded up the van in record time with as much as we possibly could – which, to be honest, was actually a lot more than we had expected to fit in. We then headed straight back to Hulme.

We had changed the locks on several disused garages in the area for our storage resources. Scotty eased the van around, so that the back doors faced the garage. We both began abruptly dumping the gear. I then instructed Scotty to dispose of the van whilst I sorted out the haul into some kind of order.

By the time I'd finished organising the goods, Scotty had returned. The two of us sat there, smiling deliriously like a couple of kids who'd just robbed the candy store. Yet this gear would certainly pay for more than just a few gobstoppers. We smiled at each other, admiring our latest successful score.

'Nice work if you can get it, eh Chopper?' Scotty winked.

I merely glared in his direction.

'I know, I know,' he laughed. 'I know that I almost got us pinched tonight, mate. It was well mad though, wasn't it,

Chopper?' Scotty had read the look pasted across my face.

As the mix of fear and adrenalin subsided a little, we both began to laugh at the thought of what had just taken place. Then he began to look at me mischievously.

'You know what I want to do, Chopper... *really* want to do, ar'kid?'

'What's that, mate?'

'Well, I reckon we off-load this gear tomorrow; Prey's crew will take most of it,'

'Keep a set of Technics though, right, Scotty?' I asked, a little unsure as to where this was leading.

'Nah, man. That's the best bit, mate,' he told me. 'We get the dough, then take a little trip back into town. We go to that Sound and Vision gaff again, only this time as customers. Then we *buy* the Technics. He's still got the display ones we left on the shop floor.'

'Y'what!' I blurted out, not exactly sure if I was actually hearing this right.

'Look. They'll let a couple of scallies like us in there tomorrow. Shit, they'll be happy to sell some speaker leads after tonight.' He began laughing. 'It just completely takes the piss out of 'em.'

'And keeps us covered legally, eh?' I added, smiling at his idea. Because, for once, it was actually a pretty good one.

FOUR

T hings began to heat up on the estate after our last few scores. The police seemed to be swarming all over the place. You see, since that Sound and Vision job, as we still referred to it, the two of us had been busy all summer. With so many of the kids being off school, it drew some of the attention away from us.

A few of Prey's crew had been busted lately and they'd found some of the stolen gear from our jobs at their premises. So they were convinced that the source to the recent spate of robberies around town was connected to Hulme.

Also, the *Manchester Evening News* was constantly roaming the estate trying to find stories. They covered all the recent stories connected to the scores we'd pulled, and they appeared just as determined to catch us as the police were. Although I imagine for different reasons.

Personally, Scotty and I didn't really give care about any of this – we never kept any of the stolen gear ourselves. And after Scotty's idea for returning to buy our mixing set-up, we had receipts for everything that we owned. The two of us hadn't been nicked in a very long while.

And since upping the level of what we were involved in, we'd become a lot more cautious. No more taking stupid risks like we had done as kids, when shoplifting was really just something to relieve the boredom. We took the jobs we did nowadays a lot more seriously, as we both realised the stakes were higher.

The only problem that we all had in common right now was that, although we were being extremely cautious, there was no denying the fact that there were way too many police in the area for anybody's liking.

The problem was that both Scotty and I were still a little naïve. I mean, there was no denying that we had respect from all the kids on the estate, and Prey's crew had also given the two of us both a lot of respect. This was obviously down to the increased distribution that we were handling (independently, of course). Prey also loved the gear we were bringing in from our jobs, and his crew always had first option on any of it.

It was also around this time we'd noticed new pieces appearing on the estate, all signed with the name – or tag as it more commonly known – 'Kezlo'. The thing was, no one was claiming responsibility for them.

Neither Scotty nor I had done any new pieces in a very long while. It wasn't that we no longer enjoyed doing them: it was simply down to the fact that our main priorities had changed somewhat. But what we also couldn't afford was to take the risk of getting arrested for something like that whilst we were more heavily involved in other activities.

It was also around this time we'd happened to notice this new kid who had moved to the estate. He was a proper funny-looking lad at that. He appeared to be around the same age as us, possibly a little younger. The reason I mention him was that he really stood out from the crowd, mainly due to the fact that he was whiter than Casper the Friendly Ghost, yet had a full head of dreadlocks all the way down his back. He must have been growing them for years. They really made him stand out from the crowd.

He seemed pretty quiet next to all the other lads on the estate, and he tended to keep himself to himself. I can still remember the day that the three of us met. It had been this one Thursday evening when Scotty and I were heading towards Sampson's to pick up some food. Sampson's was actually the taxi rank above a place known as Sam-Sam's Fried Chicken. It was also a twenty-four-hour convenience store that had more security surrounding its goods than a bank. Anyway, everybody and anybody referred to it as Sampson's Chicken. Just like we'd all picked up our nicknames, it would appear that Sam-Sam's had been blessed with its own. I wasn't sure what the actual owners thought of this though.

As we approached, we'd noticed this fracas going off outside the store. Three lads, who we both knew well and who bought from us on a regular basis, were battling away with the dreadlocked kid that we'd seen knocking around the estate. And it has to be said that he was fighting all three of them with sufficient ease, refusing to back down. He seemed to be taking them all on by himself.

'Ere'are, Scotty, check this lot out,' I said, nodding in the direction of the fight.

The three lads were Tommo, Paul and Neil.

'What the fuck's going on there?' Scotty asked cautiously. 'You reckon that we should jump in and give the lads a hand or what, Chopper?'

'Nah, fuck that,' I protested. 'It's three to one odds 'ere, Scotty.'

'Just give us your money and we'll leave yer be, eh?' shouted Tommo as we watched the dreadlocked lad swing out and catch Neil in the left-hand side of his face, sending him crashing straight into the floor.

'Makes it a little more even now,' I laughed.

Just then, dreadlock swung a huge upper cut that landed squarely on Paul's upper torso. He then crumpled to the floor. I heard Tommo scream some obscenity at him as he kicked out, catching the lad in the side of his left kneecap.

'Oh shit,' declared Scotty. 'That shit must have really hurt.'

We saw Tommo charge at the lad once more, despite his weakened condition. But just as Tommo lashed out wildly again, the lad jerked forward with what can only be described as lethal accuracy, smashing straight into its target: Tommo's nose exploded. We both grimaced at this, as even from the distance at which we stood across the street we not only heard Tommo's nose crack but saw the flesh and bone shatter.

'C'mon,' I said, jogging over the road and picking Tommo up off the floor as Scotty helped Neil to his feet.

'You two fuckin' want some of this as well?' he demanded as I laughed.

'Hell no,' I declared. 'I just don't want you to end up putting any of our customers in casualty.' I smiled at him and Scotty grinned at me.

'Just what the fuck was going on?' asked Scotty of Tommo, who I was having to hold up whilst young dreadlock merely stood there, brushing himself off and glaring at all of us.

'Apart from the three of you taking a proper kicking, that is,' I added, still amused by the entire matter.

As I said this I clearly perceived a glint in this lad's eye that told me he wasn't going to take any crap from any of us. I could honestly say that hand on heart; this kid was more than willing to fight the five of us. I couldn't help but let out a little laugh, and I found myself taking a liking towards the kid. There was something about the lad that I seemed to instantly relate to. I wasn't quite sure what it was at the time. But whatever it was he was all right in my book.

'Fucker wouldn't give us his cash,' added Paul, who was climbing to his feet.

Turning to Tommo, I glared menacingly at him, as I knew that he headed up this sorry bunch of so-called bandits. 'And just why the fuck should he give you lot his dough, Tommo?'

Scotty now had hold of the other two. 'What you two got to say, eh?' he asked.

They all just shrugged sheepishly. They knew that they'd lost the battle and were more than likely feeling the embarrassment of having the two of us bear witness to it all. The fact of the matter was we didn't know this lad from Adam. We'd only seen him knocking around the estate. But like I said, you had to give him respect; they'd tried taxing him and he wasn't having any of it.

'Go on… Get the fuck out of 'ere,' I snarled menacingly again at them as Scotty released the other two.

'Cheers for that, lads,' the kid responded, walking casually away.

'No problem,' I replied, walking towards Sampson's to deal with the ache I felt in the pit of my stomach.

And that was pretty much that. We didn't actually know at that time that the lad was Kezlo, whose pieces had been popping up all over the estate. But over the next few weeks (through business, of course), we became friendlier with him. And before any of us knew it, Kezlo had literally turned the two of us into the three of us.

We became pretty much inseparable. Kezlo also had a natural talent for mixing. He loved the whole hip hop scene more than we did. Once he got started on the decks, neither Scotty nor I could pull him away from them. He was always pushing himself harder, mixing better and better.

It had got to the stage where he was now teaching the two of us how best to mix. Before now, we'd really only messed about with it, but, for Kezlo, it was a different deal altogether. He had what can only be described as a real infatuation for putting together some great mixes.

Almost immediately we'd started to cut him in on our business side of things. I'm not even sure why: it had just seemed like the most natural thing to do, despite our only knowing him for such a short space of time.

And it was both of our businesses for that matter – the nocturnal jobs, which we were still pulling around town after hours, and the day-to-day running of the weed business on the estate.

Between the two of us we'd introduced Kezlo to everyone we knew around the estate and town. Prey also took a real liking to him. He thought that he was a crazy-looking character with all his dreads set upon his 'white boy's head' as he put it, in a strong Jamaican patois that would have made his grandmother very proud – had it not been so heavily Mancunian.

He also appreciated the fact Kezlo seemed interested in subjects that none of us cared about. Kezlo actually liked to read. And yes, that did include more than my extensive library of Silver Surfer and Batman comics. I mean he actually *enjoyed reading books* with no pictures at all inside them. Honest. No really!

And he was a lot more intelligent than he first appeared. You'd find both him and Prey huddled in some corner of the local pub where we drank, or else in his flat, discussing with each other whatever they had both recently read or some music that had been recently released or that they'd heard somewhere. That was also a big factor in Prey's life.

Pretty much the same as me and Scotty, Prey had not attended school, but he was always reading up on different subjects, constantly informing you of the latest thing he'd just finished reading. He used to always inform us that an educated crook was the most dangerous of villains.

He also continually informed us that it was easier for the police to label us through their own perceptions – as dense-minded, uneducated, low-life scum with no goals in life. He told us that if we used our noodles, we'd go far in any area we chose.

I think he worried that, as we never went to school, we were somehow missing out. He felt it was his responsibility to educate us, for some bizarre reason. We appreciated this, but all the same we had our own game plan in life. The things that we were getting up to now were more important to us than anything else.

However, in the years to follow we would realise just how vital the information that Prey had continually bombarded us with was. It would stick deep within our minds. It was like I keep saying – we got our education on the streets. And for us, it was by far the greatest education system in the world.

FIVE

The three of us had been asked to attend Prey's immediately. Two of Prey's top 'lieutenants', Sean and Parksey, had appeared from nowhere and, smirking knowingly, they informed the three of us that they had a request from Prey and that he wanted to see us straight away.

When we arrived at his flat we found Prey was sat reading a book on the Prohibition era in the States back in the twenties. He was rocking contentedly back and forth in his black leather La-z-Boy chair. I really wanted one of those chairs for myself. One of Kezlo's newly mixed tapes was throbbing from the Technics stack system located on the glass wall unit.

It wasn't one of ours though. Prey knew better than that. He never kept stolen gear around his gaff. Anyway, with the sort of money he made, he had no need to.

Although the gear his crew bought was on Prey's authority, he had many clients for the gear we stole. None of our gear was ever second-hand like the junk that the smackheads used to swap for ten-pound bags of gear. If they weren't so wasted on smack all the time they could probably pull down some pretty decent scores. I mean after all, they were resourceful enough; there was no denying that. However, it was really only the gear driving them to steal from the helpless anyway. I really hated heroin. It was by far the worst drug – I'd witnessed the effects first hand. Over the past two years we'd seen proper dependable lads that we had known for years become caught up with the drug. We had seen them progress from merely smoking or chasing it to eventually injecting themselves, all the while their bodies becoming more and more dependent on the daily hit that constantly increased, day by day, until it took over completely.

This isn't to say that I was anti-drugs in any kind of way: I just knew my limits. I mean, after the last time, over two years ago, I

49

had never touched glue again. Not since that crazy day in Salford. I still smoked weed on a day-to-day basis. I mean, I even did coke, or charlie as we knew it, so I was not perfect. But I never entered into the realm of heroin.

Saying that though, looking around Prey's flat, there was no hiding the pure and simple fact that there was one hell of a lot of cash involved in it.

Prey finally looked up at the three of us stood there. 'Well, if it isn't three of my favourite lads from the yard. How you lads doin' today? Why don't you sit down, eh?'

He smiled at us knowingly, although I'll be the first to admit that I found his smile a little unnerving right now. Still, we did as we were told. Prey had never demanded to see us like this before. And we were all curious to know what the hell it was all about. So I finally broke through the apprehensive atmosphere.

'So what we gone and done then, Prey?'

He let out a little laugh. 'Don't worry yourselves... We'll get to that later on. You lads want a drink? Of course you do... You want some of that Guinness punch from Sampson's? How about some scran? I bet you're hungry, ain't you, eh? Yes, that's it. I'll prepare some food for us. What you lads feel like eating? No, don't worry. I already know.'

He was answering all his own questions, which seemed a little weird. Or maybe we'd just smoked too much that day and the paranoia was starting to kick in. We just sat there watching him go on with himself. About the only certain thing at this point was that this was all becoming very bizarre.

He continued once again. 'How about some fried chicken, rice and peas – fried dumplings, of course.'

Kezlo's eyes lit up. 'Sound, Prey. That sounds double sweet. That spicy gravy of yours that I've heard so much about as well, eh mate?'

''Course,' he replied, rising from his seat.

'Are we in the shit or what?' Scotty asked, also feeling a little apprehensive at Prey's nonchalant attitude. He just laughed again, but didn't say a word.

'Yeah, mate,' I stared at him. 'The suspense is killing me. We gone done something to offend you, Prey?'

He flashed that devious grin of his again and winked knowingly. 'Stop being so fucking paranoid, lads. Shit – you need to lay off smoking so much weed. You've all got these crazy fuckin' conspiracy theories knocking back and forth around those heads of yours.'

We all just sat there staring at him, knowing that in truth he was probably right.

He smiled directly at me, shaking his head slightly. 'Look – first we eat. You lads haven't got anywhere to go, have you? Look, we just need to go over some business arrangements. That's all. You know, with all this heat roaming the estate, we just gotta talk about it. Reason some things out, that's all,' he informed us.

He disappeared into the kitchen to prepare the food. Prey's Jamaican grandmother had taught him how to cook, and it was well known that he was great cook. Yet another thing he'd stress was important in life.

I too had a great fondness of cooking – not that anybody knew though. But I loved to get involved in the kitchen when the chance arose. With these thoughts in mind, I left Scotty and Kezlo building themselves heavily loaded skunk spliffs, and I set off in the direction of the kitchen.

It was there that I discovered Prey tossing pieces of fresh chicken that had been coated with beaten egg in flour and spices.

'God, that smells well nice, Prey. What you got in it?'

'Ah… someone who appreciates a good scran, eh? You like to cook, Chopper?' he asked, still tossing the chicken pieces.

'Yes, mate. Well, when I get chance that is. No fucker knows though.'

'Why not? You should be proud if you can cook, mate.'

'Hardly ever get chance anyway,' I informed him. 'My old man never likes me being around the flat. I only really get chance if he's down at the boozer. Plus we've got a shite kitchen at home anyway,' I said, whilst observing the lush surroundings of Prey's newly fitted kitchen.

I continued watching him as he dropped the chicken into the blistering oil; it sizzled away, the aroma grasping hold of the air.

He turned the heat right down to allow the chicken to cook without the spicy coating burning. He then began washing his hands. 'What sort of food you like to cook, Chopper?'

'All sorts, you know. I don't ever use recipe books. Going more off instinct than anything.' I smiled. 'Way I figure it is, if it smells good to me then it'll taste good to someone else.'

'That's an interesting theory you got there, Chopper,' he said, nodding at me. 'You know what? I'd like to taste that theory of yours sometime. Obviously, you'll get full use of the kitchen.'

'Fuck that, Prey! You're a proper top cook,' I said, staring at him in disbelief. 'I can't cook up to your standard, that's the truth.' I was taken aback by what he'd enquired of me.

He glared right at me. 'Nah, fuck that, man. That's a shit attitude to have. I tell you what, next weekend, you can cook for all the crew. Your lads also, obviously,' he said. 'C'mon, Chopper… You know you should have more confidence in yourself.'

I thought about this for a minute. 'Ah fuck it! Why not, then? It's not like I've got much say in the matter anyhow, is it?'

'That's more like it, Chopper,' he announced gleefully, stirring the deliciously spiced gravy as he did.

'Just hope I don't disappoint you, Prey… That's all, mate.'

'You never do, Chopper,' he replied casually whilst continuing to stir the gravy. 'I got big plans for you lads,' he said with that devious look yet again.

I helped carry the food through to the living room, setting it down on the smoked glass table. Prey had prepared jerk chicken, rice and peas, and fried dumplings, with the most delicious spiced gravy I'd ever tasted.

Scotty and Kezlo were already pretty stoned by the time we returned.

'All right, you two. Let's eat, then,' Prey said as he placed the last dish of chicken down.

We all tore into the food before us. It really was delicious; we'd almost finished the food before us as Prey began to stare at us once again.

'Right, lads… You're obviously wondering what you've been called 'ere for,' he said, looking around the table at all of us.

'Yeah. We in the shithouse over something or what, Prey?' Scotty asked between mouthfuls of chicken.

Prey was still chewing on a tender piece of dumpling and

gravy. 'Not exactly. We've just got ourselves a bit of a problem.'

'With what, Prey?' Kezlo asked.

'Your scores that you've been pulling recently,' he said.

'What about them, eh?' I asked, automatically on the defensive, whilst all the while wanting to know more. I placed my piece of chicken on the plate before me.

'Basically you lads have attracted a lot of unnecessary heat to the area in the last several months,' he said, staring at the three of us. 'Now don't get me wrong: we appreciate the gear you bring in. I mean, you make good money for yourselves and for us. You also, let's not forget, make good money from the gear you knock out for us, which you know I appreciate.' He continued chewing as he talked.

'So what you saying?' I asked cautiously, not liking where this was leading at all.

'Look, you got things set up nicely. You've organised your side of things well. I mean, c'mon for fuck's sake. The three of you only just turned sixteen!' He laughed out loud. 'I suppose you remind me of what I was like at your age. Not that long ago either, before you cheeky little runts say anything.' He stared at the three of us, shaking his head, all the while still smiling at us knowingly.

We all listened, filled with a mixture of curiosity and caution, waiting to hear the outcome – although I thought I already knew the answer.

He stared at us all one by one. 'All right. What I'm saying is you've got to knock your scores on the head for a while. Just until the heat—'

'No way, Prey,' I blurted out before he had chance to finish. 'No disrespect to you,' I quickly added, staring at him as intensely as I dared, 'but we've got this wired. We're making too much money from—'

'Now listen up.' His eyes became fierce as he looked at us one by one. 'I'm not asking you: I'm telling you,' he said in a stern voice.

'C'mon, Prey,' Scotty pleaded, knowing that if Prey told you that you had to stop doing something, then you did.

'Listen up,' he sighed. 'Like I said before, I consider you lads like my own, so to speak. You do top graft on the estate for my crew. So I've made a decision.' He stopped himself as the living room door opened.

We hadn't even heard the front door open, and in walked Sean, Parksey, Knieldy, Johnny and Diamond. They all stared down at us, carrying with them the kind of mean looks that would have any fully grown men quaking in their boots.

At that precise moment, I reckon that all three of us felt more than a little flutter in the base of our stomachs. I could sense that Prey knew this, as he just sat there silently whilst the rest of his 'lieutenants' stared down in that impenetrable way.

Jumping out from my seat, I honestly did not know what the hell I was going to do if they went in for the attack against us. The only thing that I was sure of was that we had to stand our ground.

'All right, what the fuck's going on 'ere?' I exclaimed.

The truth of the matter was that I wasn't at all comfortable. It wasn't pure fear that I felt though – my mind was pretty clear. Although it had a thousand and one questions filtering through it at a million miles an hour. I mean, what had we gone and done? Had we gone and upset Prey that much? Were we even going to make it out of here?

Kezlo and Scotty also stood up with clenched fists. Just then Prey leapt out of his chair straight at me. I still stood my ground – but to this day I don't know how I managed it. I honestly didn't know what I should do next. He then just flung his arms around me and began laughing.

'What—' I began to yell at him. 'What's so fuckin' funny?' I asked, calming down slightly.

'Your faces, that's what,' he laughed. 'I've made the decision that the three of you are to be made full members of the crew.' He laughed even louder now. 'And before you start trippin', Chopper, about not wanting in, hear me out first, ar'kid.' He chuckled, amused by his own game.

He'd always tried to bring us in as foot soldiers and knew that we just weren't interested. 'Go on then,' I enquired with a certain amount of caution.

'Look, despite your young age I'm making you chief lieutenant over Scotty and Kezlo. I know you're not keen on the title, kid, but it goes with the job.' He looked at the other two. 'As for you two, you'll be both Chopper's and my lieutenants, all right? You all sweet with that? Y'know it's a cracking offer, lads.'

The three of us finally exhaled and slowly nodded at one another. We all knew it to be a great business opportunity – despite this whole chief lieutenant or lieutenants thing that Prey seemed kind of obsessed with, although it had worked well for him so far. However, at the same time I kept wondering why it was that I was to be put above the other two. I put the thought to the back of my mind for the moment and stared at Prey.

'You're a fuckin' twat, Prey,' I declared joylessly. 'I proper crapped myself then.'

The mood both immediately and dramatically lightened from moments ago, as everybody began shaking hands.

My head was banging when I finally awoke the following day. It was Sunday afternoon, so the old dear hadn't mithered me at all. Although back when we were supposed to attend school, she used to try and wake me relentlessly. She knew that we never went. However, I think trying to get us to go eased her guilt somewhat. I lay there half asleep and thought over the previous night's events.

We had all drunk champagne and snorted what seemed to be never-ending lines of charlie into the early hours of Sunday morning. All of us had been in high spirits. I'd felt really proud to be part of it all. The only thing that had really fucked me off was having to knock the scores on the head. I really got off on doing them. In fact, I had been stood in the kitchen by myself thinking about this matter that previous night as Prey walked in.

'Don't worry about them, Chopper,' he'd told me. 'I know exactly what you're thinking, mate. You can go back to them, Chopper – just once the heat gets the fuck out of Dodge.'

I couldn't believe what I'd heard. Could this guy read minds or what? 'What was th—'

'I said not to worry about the scores,' he'd said to me.

'But how'd you kn—'

'I could read it all over your face earlier, Chopper. I know you love doing them. Fuckin' good at it too,' he'd said, smiling at me.

'Look, I got a sweet set-up for you lads, you hear. Top money to be made from it. For all of us, kid. You can have the scores back, just as soon as the timing is right. I promise you that, although we'll have to rearrange the percentage side of things. You know, now that things are different.'

That's what he'd said to me the night before and for some bizarre reason it was the first thought I'd had as I struggled to wake up. Reaching over for the alarm clock that hadn't been set since God knows when, it had just gone three o'clock in the afternoon. We had arranged to hook up with Prey at five o'clock down at Spinners, our local pub. So, rolling out of bed, I headed for the shower.

The hot water felt so good. I could literally feel the charlie sweating out of my system from the previous night. Pressing my head against the off-white tiled shower wall, I let the hot stream of water cascade down my back. Damn, it felt good. But then again, so had last night.

The charlie had been snorted relentlessly. And if we weren't doing that, then we were rolling skunk and charlie joints that were mixed together in their pure forms. That was one hell of a potent cocktail that ended up battering your senses as if your head was merely a tennis ball being banged from one side to the other.

The rest of Prey's lads seemed all right about us being brought into the action. We still had no idea what Prey had set up for us though. He just reassured me that it was proper worth waiting for and that we'd know more today.

I finally managed to drag myself out of the shower. I slid into my navy and white Kappa tracksuit, along with my new Adidas Gazelle trainers. I was always blowing the money we made on new sports gear.

I had already phoned Scotty and Kezlo to make sure they'd both dragged themselves out of bed. To be honest, they were worse than I was, but we had business to take care of with Prey.

The three of us hooked up on the bridge that crossed Bonsall Street, making our way to The Spinner's pub. We were all in good spirits, each of us as eager as the next to discover what Prey had arranged for us. Who needed school or a job anyway, right?

As we walked through the front door to the establishment, we could already see all the others sat at the back area. Spinner's had one hell of a reputation for drug deals. It was sold so openly it was almost like asking for a Mars Bar at your local corner shop.

I turned to Scotty and Kezlo. 'You two get a round of drinks in. I'll be over 'ere.'

Scotty merely nodded at me and I swore that he gave me a look. I shrugged it off as the two of them sauntered off to the bar whilst I headed over to the rest of the lads. Prey was laughing as he noticed me and nodded.

We stayed in there drinking and enjoying ourselves until the early evening drew upon us. I found that I was overcome with a sensation that I had never experienced before: it felt as though I was suddenly part of this really secure, close family, which I had previously never been included in. It felt really first class. I sat there smiling to no one but myself, as Prey turned to me and simply smiled without saying a word. Once again, it was like he knew exactly what I was thinking.

We finally split off into Prey's black 3 series BMW and Sean's metallic silver VW Golf GTI. We screeched out of the car park, and within minutes found ourselves pulling into the car park across from Sampson's.

Climbing the graffiti-covered stairs that stank of years of abuse and piss, we eventually arrived at the top floor, stopping outside of Flat 365.

Prey grinned at us. ''Ere'are, lads,' he said, tossing me a set of keys.

I opened the flat door and we all stepped inside. We just stood there, looking around at the newly furnished flat.

'What's this then, Prey?' asked Scotty, who was walking about with Kezlo.

'This lads, is yours,' he announced proudly.

'You serious, Prey?' Kezlo responded.

I merely stared back at him. 'All right then, Prey,' I enquired. 'What's the story behind this gaff then, mate? So what's the business that goes with it, eh?'

He began to laugh. 'Always business with you, in't it, Chopper.'

'So?' I shrugged. I was not unintelligent. Things like this did not land on a silver platter every day.

'Look, the gaff goes with the job,' he informed me. 'You lads can bed down 'ere or you can stay at home. It makes absolutely no difference to me. But you treat this gaff as your office, so to speak.'

Kezlo and Scotty were already making themselves right at home by playing about with the stereo and TV, whilst the rest of the crew just made themselves comfortable on the sofas.

'Look, Chopper,' he sighed, staring at me, 'let's go outside and talk, mate.'

As the two of us stood leaning against the balcony, we observed everybody scuffling about down below. Despite it being Sunday night, the estate, as usual, was still very much alive, with it being a warm evening.

There were children of all ages running about or chasing each on their bikes. The local drunks fell about and you could clearly hear the cackles of their demented laughter all the way up here. And, of course, Prey's workers were all over the place. They stood out from the others. They somehow appeared more alive, almost like electric sparks in a frenzy of bees working away in their hive, ensuring that they kept the queen happy with their flurry of activity.

'OK,' I said, finally breaking the silence between us.

'OK,' he repeated. 'Here it is then, kid. You see, Chopper, the smack business is taking off like you wouldn't believe.'

'Fuck!' I exclaimed. 'You're setting us up in the smack business or what, Prey?' I was staring at him in disbelief, not quite sure if we were ready to be promoted to being heroin dealers just yet.

'Fuck that. No fuckin' way, Chopper.' He shook his head sternly at me. 'I don't want you lads anywhere near that at your ages. No, I want you lads to take over our weed business – just on the estate, but all over town. You know, so we can concentrate on the rest of our affairs.'

He was watching for a reaction from me, staring down at me with intense eyes. Finally he spoke. 'You in or what, Chopper? I need to know before I disclose any more information to you.' He was still staring at me with those scrutinising eyes.

'Are you kidding, Prey?' It was my turn to shake my head at

him. 'Do I look like I'm fuckin' stupid or what?'

He just stared at me, not knowing what the hell to think right then. I enjoyed the moment a little longer, allowing it to linger before finally speaking. 'Of course I'm in, Prey.'

'You little shit, Chopper. I didn't know what to think then! I thought that you were going to back down on me!' He laughed with me as we both enjoyed the moment.

'All right, there's another flat around the corner. Number 464. Now, you can't get a visual on it from the street as we picked it out carefully. No matter where you are at street level, you can't see this gaff. We had the neighbours – how can I put this – *relocated* so to speak, for ar' convenience. You and Sean are the only ones with access to it. Even I don't cross the doorway. That's how fuckin' serious we are with this shit. It's a big responsibility that I'm handing you 'ere, Chopper. But if you're gonna do this shit then you're gonna need access to it twenty-four-seven. We keep the gear stashed there. For the next couple of weeks Sean's going to work closely with you to show you how things go. He'll go over everything with you, and you'll be introduced to all the contacts around town that we've got. After that it's down to you and your crew to handle things. All I'm interested in is that you make it run properly and we all benefit from the profits.'

'All right,' I nodded. 'What about the money side of things, Prey?'

'Like I said, Sean will go over all the details with you in the next couple of weeks.' He looked me in the eye. 'You do realise how much weed is sold each week, don't you, Chopper? You'll be working with the big boys now, you know. None of this couple of ounces here and there.'

'That's sweet, Prey,' I smiled at him. I was still unable to fully believe the opportunity he'd given us; it was overwhelming to say the least. 'I won't let you down. I'll make you proud of us all, Prey.'

'I know you will, Chopper. Why do you think I picked you for the job?' He smirked at me. 'Also, it keeps you away from the temptation of the smack business. You've got to be strong-willed before entering into that arena. One day you may move into it, just not at this moment in time.'

He suddenly grabbed my shoulder and stared directly at me. 'I tell you – if I ever hear that you're fuckin' about with that shit on a personal level, I'll cut you off completely.' He was serious.

I gazed back at him. 'C'mon, Prey... You know I hate fuckin' smackheads.'

'Just one more thing, then: you keep your crew in check. No fuckin' about. Oh – and if you ever try to fuck me, and I mean ever, then I'll...' He just left the rest to my imagination.

Then he started to smirk at me again before leading me back into the flat and through the side door before entering the living room.

'I almost forgot, Chopper... Just take a look at what you got in 'ere,' he announced joyously, witnessing the look upon my face that could only be described as utter ecstasy. Because he had led me into the kitchen, and it was an exact replica of his own that I had admired so much.

SIX

N early twelve months had passed since Prey had set us up in Flat 365. Business had commenced almost immediately, but for the first couple of weeks, as Prey had promised, I had Sean going over and over the set-up, covering every aspect of running a tight crew. He taught me how things were supposed to run, who to trust, who not to trust, the low-down on all the main heads in and around town, which ones were all right, which weren't all right, and who were the best wholesalers around to deal with.

Thinking back, we must have travelled every inch of town in that time. Sean introduced me to everyone; all the contacts that we would need to use. He reassured all of them that I was one of Prey's lieutenants, so not to go messing with me, thinking I may be some sort of an easy target.

Sean showed me all the best means of transport for carrying the gear around, informing me it was always best to use public transport or taxis to get about. We covered the best bus routes to use and the best taxi ranks to use (it was always best to try and use Frank from Sampson's taxi rank whenever possible, as he knew the score and was on the payroll). As it would turn out, taxis would become the best means of transport to use – I've never once been caught in a taxi.

And although we travelled all over town visiting different sources, it would turn out that Wythenshawe was the most reliable source for weed. Our contact there was one of the older heads named Batty. Doing business with Batty was very cool, as Wythenshawe was so close by with easy access from the Parkway. On a good run with Frank, business could be dealt with, all in all, in about an hour's time.

Sean tested my knowledge on a daily basis. He was keen to hear my ideas on how I wanted to run things. Each idea was covered in a professional way, weighing up the pros and cons of every aspect.

It was safe to say that by the end of the training my head was properly spinning, not knowing whether I was coming or going as I tried to take everything in.

As appointed chief lieutenant, there was one aspect that had bothered me – how it might affect me and Scotty. You see, there had never been any competition between the two of us, ever. I kept thinking that he'd be annoyed at me for being appointed to the position, knowing that he'd not been given a mere foot soldier's job and was still one of Prey's so-called (and also mine as well, I suppose) lieutenants. I was also holding my own ideas on what I wanted to do with him. Kezlo too for that matter.

It had also been one of the first times that we hadn't seen each other every day since being kids. The time I had spent with Sean had been so busy, the busiest time of my life in fact. I supposed that was also one of the reasons for my worrying about Scotty's feelings on the situation.

As it turned out though, Scotty didn't seem to care about it. He told me that he always considered that I was the one to follow. Although I was pleased his feelings weren't hurt, what he had said confused me. You see, I'd never seen it that way before. So I eventually brought up the subject with Prey.

He explained to me that he had also always felt that I'd held true leadership skills, as he referred to them. He also told me that the fact that I'd never seen it in myself before only heightened the appeal to others around me. Well, that was Prey's theory on the subject anyway. He told me, 'It will be your true making in life one day, Chopper.'

Those words would stick with me for years to follow.

So, following that intensive training, I was then faced with training Scotty and Kezlo, filling them in on all the aspects of what they needed to know, but never letting them in on everything.

Sean had told me that that was the way it needed to be, saying it was necessary that no matter how much you considered people around you to be the best of friends, business was business and mates were mates. He informed me that you should always remember that, no matter what the situation was.

I'd mentioned to Sean that I felt we needed to have our own foot soldiers around both the other two and myself. He also agreed with me on that score, saying he was pulling more into the smack business.

So our first job in hand was to put together our own crew of trusted soldiers. Between the three of us we debated until the early hours as to who was ideal and who didn't stand a chance. Finally we got our crew together.

With Scotty and Kezlo being lieutenants, they worked directly for me with the distribution side. So first off we enlisted Jonah, who both Scotty and I had known for some time now. We put him in charge of all of our street crew (we preferred such a name rather than Prey's military theme).

You see, Jonah carried the look of a public school boy; his image was great. He would just pass you by in the street without a second glance. It was an excellent quality to have. But in truth, Jonah was just as ruthless as we were. Growing up on the estate with his clean looks, he'd always been in and out of fights, usually getting the upper hand. Nowadays it was very rare that any man on the estate wanted to fight with him.

Eight other lads from the estate were brought in to handle the street: Joey, Paul, Darren, Tommo, Chods, Neil, Dougsy and Kirk. We also brought in two girls, which went completely against the rules; they were Sharon and Janine.

Sharon was this skinny little white girl from the estate, who often used to bunk off school with us. As skinny as she was, she carried a huge pair of breasts that Jonah had the pleasure of playing with every night. Being Jonah's girl, we knew that no one would go messing with her. Also she knew of the people on the estate who would be of value to us.

As for Janine, she was more of a woman than a girl. She was Prey's age and completely gorgeous. She was of mixed race and blatantly knew that all the lads on the estate fancied her. Not that it was any use though, as she was gay and very proud of it. None of us gave a shit though, and secretly we all had fantasies of threesomes with her and her lovers…obviously!

The thing was, whilst growing up, Scotty and I had always looked up to her as kind of an older sister. She was a top girl, who carried good connections at the gay clubs in town itself, rather than the estate. So not including her would have been daft.

Although the decision to include these two had made Prey a bit dubious. I spoke with him for hours on the matter. He finally respected my decision.

So with the crew put together we had gone into business for Prey.

Within a short period of time we had all made quite an impression, both on the estate and in town also. It was fair to say, between all of us, we were attracting more and more business each week, working hard and opening new channels, all the while trying out new ideas to increase revenue.

Prey loved all of it, as well he might, as within that twelve-month period we managed to double the sales and distribution of the weed.

It was also around this time that Prey kept his promise to me about the scores we'd previously been doing: he finally raised the ban on them. Truth is, he missed the gear we'd been bringing in. Like I've said, it was always quality gear.

In truth though, Scotty, Kezlo and I didn't need the money like we used to. All of us were making a lot of it from our recent activities. The thing was, I was itching like crazy to get back to it and couldn't wait to check out all the new so-called top-of-the-range security systems; we always loved pulling off those jobs back then.

The problem we encountered now though was that all three of us were so busy with the weed business each and every day.

It makes me laugh, this image people have of us from the movies. You know, the one where we sit around, doing nothing at all, and the money just makes itself. Well, the reality isn't quite the same. Running a business like we did consisted of a lot of hard work, much like any legal operation. In fact, it's twice as hard as you've got to cover yourself to make sure the security is even tighter.

You see, we were aware that the police knew of the activities on the estate – it's just in a court of law they need to prove without a doubt that they are positively right. Or at least that's what they're supposed to do. And they just couldn't prove anything against us. We had it set up so that when they snatched any of our street crew they couldn't charge them with anything more than possession for personal use.

They were also constantly trying their best to turn our workers into snitches with offers of good money and even free drugs, if you can believe such audacity. Our crew always laughed off these situations though.

So we ran a tight ship that always required the security aspects to be reviewed, and therefore business to be changed frequently, not only to keep ourselves on our toes but also to keep the police on theirs. That way it went in circles, keeping all of the crew on their toes. And, more importantly, they were not entirely sure as to how things were actually being run. Ever!

With all this in mind we came to the conclusion that we couldn't pull down scores the same way we used to. So I'd suggested that what we did then was to only pull a job once a month. That way we could still pull them, but it wouldn't go attracting the heat back to the area. And with all the new contacts we'd acquired over the past twelve months, we could keep the gear well out of Hulme anyway.

For the first score, we decided on one of the wholesale electrical warehouses over in Cheetham Hill. Rasheed's was the biggest wholesale operation in that area, run by two Asian brothers. We definitely needed more than just a transit van for this job.

Scotty, shrewd as ever, had already worked that side of things out. The only thing was that we just had to wait a couple of weeks. A couple of months back, Scotty had met this young girl from Macclesfield, who he was sleeping with. He referred to her as his 'bit of country fluff'. The real bonus with this girl was that her family owned and ran Smiths Removals, which was situated on one of the estates over that way. The even bigger bonus was that they were going on holiday to Spain in two weeks' time, leaving us the opportunity to 'borrow' one of their removal vans. So we left that side of things to Scotty.

Kezlo and I spent the previous week going over how best to go about the plan. The two of us had looked over Rasheed's alarm system, having to admit it was a very good one. They had it so that if it tripped out no bell would sound. It was wired to trip silently, crossing through the phone lines directly to the police station. I'd only ever come across one of them before – on a jewellery score we'd pulled just before Prey had put the ban on the jobs. We'd only just made it away as the police turned up in full force.

Anyway, it had baffled the hell out of me, so I returned to the store a week later, as I needed to know whether it had been pure coincidence them turning up or whether it had been something else. The alarm system hadn't seemed to be anything out of the ordinary. I was trying patiently to fathom it out, and an hour later I was still baffled. That was until I eventually discovered the alarm system was wired onto the phone line. Then it all came together.

So the three of us returned once again a week after this recent discovery and robbed them again. Only this time, we bypassed the phone line so as not to trip the alarm.

The score was set for Saturday night. Sunday, believe it or not, was always Cheetham Hill's busiest day. And seeing as we were not dealing in cash, we'd be guaranteed they'd be fully stocked up and ready for trade that day.

We arrived at the back of the warehouse at precisely ten o'clock. All three of us were wearing Smith's overalls, along with ski masks, as we clambered out of the removal van into the cool night air. Scotty immediately went to scan the area for any signs of security, whilst Kezlo waited on standby with the bolt cutters.

I headed straight for the telegraph pole, hitching myself up with spiked heels that I'd fitted to the back of my boots. I'd picked the spikes up from some smackhead on the estate – he'd robbed them from some unsuspecting British Telecom worker, high up his telegraph pole. The smackhead didn't have a clue what he was going to do with the loot, just that it was there for the taking. However, I arranged for the transfer of a ten-pound bag in exchange for the bag of useless goods, bar the spikes.

Bypassing the alarm in three and a half minutes, I was a little off time, but hey, nobody's perfect. Kezlo had dealt with all the locks by the time I'd descended from the pole. Scotty was still scanning the area, whistling soft signals as Kezlo and I eased back the large, heavy, solid steel loading-bay doors. God, they weren't half stiff. Just then, Scotty raced between the two of us into the darkened warehouse and headed straight for the forklift truck.

He began to work out the forklift truck as Kezlo and I both scanned the warehouse for the stock which would bring in the best returns.

'Chopper, check this lot 'ere, mate,' Kezlo said.

Flashing my light over to where he stood, I saw Technics stereos and turntables stretched from floor to ceiling. *Trust Kezlo to find those*, I thought, smiling to myself. 'Sound, mate. Carry on checking. We'll still take all of those though.'

Just then we heard the forklift's engine come to life. As I turned I could see Scotty beaming at me.

'Bag of piss, mate,' he smiled as he manoeuvred the forklift truck with precision and ease. 'Right, what's first, Chopper?'

I shone my light at the pile of Sony boxes. 'Those boxes there.'

As Scotty swiftly and expertly manoeuvred the forklift, I returned back to the rear of the removal lorry, opening the doors. Climbing up into it, I hadn't realised just how spacious the holding area actually was. Scotty appeared with the first stack of stereo boxes.

'Scotty, we'll fit shitloads in 'ere. Tell Kezlo to pick some of the top of range Sony Trinitron TVs... No, on second thoughts, just tell him to come stand guard. You'll know what to pick up, won't you?'

He just smiled back at me. ''Course, mate.'

Scotty quickly disappeared back into the darkness of the warehouse. Moments later, Kezlo appeared. He was smiling away through his ski mask.

'This is double sweet, Chopper. We're going to make top bees off all this gear,' he announced.

'Bees', as he referred to them, was our term for money. It was short for two things: bumble-bee, relating to the buzz you got from money obtained through these kinds of deals; and also the letter B, which quite simply stood for bucks, as in slang for dollars.

Scotty was already returning with the first consignment of gear. 'All right, lads, I'll sort this lot out. Scotty, you just keep it coming,' I glanced at Kezlo. 'And Kezlo, you go have a look about; check the area is still safe.'

Both nodded their understanding. It took just over half an hour to fully load up the back of the lorry. As I leapt back down from the lorry, Scotty was running back out of the warehouse, his smile beaming through his mask.

'Go join Kezlo in the front. I'll finish up 'ere, all right, mate,' I said, easing the steel doors down.

'Sweet, mate. Fuck yes... Yes, mate! Chopper, it feels proper good, doesn't it?' he said, running past me. 'I've missed doing these jobs.'

I returned his smile, knowing exactly how he was feeling. My adrenaline was pumping too, from the job we'd just pulled off. Christ! It felt really good. In fact, better than good: it was fantastic. I certainly had missed them.

Easing the large steel warehouse doors back together, I then returned to check the lock on the truck once more, pulling on it to make sure it was secure before checking my watch. It was 10.46. *Good timing*, I thought. Just as I began to turn, I suddenly noticed something to my right-hand side move sharply... a shadow... but not mine, that was for certain... It was somebody else's.

Just then a light snapped on, blinding me.

'Oh shit! Why on my fuckin' shift?'

It was the security guard.

Time seemed to momentarily stand still, although immediately my mind cleared of all reasoning. Nobody was going to stop us now. Especially, I might add, some security guard on minimum wage. Without hesitation, I swiftly flipped open my butterfly knife.

His light bounced brightly off the steel blade and I briefly caught a view of his face. He looked whiter than was normal: scared, shocked and fearing for his life. But he was also the one that stood between me – us – and our haul.

I leapt straight for him with the blade aimed straight at his throat. I heard his hopeless last cry for help as he tried to back away from my attack.

'No, I don't—' was all that I heard as his voice just trailed away into the dead of night.

The blade tore through into his throat, slicing his jugular wide open. I continued to slice upwards into his face. The sound of tearing flesh was all that could be heard. As both our bodies crashed to the floor, blood sprayed extravagantly into my face as I stuck the blade into his security blazer. I cleanly sliced the material away, forcing the blade into his chest area.

The guard had fallen silent, yet his eyes were still bulging maniacally at me. Then there was nothing: no movement, no breathing; just stillness. He was dead all right. And did I feel guilty? Hell no! My only feeling was of anger at being forced into this situation.

Just then, I felt myself being dragged away from the body. My bloodied victim lay still beneath me, his face frozen in an expression of shock and bewilderment.

It had been Scotty hauling me from the floor. 'Fuck me, Chopper… You've ju—'

'Is he dead?' a traumatised Kezlo interrupted.

Just as before, my mind suddenly cleared completely. We needed to deal with the situation at hand. 'Right, listen up… I'll dispose of the body. Kezlo, get back inside; look for something to cover the blood with.' Observing his dismayed face I said, 'Don't bother with water. Find something dark – oil from the forklift, something like that. But make sure that you bring me some water to try and clean myself off. Scotty, go and scan the area. Last thing we need is any more fuckin' surprises like that.'

I gave out these instructions with extreme calmness, which, to be totally honest, I had no idea where I was finding such tranquillity given the situation in hand.

'But, Chopper… you've just…' Kezlo began to say.

Scotty began to come around from the initial shock. 'Kezlo, do as Chopper said. *Now*, Kezlo.'

Kezlo disappeared back into the darkness of the warehouse, looking a little lost as he left.

'We got to move quickly 'ere, Scotty,' I said.

'What you going to do with the body, Chopper?'

'I saw some sheeting in the back of the removal truck,' I replied, staring directly at him. 'Go get them for me. And remove those overalls, Scotty. I need to get out of these ones; they're covered in his blood.'

As Scotty clambered up into the back, I began stripping myself naked apart from my gloves. The guard lay there; blood still seeming to seep from the open wounds. Or maybe that was merely my eyes playing tricks on me. Just then, Scotty returned with two large plastic sheets and a large cloth one.

I began to unravel one of the plastic sheets. 'Scotty, go see what Kezlo's doing, will you? I'll sort the body out and dump it somewhere. Just make sure that you keep hold of the rest of the sheeting. I'll keep hold of this so we can get rid of it all afterwards.' He looked at me, confused. 'If I carry him over there as he is, there'll be blood all over the place.' I looked at him. He seemed to understand. 'We need to get the fuck out of 'ere double quick, Scotty!' Whilst I was saying this, he was half laughing. 'What's so funny, you twat? This ain't the time for joking about.'

He was still grinning away. 'Sorry, Chopper mate,' he said, trying to control himself a little. 'It's just… Well, the sight of you naked with just a pair of gloves on mate.'

I glanced down at myself and half smiled.

'Go on, fuck off, you dick. We need to hurry this the fuck up.'

As I rolled the guard's body into the plastic sheeting, I noticed that his uniform was caked in warm, sticky wet blood, making it harder for me to ease him into the sheeting. I have to admit that I was trying my best to not look at his sliced face. I mean, after all, it hadn't been personal. It had merely been a case of not hesitating. That's all it was (so I kept telling myself). It was business, pure and simple. He'd just been in the wrong place at the wrong time.

Being sure to use both lots of plastic, I then hauled his body onto my right shoulder and headed in the direction of the empty car park on the other side. There were three large industrial steel dustbins in the left-hand corner, by the wire fencing.

My breathing was becoming faster and heavier as I finally reached the bins. Easing his body over the side of the furthest dustbin, I was suddenly filled with a massive pang of guilt for what I had done. As his dead weight unravelled from the sheeting, it hit the steel base of the bin and echoed loudly into the dead of night.

Paranoia hit me, and I forgot instantly about the guilt. I struck the cold concrete floor hard; my naked flesh began to shiver, and goose bumps rose. I was scanning the area for any movement, any sign, to indicate more security, or even police for that matter. But there was nothing, nothing whatsoever to alarm me. So I quickly shot off, still fully naked apart from the gloves, in the direction of Rasheed's, carrying the bloodied bundle of sheeting with me.

Scotty and Kezlo had eventually found a large container of grease, and between the two of them they were smearing it everywhere. Not just on the bloodstained floor, but also on the walls, the doors – just about everywhere.

'What the fuck are you doing?'

Scotty smirked at me. 'Well, they'll just presume it was mind-less vandalism, won't they?

'Ere'are, Chopper. Wash yourself down. Scotty's overalls are over there too.' Kezlo pointed to a container he'd filled with water, in the rear of the removal van. He appeared to be a lot calmer, and I remember feeling glad about that at least.

'Stick your gloves with the pile of clothes there,' he added, still smearing the grease and nodding towards the removal truck.

They'd bundled my bloodied clothes and the bloodied plastic sheeting into the cloth sheeting. I quickly washed myself down as best I could. Then I began changing my clothing before returning to the others.

'You lads finished or what? We need to get the fuck out of 'ere.'

'Sound, Chopper. From what I can see, the blood has mixed well with the grease. It seems to have turned pretty black,' Scotty said, throwing the container of grease to one side.

'Right then, let's go. Work out what the fuck we're going to do,' Kezlo declared.

'I think I know what we'll have to do,' I told them both. 'C'mon, let's just get on the road.'

SEVEN

My head was amazingly unclouded (although it *was* spinning) as we made our way back through town. I told Scotty to stick to the main roads, as taking backstreets might raise suspicions, plus it was still relatively early and traffic still roamed the streets. The last thing we needed was to get a pull, because not only was all the gear in the back of the van, but also a bundle of bloodied evidence.

Scotty looked at me. 'All right, Chopper, where do you want me to head for then?'

'Sandbach Services,' I said.

Kezlo turned to me. 'Are you trippin', Chopper, or what? That place'll be crawling wall to wall with coppers.' He sounded alarmed at the very prospect of it.

'It'll be sweet. We're not going to stop off for coffee and Danish or whatever, Kezlo.'

'All right, Chopper. You want to tell us why though?' Scotty asked.

My mind was working overtime. 'Look, I need to contact Prey. He'll know what to do. Plus I've already got an idea of what he'll have in mind. Sandbach Services is on the way.' I smiled at them both. They appeared bemused.

We arrived at Sandbach Services without a hitch, making good time. It was 11.52.

Jumping down from the front cabin, I turned back to the other two. 'I'll be back in about ten minutes, all right? Scotty, you best check the fuel situation out. Kezlo, look for a road map; there should be one around 'ere somewhere.'

Kezlo looked at me. 'Chopper... Just be careful, man.'

Smiling and nodding at them both, I turned and ran over to the phone boxes.

I dialled Prey's number, slightly out of breath. 'Prey... I need to speak urgently,' I blurted out.

'What the fuck's up, ar'kid?' he asked anxiously, sensing immediately that something was wrong. 'You ain't been pinched, have you?'

'No… no, it's not that. Just go to the other line. I'll call back,' I replied, replacing the receiver.

We'd hooked a separate phone line up in this old lady's flat near Prey's. She'd known and loved Prey since he was a young child, never ever judging him like some people did. So Prey was always looking in on her to make sure she was all right for food or warm clothing. He was always helping her in any way that he possibly could. So when he'd offered to put her a telephone in and pay the bill, she was over the moon, only too happy to help.

After five minutes I dialled back through to the separate number; he answered immediately. I relayed the entire story to him.

He fell silent for a minute. 'Fuck me, Chopper… All right, listen; you done well up to now. You've still got all the gear as well, you little bastard,' he half laughed. 'Look, I've got to make a couple of calls, see what I can sort out. Give me your number, and then go get a pen and some paper. About ten minutes, all right.' He hung up.

After what seemed to be a very long ten minutes, Prey returned the call. 'Right, it's your lucky day, boy. You got that pen and paper handy 'cause I'm only telling you this one time.'

'Sound, mate. You've got my full attention.'

'Head for southeast London. Find your way over to Grove Park. The roads should be quiet so it's safe to say that you'll arrive easily by seven in the morning. Find Baring Road. Apparently it's easy to locate. Also you'll need to find the train station there. There are some shops across from the station, so park the van round the back of them. My guy down there is Sleeper. He'll phone you at 7 a.m. precisely, so make sure you're there on time. He'll have further instructions for you. I was lucky: he was just on his way out the door when I called him.' He paused, as if thinking of his friend.

'He says if the gear you got is as good as it normally is then he's going to get on the blower tonight. Says keep your fingers crossed and he should be able to off-load a majority of it for you tomorrow. You'll have to accept a bit of a loss though, Chopper.

Anyway, you just make sure you three make it there in one piece, brother.'

'All right, mate. What about the transport and bundle?'

'Don't worry about it; Sleeper will take care of everything.' He sighed his concern down the phone line. 'You lads got enough dough on you?'

I hadn't thought about that, but checking my pocket I could see at least a couple of hundred on me. 'Yes, mate, everything's sweet.'

'Oh, one more thing, Chopper: don't you worry about shit back 'ere. I'll take care of things personally for you. You take it easy, ar'kid,' he informed me. 'I'll speak with you soon enough.'

Just then the line went dead, before I'd had chance to thank him.

We made it to Grove Park with quite some time to spare. As Prey had said, the phone rang at exactly seven o'clock. 'Chopper?' was all the voice at the other end enquired.

'Yes, mate. Prey sent us.'

'All right, turn around and look over to the newsagent's. You'll see a silver motor,' he instructed. Turning, I could see him waving at me. 'Suppose you better come over, then.'

Making my way over the road towards where he was waiting, Sleeper was climbing from the silver Mercedes. He leaned back against the car, watching me. Sleeper was a slick-looking character, dark in complexion with a slight Oriental look about him. His dress sense was sharp, and gold dripped from everywhere. He looked like he'd take no bullshit.

'All right, Chopper, I'm Sleeper, mate,' he said and shook my hand firmly.

'You all right, mate... You know this is well appreciated, Sleeper,' I told him as a slight shiver ran through me. For this character's eyes held something else deep within them. They looked liked they had returned from years of depravation to seek out revenge against all those who had wronged him. I shook off the thought as I smiled at him. 'Prey said you'd take care of things for us.'

'Certainly will do,' Sleeper smiled at me, temporarily dispelling my fears. 'Come on, let's go meet the other two,' he said, climbing back into the Merc.

We made the very short trip around the back of the shops to the car park. I introduced Scotty and Kezlo to Sleeper.

'All right then. First things first, boys. How much gear did you manage to get last night?'

'The van is full. That's about all we can tell you,' Scotty said.

'That's all you know,' he laughed.

'Things kind of got a bit rushed last night. We're not entirely sure, Sleeper,' I told him honestly. 'I think I can remember most of it though. Pretty roughly anyway. I packed it up.'

'All right then. Chopper, you come with me. I've got some clothes for you anyway.' He glanced at Scotty. 'Scotty, you put his overalls on. Last thing we need is to arouse suspicions. You don't go doing anything fancy either; drive at a moderate speed behind me. If by chance we get a pull, then I'll stop and handle it, all right?'

'You think we'll off-load it all?' Kezlo asked.

'Just keep your fingers crossed. If it's as good a haul as Prey's made out, then you should be all right. C'mon, Chopper, follow me, mate,' he said, heading off towards the silver Mercedes.

Whilst I followed him, I kept thinking just how much the car suited him. 'It's a don' motor you got there, Sleeper,' I informed him as he popped open the boot.

He grinned at me. 'Oh, I suppose it gets me from A to B and back again.' He now laughed with an ease that made me feel welcome. I imaged that it was one of his main traits though: perhaps he put anybody who crossed him at ease before striking like a deadly viper. 'Here, Chopper, put these on.' Sleeper threw me a navy Lacoste sweatsuit along with a pair of Reebok classics.

'Sweet, Sleeper. Fuck, I needed these.'

As I was pulling the clean sweatsuit on, I noticed that Sleeper was staring at my bare chest. Glancing down to where he was looking, I noticed that the right-hand side of my chest was still covered in the security guard's blood.

'That's not yours I take it,' he stated sternly. 'You're not bleeding are you, Chopper? You're not hurt, are you, kid?'

'No... I... er...' I wasn't quite sure what to say.

'Don't worry, Chopper.' He smiled broadly at me. 'I was just worried that maybe you hadn't realised you got hit as well last night.'

'I'm sound. Thanks for the concern.' I returned the smile as I realised straight away that he wasn't prying and it had been a case of genuine concern.

'Size ten, right Chopper?' he said, grinning at me as I began to pull on the trainers, changing the subject totally.

'Er…yeah… How d'ya know?' I asked, confused.

'Prey told me. The two of us go back along way, you know. He's told me all about you, mate. And I'm not just talking about last night,' he said, looking directly at me as I changed into my new gear. 'He tells me I'm to give you nothing but star treatment whilst you're down here. He's got one hell of a lot of respect for you, Chopper, you know that? I ain't heard Prey sing praises about someone like you in a long time.'

'It's likewise, Sleeper,' I added, not fully taking in what he'd just told me.

Sleeper had arranged to off-load the gear in Lewisham. He told me that his contact over that way ran a legit business (on the surface, that is). I informed Sleeper of what I could remember from last night's haul. He told me that he'd take the Technics over to Brixton, as his other guy over there would definitely take them.

I was curious to know just how much Sleeper actually knew about last night, as I didn't want him thinking I was some cold-hearted killer.

'What did Prey tell you about last night, Sleeper?' I asked him, as I was unable to think of a more subtle way round it.

He just looked at me. 'He didn't tell me jack, Chopper. There wasn't any need to, kid. Fact is, something turned pear-shaped, right? That's for sure, or you lads wouldn't be down this way,' he smirked. 'I mean, aside from the fact you lads have had to travel all the way down here straight away… I know that Prey could and would want to bring you a much better return on this gear up there. I think that he's proper gutted that I've landed your latest score down here instead of him getting his dirty mitts on it first, eh?' He laughed.

I smiled. He was clearly enjoying the fact that he, not Prey, would be handling the gear we'd stolen. But I didn't think that there was anything malicious in it. It came across more like boyhood rivalry. All that aside though, I still needed to be certain that everything was going to be disposed of properly. However, I still didn't let on about what had gone down the previous night.

'Did he say about disposing of a bundle for me, Sleeper?'

'Look, Chopper, don't worry about a thing. I know as much as I need to know and nothing more. It's not my business what went down and I don't particularly need to know – if you know what I mean, brother.' He flashed me a smile that basically told me what I needed to know. 'Prey's instructed me on what he wants me to do,' he then informed me. 'After we off-load this gear this morning, I've got another guy whose going to meet us to take care of everything else. All right, Chopper?' he said, looking straight at me.

'Sweet, Sleeper. I just wasn't sure how much you knew, that was all, mate.'

He grinned at me. 'One other thing you should know, Chopper.'

'What's that then, Sleeper?'

'You're to be my guests for at least a week.' He watched for my reaction.

'A week? Are you trippin'?' I blurted out.

Sleeper began to laugh loudly at me. 'It's funny, you know. Prey said that you'd stress over that part.' He controlled his laughter. 'Don't worry about a thing, kid. You'll be staying at my gaff here in London.'

'A week though,' I sighed whilst staring at him. 'We got shit that needs taking care of back home.'

'Prey told me to tell you that he's going to take care of things personally for you. You won't miss out on anything. C'mon, Chopper… we both know what he's like. If he says stay put, then that's what you do. All right, kid?'

'Sweet then, mate,' I finally gave in. It was useless arguing, knowing he was right. 'Look, you know it's not that I don't appreciate it, Sleeper: I do. It's just—'

He cut me off. 'No need to explain how it is: I know, mate. Look, Chopper, I'll do my best to get you lads the best possible return that I can. Twenty per cent gets kicked to me of course.' Sleeper watched for my reaction, as he knew that it was way over the top. But he also knew that we had our backs to the wall.

Gazing at him and smirking, I said, 'Whatever, Sleeper. Sweet, mate.

Besides which, I'd taken to Sleeper almost straight away – well, almost. There was that look in his eyes. I knew that he could be counted upon, but by the same token I also knew that if I were to ever cross him it would be the last mistake I ever made.

The score had turned out to be a lot bigger than we'd ever expected. Sleeper's contact was this cockney arse (also dripping in gold) called Trevor. He was a proper cockney, and it was safe to say that I took an instant dislike to him. However, he did have the cash for all the gear. Trevor ran a large wholesale warehouse just outside of Lewisham, which was supposedly legit, but you got the feeling that his custom was probably as dodgy as he was.

All in all though, we managed to pull back almost £30,000. And that was *after* Sleeper took out his 20 per cent. We knew the gear to be worth a hell of a lot more, but it was the best that we were going to get at such short notice. Besides which, it had taken Sleeper almost an hour of bartering with Trevor for that price. The cockney arse had wanted to give us next to nothing for it.

Plus we still had the Technics that Sleeper wouldn't allow Trevor to have, saying he would get a better return elsewhere. We reckoned it was more that he wanted his friend in Brixton to have first option on them.

As we left Trevor's, another of Sleeper's associates had arrived. No introductions were made. Only Sleeper communicated with him; the three of us just watched as he clambered into the removal van and started her up. That would be the last we would ever see of the removal van or its contents ever again.

Sleeper just winked at us. 'Nothing but a lump of charcoal by tonight, lads.' He smiled knowingly. 'C'mon on then, you lot. Let's get you back to mine.'

'Where's that then, Sleeper? Your gaff, that is?' I asked him.

'It's right in Central London. You have been to London before, haven't you?' he asked, looking a little bemused at our confused faces.

We all shook our heads. 'Nah, mate. We're pure Mancs,' Scotty stated proudly.

'Manc scallies, that's what you lot are,' he laughed.

'So you gonna show us your manor then, Guv'nor?' Kezlo enquired, attempting to mimic Trevor's accent. We all laughed.

'God yeah. I can't believe you lot ain't been down here before.' He looked at us all and laughed. 'You do realise it's the capital, don't you?'

'Nah, mate,' I stated, smiling at him. 'That's just what you like to think it is. Manchester is the centre of everything, mate.'

He roared out in laughter. 'We'll see, boys, we'll see,' he said, opening up the car for us to get in.

On the way to Sleeper's I stayed quiet, just thinking about last night's events as they raced through my mind. Truth was, it had been the first time I'd even given any thought to the dead security guard. I wondered if they'd found his body yet. They would obviously have discovered the fact that Rasheed's had been robbed.

I was wondering just how well we'd covered our tracks. I'd acted fast without giving much thought to anything other than getting away and buying us as much time as possible. Although I had to admit, in all honesty, that I felt nothing towards the security guard. But I was not sure whether I wasn't feeling anything due to the fact that it hadn't hit me properly yet.

But it probably wasn't that. Truth be known, I felt pretty normal considering the circumstances. But I think that that scared me a little more than the fact I had actually taken another person's life the previous night.

Scotty and Kezlo hadn't mentioned it either. I reckon that they'd laid it to rest for now. Well, at least until we had a clearer picture of what was going to happen.

My mind raced with what prospects we faced if they were on to us. I knew that I had quite a bit of money stashed away back in town. We had also made a good bit of cash from the score last night.

Although not sure how well off the other two were, I also knew that that would not matter. If we were faced with the fact we had to leave the country and go somewhere, then I'd see them both all right.

But the thought of having to leave Manchester, never mind the bloody country, actually scared the hell out of me. The last thing I wanted was to move away from Manchester. But there was the possibility that we'd have no choice. Well, myself more so than the other two, of course.

There was nothing we could do now; it had all been done. All we could do now was keep our fingers crossed and wait to hear from Prey. I made a decision right there and then that I'd do my best to try and not think about it until we knew more. One thing was for sure though – it wasn't going to be an easy task, to say the least.

Suddenly Sleeper broke the silence. 'All right then, you little scallies – we're here,' he announced, easing the car into a parking space.

As we all clambered out of the vehicle we gazed around with open mouths. 'Fuck me. It's big houses round 'ere, ain't it, Sleeper,' Scotty said, in response to the view.

Kezlo laughed. 'You think that any gaff is big if it ain't a flat.'

Looking around at the large old buildings surrounding me, I had to admit that I was very impressed. I'd been so used to housing estates, blocks of endless flats and high rises. This had a certain class about it, I had to admit.

'You live 'ere, Sleeper? Whereabouts's this?'

'It's Marylebone, Chopper. Central London, mate.'

'Sure beats Hulme,' Scotty exclaimed.

I stared at him, then, suddenly defensively, snapped, 'Yeah, but that's ar' back yard, mate. It's where we're from. Always remember that.'

'That's the truth, brother,' Kezlo also announced proudly.

Sleeper just laughed out loud. 'Hey, believe me, lads – London's full of shitholes and estates. I should know. I lived in them for long enough. C'mon, the apartment's down here,' he said, heading towards some basement stairs.

Sleeper's basement flat was fantastic: completely furnished with style, all the latest gear. This I liked immensely. And that's when Sleeper introduced us to his woman, Lisa.

She was something else to look at. She was over six foot easily, with the most gorgeous thick black curly hair that was casually tied up upon her head and held in place with pencils. Her figure was slim. Basically, Lisa was stunning. She exuded casual unselfconsciousness about this. I'll openly admit right here and now that I was bowled over by her instantly. Nobody of the opposite sex – and I mean nobody – has ever had that kind of effect on me.

'So these are our guests, eh Sleeper?' She smiled warmly, winning us all over instantaneously. Jeez, I thought maybe *I'd* died the previous night – not the security guard – and had somehow found my way to heaven. 'Hello there, lads. I'm Lisa.'

I didn't even need to look at the other two, who I'm sure were as taken with Lisa as I was. Sleeper made the introductions, watching our gawping expressions as he did so with a little smile on his face, before showing us to our rooms. Scotty and Kezlo had a shared room, and I was given my own double room.

Sleeper did exactly as he said he would, taking the best of care of us. Thinking about it though, you could see that he was actually enjoying it. Both he and Lisa seemed to enjoy having us about the place. He still couldn't get his head round the fact that we'd never been to London before.

With that in mind, the two of them took us all over, showed us the sights, so to speak. They took us into the West End, shopping and into Soho, which was proper mad. There were peep-shows and gay bars everywhere; sex shops offering all kinds of weird and wonderful contraptions; girls readily available in upstairs flats.

London was all right – but it was just too bleedin' big though. It took forever to try and drive anywhere. If you weren't driving, then you had to use the Underground. And that was a nightmare in itself.

Sleeper took us over to Brixton to meet his guy over there, the one he wanted to sell the Technics to. We arrived at the Boom-BasticSounds record store. We were introduced to the owner of the store whose name was 'Eazy'.

Now, I've seen some big guys in the past, but nothing that prepared me for this character. He was a huge man. His head was just... Well, it was just so big and so round and shiny. Indeed, it actually resembled a huge bowling ball. But despite his imposing appearance, I don't think I'd ever come across a more sound guy. As soon as he spoke in that deep, resonating voice, and automatically laughed straight afterwards, he reassured us all that he was more than all right. Yet as friendly as he came across, his mammoth frame was so imposing, I decided that I'd never like to bear witness to his anger.

Kezlo and Eazy were like two lost brothers who'd just found one another again. We'd all been sat in the back of the shop for a couple of hours now, just chilling out, listening to tunes. Eazy was into exactly the same sort of music that we all listened to, and with Kezlo in his store, rooting through his stock, he resembled a kid on Christmas Day opening his presents.

'So you already got these ones, Kezlo?' Eazy's large voice boomed.

'For pure time now, Eazy. Between the three of us, we got ar'selves a proper nice collection.' He looked enthusiastically at the two of us, smiling away, all excited. 'What else you got for us?'

I couldn't help but laugh out loud at the way these two were carrying on. 'Have you seen these two, Sleeper?' I said, passing the freshly rolled spliff to him.

'I know. Eazy thinks that he's the only one who brings this shit into the country. Doesn't realise that you can buy imports elsewhere.' He smiled at his friend, who looked up at the mention of his name. 'Kezlo sure seems to know his shit though,' he added.

'Tell us about it. We got this set-up back at ar's, you can't get him off it,' Scotty said. 'Both me and Chopper bought it pure time ago. Got to admit though, it was already starting to gather dust when Kezlo arrived on the scene.' He drew back deeply on his spliff, allowing the smoke to drift aimlessly above his head.

'So are you going to take all of them, Kezlo?' Eazy responded enthusiastically.

'Of course. You got some old tunes in 'ere I've been after for ages. Besides, Scotty and Chopper will be buying with me also, won't you?' he said, turning to us.

'Is that right, Kezlo? Why the fuck me and Scotty always putting bees in to buy records when it's only you who fucks about with them?' I laughed, joking with him; we always split the cost of it. Well, we had to. If we didn't, who else would put our tapes together for us, eh?'

Scotty laughed, getting in on the joke. 'Yeah... Fuck you, Kezlo. Pay for them yourself.'

'C'mon, lads.' He stared at us with what can only be described as pleading in his eyes. 'I owe Eazy a small fortune 'ere, lads. And they'll be great additions to ar' collection.' He was not seeing the joke.

'You heard any of this Detroit or Chicago house music that's being imported at the moment, Kezlo?' Eazy enquired.

Kezlo looked at him. 'Don't you think you've already got me trying to spend all of my dough, Eazy?'

The afternoon carried on like this until it was time to close the store. Between the three of us we spent a small fortune in there that day, although Eazy did sort us out discount-wise, big time. The house material that Eazy supplied was also very good. We'd never really listened to any of it before. It was kind of different from our usual taste in music.

That evening, Eazy took us to some of the estates to show us the pieces down that way. We all came to the conclusion that we'd have to return to show them how to really bomb a wall properly. Saying that though, I couldn't honestly remember the last piece that Scotty or I had done. I knew that against my will, Kezlo still went out in the middle of the night now and again, and the next day new pieces would appear on the estate. I knew that he still loved all of that side of things.

By the time we left that night, Eazy was sorry to see his 'bleedin' northern scallies' leave, Kezlo more so than us two, I think, as they both appeared to share the same passions in life. However, we all promised to keep in touch no matter what happened.

That was hoping that everything was all right back home. Prey still hadn't phoned and it was Thursday already. I was becoming more than a little anxious to find out what had happened, but Prey had left instructions with Sleeper not to contact him and that he would contact us when the time was right.

After a whole week and the arrival of the weekend, we were beginning to long for Manchester. Don't get me wrong: London was all right. It was just so big though, and everything moved too fast. I kept thinking to myself that these damn cockneys would all end up having heart attacks.

Prey still hadn't called though. Sleeper just kept reassuring me that we shouldn't worry. He told us all that he was actually enjoying us being there, as was Lisa. That part, he said, he really enjoyed, as it kept her from nagging him so much. We were told that we were welcome to stay as long as it took for things to cool off back home.

I mean, it wasn't that we didn't appreciate it: we truly did. The truth was, though, that none of them had spoken about the events of the previous Saturday night, and to be honest, I didn't think we ever would, unless it was absolutely necessary. But not knowing anything was starting to take its toll on me.

Being in London also meant we'd seen no local news. We kept watching the main news, but nothing came up. Surely if there was anything, it'd be on local news.

The following Wednesday arrived and so too did the call we'd all been waiting for. I remember thinking impatiently that it was about time too.

Sleeper answered the call, talking with Prey for a short while. 'Chopper, you better take the call in my bedroom, mate.'

As I stared at the telephone on Sleeper and Lisa's bedside table, I was filled with an array of conflicting feelings. One side of me was happily overwhelmed by the call; the other side was full of dread as to what the news would be.

Without another thought I quickly grabbed the receiver. 'Prey,' I answered cautiously.

'You all right, Chopper? How you and the lads doing, then? Is Sleeper taking good care of you?'

'Yeah, double sweet, mate. Look, I need—'

He stopped me. 'Hey – sorry I've not called you. I just wanted to be sure of everything before phoning you, that's all.'

'We're all itching to get back to the yard, y'know… How's things been?' I asked cautiously.

He just laughed down the line. 'Well, you better get your arses back then if you're missing it so much, Chopper.'

I held my breath. 'So it's all sound, Prey?'

He was still laughing. 'I tell you what, Chopper: if you lads had planned it, you probably couldn't have done a better job. I tell you, Chopper, I reckon some fucker up there looks down over you, boy.'

I found most of the week's anxiety ebbing away. Things began to sound a little better. 'So are we in the clear? More to the point, Prey, am I all right or what?'

'Just listen to this, Chopper. The guy worked for Wilson Securities over in Salford.' He chuckled at the information, confusing me. 'Well, check this out then – they hadn't done a tight background check on him. His name was Martin Grimes – Peter Martin Grimes. He'd blagged it with his middle name so to get the job. That's not the best bit either,' he laughed.

'What is then, Prey?'

'Well, to be honest there's a few things. Just bear with me 'ere, Chopper.' He sighed deeply before starting. 'Listen, you're not going to believe this. He just got out of Strangeways a couple of months back.'

'What the fuck for though?' I asked. This was becoming more interesting.

'Aggravated burglaries; several of them.' He roared with laughter at the mere thought of this. 'And, 'cos this firm is now in the limelight over what's gone down, the police do a check into all its personnel who are on the payroll there. Guess what they find. Over half the company's personnel has been convicted of one thing or another. Most of them cats done bird also,' he said, roaring even louder with laughter.

By now I was intrigued. 'C'mon, Prey… Tell me everything.'

'Well, it turns out that only a report of burglary and vandalism was called in. So none of the uniformed coppers even clocked all the blood. Apparently all they'd found to be strange was that the job obviously wasn't kids, so they didn't understand the vandalism.' He chuckled down the line.

'So anyway, it's not until that night they realise that this guard is missing. Apparently he was a guard for that entire area of warehouses, not just for that gaff. So when they realise he's missing, they immediately run a check on him and all the shit on him crawls out. So CID gets themselves involved now, as it's

Monday and they're back in the office after the usual weekend off. They reckon with this cat's background they're well onto a good lead to the score. As soon as they arrive though, they automatically clock the blood that you lads tried to cover up, albeit Rasheed's had someone try and clean that shit up. So the uniformed boys in blue somehow managed to miss this shit, although by that time forensics would have been pulling their hair out, as pretty much everything would have been destroyed. Evidence-wise, that is.' He was chuckling as he said this.

'So they found the body?' I asked, almost in a whisper.

'Yeah, almost immediately after they closed off the area on Monday. But check this out; it's been all over the fuckin' papers up 'ere. It seems that this guy was heavily into some of the main heads over that way – both for dough that he owed and gear that he'd taken on tick. He was a fucked-up character. So they rounded up half of fuckin' Salford. Obviously the police got their info through the usual snitches and grassing smackheads. You know, usually I hate them with a vengeance, only this time it looks as though they done us some good.'

'So how do you know we're clear?'

'Well, obviously they've got him tied into the robbery itself. Only now it's looking like things turned sore for him. You see, from what I hear, he owed a lot of dough out over that way to some pretty heavy characters. Looks like they're determined to catch the culprit over Salford way, Chopper. Like I said, you couldn't have planned it better if you tried,' he sniggered.

'You sure though, Prey?' I was still wary.

'Since you lads ain't been pulling down scores for a while, it doesn't even look like they got a connection to ar' yard. I tell you what, come back, and if things look a bit dodgy, then I'll ship you out again. That sound all right with you, Chopper?'

'All right, mate. Look, Prey, I just wan—'

'Don't, Chopper. You're like family, mate. You'd do the same for me, ar'kid. I know you would.'

'Cheers, Prey. For everything, brother.'

'Couple of other things though, Chopper. First off, there are precisely four people still around who know exactly what went down. Now that stays that way; I mean it. As far as everyone back 'ere knows, you've been out of town doing a job for me. That goes for Sean also. Nobody else knows shit about it. We never bring it up, unless it's an absolute necessity. You hear me?' he asked sternly.

'Crystal, mate,' I replied in a mockney accent. He laughed.

'Just one other thing I need to know,' he said. 'How are you holding up, ar'kid? I mean, after all, it was down to you. How's your head coping?' His voice held a softer tone than usual.

'You know what, Prey, I have thought about it, but I'm not bothered.' I sighed with pure relief at being able to talk about just how I felt. Also, hearing the words out loud made me feel a little better, so I continued. 'I don't want to come across as some cold-hearted tosser 'ere, Prey. But I was backed into a corner. So I didn't hesitate. Not for a single second. I don't feel sorry, because it was a case of him or me at that moment. He should have just stayed out of it and not gone shining his fuckin' light into my face like he did. I'm fine, mate, really I am.'

'That's the cold truth you speak there, brother, I tell you. You did what you had to do without hesitating. That's a true lion's heart you got there, Chopper. You know that… true lion, brother. All right then, after this, like I said – no mention of it to anyone.'

I felt a huge burden lift from my shoulders. 'See you soon, Prey.'

'Chopper, just put Sleeper back on the line. I'll get him to bell me when he knows what time you'll be arriving. You take it easy now, Chopper.' He laughed joyously, obviously pleased that we were to return home to Manchester.

And at that very moment I knew one thing for certain: he wasn't the only one.

EIGHT

There was good reason to be lying there in bed that morning, enjoying the heavily loaded skunk spliff. The date was 10 August 1987: my eighteenth birthday had finally arrived.

Something had triggered a memory of the incident that had happened almost a year ago now. It was very rare that my thoughts wandered back to it, but something Prey had said to me back then about having a true lion's heart had stuck with me. And as I lay there smoking away, I'd been thinking of my star sign, which happened to be Leo. It must have been that which had triggered the memory.

Maybe. Or maybe with it being my birthday, I was just thinking about my life or just life in general. I was brimming with thoughts of just how crazy my life had been already, the most significant thing being that I was only just was turning eighteen.

We'd always lived our lives to the full. Life, in its own perverse way, had been good to me. We survived day to day by any means necessary.

Although the police had never come near us on the Cheetham Hill score, I had to admit I'd been more than a little paranoid for a while when we returned to Hulme. As far as I knew, no one had ever been prosecuted for the murder of the security guard.

Prey had heard that they pulled some young Salford lads in for it though. Some snitch had given them in. The case had baffled the hell out of the cops. And by the time they arrested these lads, it was obvious they were merely clutching at straws. Their briefs had seen to it that the case was kicked into touch before any of the taxpayers' money was wasted on a trial. So it was just thrown out through lack of evidence.

The last anybody had heard about it was that it was an 'on-going investigation', as they liked to put it. The truth of it was that they probably didn't care. He'd been a crook anyway. However, they still had to appear to be doing something in the public's and the guard's family's eyes.

Despite that score getting so messed up, the three of us still longed to pull them. So around six months later, we began to organise them on a regular basis. The scores really got our juices flowing; none of us could truly explain why. The rush that we experienced when pulling them off was almost better than sex. Almost.

None of us needed the bees these days. Not since way back in the day now. But between the three of us, the money was really only part of it. Obviously it was a nice bonus to have, but in truth it was the adrenalin rush that we associated them with that did it.

Business on the estate continued to expand each week. Since starting the initial operation over two years ago, it had expanded beyond any of our expectations. Our street crew had almost trebled in size. However, it was Jonah who still controlled them. And he continued doing a very good job of it indeed.

Scotty and Kezlo were still the ones responsible for the distribution side. I liked to think of myself as a general manager, so to speak. And apart from Prey, there was only myself who knew how things actually worked with our side of the operation. There had been so many changes since the beginning. In my own way, I felt proud of what had been accomplished with business.

Earlier that year, some of the younger lads from Moss Side had tried to muscle in on our operation, tempt trade away from us. We hadn't stood for any of it. They had their own area to control and we all knew that, them included. So in that way it was an expected issue.

You see, violence was associated with the business we were involved in. You could hardly turn to the local authorities if someone was trying to take over your business, could you? Not a chance. The only thing that you could do, and had to do, was to deal with it yourselves.

All of us were in and out of battles for months. Then they'd made the fatal mistake of trying to muscle in on Prey's smack business. That was when things really heated up. Prey had taken about as much as he was prepared to. Up until this point I'd kept control of the weed side. He'd wanted to step in when it first started to happen, but I'd kept on telling him we were capable of sorting it, which, I honestly believed, we were more than capable of achieving. But when they tried to hit the smack side of the business, Prey lost his patience. He hit back with serious force.

And to cut a long story short let's just say that more than enough people ended up in the emergency ward and coroner's office around that time. It wasn't doing any of us any favours, as it was attracting a lot of extra heat to both areas from the police.

So eventually some of the older heads from over that way sorted it out with Hulme. After negotiating a deal with Prey for an end to the violence, things calmed down almost instantaneously.

The trouble with the younger lads over that way was that they didn't respect that they had to work their way up through the business. The main problem with Moss Side was that different crews controlled different areas. So the younger lads had tried to move in over our way to compete. There had been no way that I or any of my crew were going to give up what we'd assembled. There was more chance of hell freezing over before I was going to allow that to happen.

Actually, talking of business, that was another thought. Prey had some new business he said he needed to discuss with me later on in the day. We had to go and meet him around five o'clock. He said that he couldn't go over details until then.

As I lay there, I wondered what it could be. Could it be something new? Maybe some new contacts? A new supplier he'd discovered? New product? Ah, God knows what it was. I suppose I'd find out later on. I just hoped he wouldn't keep me long though, as the lads and I had arranged to go to Seventh Avenue tonight. A DJ from the local radio station named Stu Allen, who ran an excellent hip hop show each week, was playing a set there tonight. And one thing was for sure: it was going to be a kicking night.

Still drawing back on the potent spliff, I felt its effects slowly clouding both my lungs and mind. I really loved to have a smoke before considering leaving the warmth of my bed, no matter what time of the day it was.

As I continued to exhale the thick stream of smoke, I could

hear immense clattering, thumping and even crashing sounds from the direction of the kitchen. It would be Scotty in there for sure. He always did this to try and get me out of my bed, so that I'd make breakfast. Seeing as I was the only one who could actually cook anything edible, they both loved it when I cooked breakfast for them. Or any meals for that matter.

Although I had to admit that I loved doing it. It was a real passion. However, passion didn't always equal talent. Not that anybody seemed to complain when I did cook for them.

The pounding continued, although I was doing my best to ignore it. Glancing over at the bedside clock, I noticed that it had just turned 11.40. I hadn't been out the previous night, as I'd been busy with business all day and was completely wasted by the time I finished with it all. Fridays were always the busiest time for me, being just before the weekend.

Just then, I heard a girl's high-pitched voice nattering away to Scotty incessantly. Another one he'd obviously managed to pull last night. He seemed to manage it with confidence, heavily sprinkled with bullshit. It had to be said, though, there was no stopping this guy. He averaged at least a different girl a week. On occasions it had been known for him to manage at least *five* in a single week.

I'd never seen anybody like him. He just had this uncanny way of breaking down their defences and saying exactly what it was they wanted to hear. Well, it had to be something like that as he wasn't any oil painting, that was for sure. I began laughing to myself at the thought of my best friend's antics.

I tried to remember who the last girl was that I'd been with. And to be honest, no one sprung to mind. I was generally pretty out of it when it occurred. This meant that each experience was usually nothing more than just a blur by the morning. I wasn't bothered though, as I was still having too much of a great time day in, night out with the lads to care in any way about finding myself a full-time girlfriend.

If it happened, then it happened. That was always the way it had been with me. Although I was still trying to remember who the last one was, and nobody sprang to mind. It must have been because it'd been so long. Well, either that or this spliff that I was smoking was messing with my head. My thing was casual sex. As it was with Scotty… only he couldn't get enough casual sex.

Rolling over, I placed the spliff end in the ashtray. Then, rolling back onto my back, I began staring mindlessly at the ceiling. Just as I was beginning to drift off into a world of my own, the bedroom door crashed open. Scotty and Kezlo came bombarding through singing 'Happy Birthday to You'.

Scotty was holding a plate. 'All right, Chopper… 'Ere'are then; we made you breakfast in bed for your birthday, ar'kid.' He proudly handed me the plate.

A single, unbuttered, burnt, sorry-looking piece of toast was all that was on the plate. 'You couple of twats,' I laughed.

Kezlo stopped singing. 'Sorry, mate, that's the best we could manage,' he smirked.

'All right, lads. I'll get up and make breakfast.' I shook my head at them. 'How many for *this* time, Scotty? Just the three of us, or four again?'

Kezlo grinned at me. 'Nah, mate. Five. Even I got lucky last night.'

'Yeah, bad fuckin' luck, Kezlo,' laughed Scotty. 'You sure she hasn't got a dick? She sure looked like a bloke to me last night.'

'Fuck you, Scotty,' grumbled Kezlo as the two of us began laughing at him.

He quickly glanced over his shoulder to check no one was there. 'She was a bit of minger actually, eh? But hey – a shag is shag, eh Chopper?'

'She was more than just minger, mate,' said Scotty, pulling his face at the thought. 'In fact, make that breakfast for three, Chop. I'm gonna go kick them out now so it's just the lads. Besides which, I honestly don't think that my bacon and eggs would stay down if I had to eat it whilst staring at Kezlo's bit of skirt from last night.'

'Twat,' Kezlo grinned as he watched me shaking my head.

'Sound, lads,' was all that I could manage, as I began pulling on my Adidas tracksuit bottoms with a little smile upon my face.

NINE

S cotty had insisted that the three of us get a taxi to The Parkway pub, which was located, funnily enough, on the Parkway that led straight out of Manchester onto the M56. It seemed pretty stupid to me, especially as we were only to quickly meet Prey about some business he wanted to discuss before heading into town for the evening. I mean, we'd all passed our driving tests shortly after turning seventeen. We'd all passed first time round, which was a bonus. I reckon driving about in all those nicked motors whilst growing up had obviously helped us somewhat. All we had to do whilst being tested was control that wild streak inside of us. Scotty had been the first to pass, rushing out that very same day to buy himself a red Escort XR3I. Kezlo had been next to purchase his: a black VW Golf GTI. Both were, it had to be said, very nice motors.

But when my time came, Prey had taken me over to see this silver 3 series BMW, which his mate was selling over in Didsbury. I fell in love with it as soon as I set my eyes on it. It had reminded me of Sleeper's silver Mercedes Benz, although it was nowhere near as slick. But hey, we all have to start somewhere. And I supposed for my first vehicle of choice it would do.

So it seemed very strange that we'd taken a taxi, seeing as we weren't staying at The Parkway all night and would soon be heading straight back over this way where we could have quite easily dumped our motors before our night out.

As the taxi eased itself into the car park of The Parkway, we exited the vehicle and thanked our driver, Frank. The other two were already making their way to the door. As always, through paranoia or sheer caution, I found myself looking around the car park. There were certainly enough cars about, but something just wasn't right; I wasn't sure what it was. Then it dawned upon me. The establishment itself was extremely quiet, especially for a

Saturday afternoon. Also, no lights appeared to be on as the other two disappeared through the side doors leading to the smaller pool area of the bar.

As I followed the others through the doors, something caught my eye. There was a silver Mercedes, parked over in the far corner of the car park. I simply smiled to myself as the memories of Sleeper, Eazy and Lisa all came flooding back. Walking through into the bar, however, I saw that only Scotty and Kezlo were standing there.

The place was deserted. There wasn't even anyone behind the bar.

'What the fuck... Where's Prey? In fact, where the fuck is anybody?'

Scotty just stared at me. 'I'm fucked if I know, Chopper.'

''Ere'are, lads, let's check the other bar out. You know, the main one,' Kezlo said, heading off towards the partition doors.

I wasn't holding out too much hope. The place was deserted. There wasn't a sound to be heard. But as the other two swung open the doors, there was an almighty yell of 'Happy Birthday, Chopper!'

The cheers were deafening and the room was filled to capacity with just about everybody that I knew. All of them were cheering as I stood there, motionless. I actually think that I was in some sort of state of shock.

I turned back to the other two. 'You couple of twa—' was about all that I managed as they both began lifting me up onto their shoulders, above their heads.

It was all very uplifting. The atmosphere was great. A heavy bassline suddenly kicked in and sounds flowed from the large system in the corner of the room. Almost immediately everybody began dancing and jumping around. I recognised everybody from the estate, plus many more. People from all over town, and even Salford, were here. I still couldn't get my head around what they'd done. Just then, Scotty and Kezlo began to lower me to the floor, and there was Prey with open arms, one hand clutching a bottle of Möet champagne.

'Happy birthday, kid,' he announced, grabbing hold of me in an unexpected show of emotion, hugging me in front of everybody.

'I don't know what to say, Prey.'

He popped open the bottle of champagne, froth spraying everywhere.

'Let the party begin!' he yelled out loud, as the entire place erupted in cheers once again.

This felt real good for sure. Just then, somebody touched my shoulder. As I turned to see just who it was, I was met with a warm, moist pair of lips that almost made my heart melt as I let them take control of my own.

Now this felt really good. My eyes had closed automatically as I enjoyed the moment immensely. Suddenly the moist lips moved to my ear and I felt the warm breath as the voiced whispered, 'Happy birthday, Chopper.'

'Lisa!' I exclaimed in recognition. 'What the—'

'Oi, scally.' Sleeper was stood there. 'Get yer filthy mitts off my woman, will you?'

'What the fuck,' I exclaimed once again, at ease at the little smile he gave me to let me know all was cool. 'Yes, Sleeper. How's it going? What you doing 'ere?' I was still taken aback by all this. I was so shocked that I was sure that it presented itself quite openly in my voice.

He just grinned as Prey refilled my glass, smiling along with one of his closest friends. 'You look a little bewildered, Chopper.'

'C'mon, scally,' said Sleeper, 'you honestly didn't think we'd miss this one, did you? Eighteen now. Young man, and all that nonsense, eh? C'mon, we've got another surprise for you.' Lisa linked her arm through mine, giving me a little sensation that I couldn't quite describe.

We made our way through the crowd of dancing people towards the DJ box. The DJ was playing some very fine tunes indeed. As he began to turn round I laughed out loud – for it was the unmistakable mammoth frame of Eazy.

'How's it going, Chopper, you little scally boy?' Even with music as loud as it was, his voice boomed over the heavy bass effortlessly.

'Yeah, Eazy... you all right, big man,' I said as we both shook hands.

'So you enjoying the surprise, Chopper?' Lisa asked.

'Fuck yes!' I spluttered out enthusiastically. 'I honestly can't believe what you guys have gone and done. This is well top.'

As the party began to really start kicking I sought out Prey and found him purchasing more champagne. 'Listen, Prey man, I just want to say thanks a lot. You know this is well sound, mate. Double sweet, I tell you.'

'Don't just thank me, brother. Your crew helped put it together also, y'know.'

I looked around for Scotty and Kezlo and, spotting them both, yelled over at them. They both raised their glasses to me as I grinned back at them. Everyone was dancing and enjoying themselves.

The whole crew from the estate must have been there. And I was more than thankful for this. Though I did wonder just who the hell was taking care of business back at the estate.

Jonah was heading towards me with Sharon by his side. 'All right, Chopper?' he asked, shaking my hand.

Sharon gave me a birthday kiss. She sure had grown up over the last couple of years. In fact it was pretty safe to say that she was a right little stunner now. 'Happy birthday, Chopper.'

'Thanks, Sharon,' I smiled at her. 'You're looking fine tonight.'

'In't it, mate,' laughed Jonah as he winked at me knowingly.

'How's business been this last week, Jonah?'

'Sweet as always, Chopper. You know I always take good care of things.'

'That's the truth,' I laughed.

'Look, Sharon, why don't you go powder your nose or some-thing?' said Jonah. 'I need to speak with Chopper alone for a minute.' He kissed her, and she scowled at him in a fun-loving way.

We both watched her leave, blatantly shaking her backside at the two of us as she did so.

'What's up then, Jonah?'

'Nowt, mate. It's just I've got a new idea for the business. Y'know, a kind of expansion, so to speak.' He was looking at me all serious.

'Tell me more, mate,' I said, somewhat intrigued.

'Not tonight, mate,' said Jonah, knowing that he'd piqued my interest. 'We'll talk this week. Prey also. It might be nothing, Chopper. But then again, mate, it could be worth top bees, mate.'

Just then Prey appeared.

'What could be worth top bees, Jonah?' he asked.

'You hear everything when there's money involved, don't you, Prey?'

'Of course I do, lads,' he shrugged.

'You want to hear it now?' Jonah looked at the two of us.

Prey just looked at him. 'Nah, mate. Save it, kid. It's Chopper's birthday tonight. We'll talk this week sometime. All right, Jonah?'

'Sound, lads,' he smiled just as Sharon returned to us.

Prey turned to me. 'C'mon, Chopper.' He winked at me. 'I've got a little something for us to try, mate.' Just then, Sean appeared.

'Knieldy says you're looking for us, boss.'

'Yes, mate. And stop calling me boss; y'know I hate it,' Prey scowled at him, heading for the main doors.

'Yes, boss,' Sean laughed.

The three of us piled into Prey's racing green 5 series BMW.

'What's up, Prey?' I asked from the back seat.

'Sleeper give us this to try,' he declared, producing a snappy bag filled with what looked to be small pieces of broken white cheddar cheese.

'Is that what I think it is, mate?' Sean enquired.

Prey stared at him. 'It certainly fuckin' is, Sean.'

'What the fuck is it?' I wanted to know more. I was more than a little confused.

He turned to face me in the back seat. 'This, ar'kid, is pure, 100 per cent crack cocaine. You lads want to try some?' He stared from Sean to me. 'No pipes or nothin', just spliff it up,' he smiled, watching for our reactions.

'Fuck yes, mate,' responded Sean enthusiastically.

'Why the fuck not,' I added, not entirely sure just what it was I was agreeing to.

'You already tried it, Prey?' Sean enquired eagerly.

'You both smoked charlie in spliffs before, right?' he asked, watching as we both nodded in agreement.

'And?' Sean asked.

'Well, times that buzz by about twenty and you're about half-way there. Sleeper says it's sweet to spliff it, but that it can get a bit messy when you're piping it.' As he said this, he gave the two of us stern looks, which sent a slight shiver through me.

'You two listen up though: this gear is strictly treat gear. You both hear me?' He stated this firmly as he broke the pieces of rock into the tobacco.

'Sound, Prey. Whatever you say,' I told him, with Sean nodding in agreement with me.

Prey completed rolling the spliff and lit the twisted end. He held the smoke in his lungs for which seemed like an eternity.

'Arhhh… Yes… Now that *is* double sweet, lads,' he sighed as the stream of potent-smelling smoke drifted from both his open mouth and flared nostrils, filling the car with its toxic density.

'Damn that smells good, Prey,' Sean said as he took the burning spliff from him.

I sat there and watched as their eyes began to blur from the drugs.

''Ere'are, mate, give us a go then,' I said eagerly to Sean.

As he passed to spliff back to me, I noticed that he was smiling foolishly away at me like a court jester who'd just got his biggest laugh of the day. I eagerly began to draw on the crack-loaded spliff.

Instantaneously my head began spinning. That's when my body began shaking, and believe me when I tell you this – it sure felt good. But the most distinctive thing about the drug had to be the taste. Drawing back ponderously again on the spliff, I continued to try and fathom out where I'd tasted it before. Damn – just where the hell had I tasted that taste? Although, in time, I soon came to realise that if you knew where you tasted it before, then you'd be a very rich man indeed. For the taste was unique. And that I found to be part of its attraction.

'What do you reckon, Chopper?'

Smiling away to myself, my mind floating, I glanced at Prey and felt my eyes half closing as the drug took complete control of me.

'I reckon we've just had a glimpse into what the future holds for us, mate,' I responded, as my whole body accelerated with the sensation.

'In't it, Chop,' Sean merely managed.

'Look, some of the lads over in Moss Side are already starting to knock this shit out,' Prey said. 'What we'll do is just see how well they do, then decide if it's gonna be right for us lads or not. This gear's just a little bit too nice. D'ya know what I mean?' he added.

'That's the truth,' I smiled, passing back the spliff to him.

My blood was rushing so much I honestly felt as if it would out-run itself at any moment. Not that I cared. For at that very moment in time the only things that mattered were the contents of the spliff and the bag that was nestled in Prey's lap. It had to be said, this gear was fantastic. I absolutely loved it. And all that aside, I still knew 100 per cent where Prey was coming from though. It was a bit *too* nice.

The three of us didn't return to The Parkway until nearly eleven o'clock. We were completely caned from the rocks we'd consumed. I was totally wired. Although I felt in total control of myself. I was filled with unparalleled confidence, striding through the crowd like a man with balls the size of watermelons. I'd lost count of just how many we'd smoked. One was being smoked as another was being rolled. Not that I was complaining in any way.

'Where you been, Chopper?' Scotty asked as I arrived back at the bar.

'Just outside with Prey and Sean, mate.'

'You looked fucked, boy,' he informed me.

'I am,' I replied confidently.

I began to rock to the thumping bass of the music. Kezlo had taken control of the decks, pumping out a large selection of both old and new tunes. As I rocked back and forth, I suddenly became aware that someone was watching me closely.

Turning to my left, I observed a large group of girls dancing. There was this one girl who really stood out from the group. She looked to be around the same age as me and was very petite in size.

But the thing that was most striking about her was her gorgeous blonde hair, pulled up on top of her head. She continued to smile at me. All the while, she never missed a beat, continuing to dance to the music.

Feeling especially confident, I resolved to wander over to her. Drawing closer, I noticed she had the most gorgeous green eyes I'd ever seen. Her lips pouted slightly and she had what looked to be a perfect body. My eyes just wouldn't leave her breasts, which swayed along to the music with her. In short, she was stunning. It was all I could think of as I drew close to her.

Standing there, I returned her smile. 'You all right there?'

'Sure am,' she smiled as I felt my knees go weak. 'This is a well top party.'

Damn, she even had nice teeth. Was there anything wrong with this girl? This was way, way too good to be true.

'I'm Chopper.'

'I know who you are. It's your birthday, right?' she said, still smiling and continuing to dance about seductively.

'Oh yeah, so it is,' I laughed. 'Anyway, how come you're 'ere? I ain't seen you about before.'

She glanced over to one of the coffee-coloured girls dancing alongside her. I recognised her immediately. 'I know Karen. She's one of Prey's friends. I came with her, kinda gate-crashed. Hope you don't mind.'

One of Prey's friends she'd said. I smiled at this. Karen was one of his 'sex kittens', as he liked to call them. 'Just here to satisfy my sexual desires… or perversions for that matter,' he used to tell me.

'What you grinning at, Chopper?' the girl suddenly asked. 'You're not having dirty thoughts, are you now?'

That last bit caught me a little off guard, but she was right though: I had been having those thoughts. I suddenly realised that I hadn't even asked her her name yet. 'I'm sorry, what's your name?'

She pouted those lips at me. 'What you sorry for, Chopper? Not asking me my name or those dirty thoughts you're having?'

This amused me; I was attracted to her open style. She was just being herself, and I was really beginning to take a liking towards her.

'Your name, I meant,' I said, laughing. 'I'm still holding on to those dirty thoughts though, until later. But the face has suddenly changed somewhat.' I winked cheekily at her.

'Oh yes, Chopper?' She winked back at me, blatantly taking the piss. 'I wonder whose face it's changed to, eh?'

'Well, hopefully we'll get to that answer later,' I said. 'But for now, how about a name to go with the dirty thought?'

She stepped forward, placing her right hand against my thigh. 'Confident tonight aren't we, Chopper.'

Her body began slithering up and down against my own as she continued to smile at me. She slid her hand against my inner thigh as she did so. God damn, this girl was something else. She was really getting me worked up. Just then she whispered into my ear. 'My name's Donna. That's if you're still interested, Chopper.' She smiled, dancing away from me seductively.

'Fuck yes,' I spluttered out at her like a complete idiot.

Suddenly her eyes dropped to my crotch area and her eyebrows rose slightly as she winked knowingly at me, giving a little click of the tongue. I suddenly became conscious of the erection she had given me. Looking at her as her body began to move in towards me again, Donna wrapped herself around me, kissing my gaping mouth both hard and passionately.

I somehow managed to calm my erection down. Although it wasn't easy, to say the least. That had never happened before to me. Ever! Although I have to admit it felt good.

The two of us continued to dance with each other, and became totally inseparable. We stayed together right into the early hours of the morning. I wasn't able to fathom out whether it was just effect of the drugs consumed earlier that evening or if this girl really was as good as I thought she was. I'd never been like this over a girl before.

The party began to quieten down as 5 a.m. approached. Donna's friend, Karen, walked over to where we were both sat. 'C'mon, girl... we got a taxi outside.'

I suddenly found myself protesting profoundly at the notion. 'Nah – fuck that shit. You're coming back to ar' gaff,' I said, with an almost pleading sound in my voice. Oh my God. What the... Damn, this wasn't right. What the hell was she doing to my head?

'I can't.' Donna just shook her head at me. 'I'm sorry, Chopper.'

'Awesome party, Chopper. Even if you didn't know about it, eh?' Karen said, but I wasn't listening to her. There were more pressing matters at hand.

Donna began to hand a piece of paper to me with something scribbled on it. 'Give us a call tomorrow, Chopper.'

'C'mon, Donna,' I said, that awful pleading sound in my voice again. Shit, this was very, very sad of me. I'd never acted this way before. Just what was going on?

Donna bent over to kiss me and began whispering into my ear. 'I really hope you ring me, Chopper... I enjoyed tonight.' She smiled at me.

'C'mon, please Donna.' This was becoming really sad now.

'Oh, Chopper, seriously: what you going to think of me if I go home and sleep with you like some cheap whore?' she said, kissing me once more before taking off with Karen. Those last words had hurt and the thing was, I honestly didn't even know why.

Sitting there alone... What the hell was she going on about? She wasn't some cheap whore. I didn't think that at all. And what would I think if she came back? Well, 'nice one' probably. What did she take me for anyway? This was all getting a bit weird now. And yes, I will say it again – this had never happened to me before!

Feeling all strange inside... What the hell had this bird done to me? I mean, that was it, she was just a bird... an ordinary girl. Right?

No, no, no. She *wasn't* just a bird at all. She couldn't be. No ordinary girl had left me feeling this way before.

What in Christ's name was going on? Why hadn't she just come back to mine? You know, like all the others had. Just what was happening to me? I was looking around in desperation for her to still be there for me, but of course she wasn't. She'd gone. Please, ladies and gentleman – Miss Donna whatever-her-name-is has just left the building!

I found myself observing Prey, who was stood over by the DJ box, staring at me. He just smiled and nodded at me in that knowing fashion of his as I shook my head. All I could think as I sat there all alone was what a great night tonight had been – but at the same time, what a very confusing night.

TEN

O ur mutual friends from the south had extended their stay for a further week at Prey's insistence. After the hospitality that we'd been shown in London, we obviously had to keep them as entertained as possible.

I'd not been able to get Donna off my mind since Saturday night, yearning anxiously to see her again. But despite that, the week had turned out to be a great one all the same. Prey really had his host-with-the-most head on the entire duration.

When the party had initially broken up last Saturday we'd originally headed for Prey's gaff, although I had maintained – very unconvincingly I might add – that I merely wanted to return straight home. I used the excuse that my head was well and truly hammered and that I just needed to make it to my bed in one piece.

And to be honest, I thought I was doing a pretty good job of it as Prey appeared to be nodding and sympathetically agreeing with my needs as he placed his hand upon my shoulder. But then he happily announced that if I wanted to return to our flat it wasn't a problem at all. And then went and invited everyone who was still up for it back there! Bastard!

It did kind of make sense though, as we had the Technics set up at ours. Though in all honesty I never used them any more. Scotty played about with them now and again. Kezlo though, was a completely different matter – you couldn't keep him off them. He was very good at it. He was constantly practising his mixing skills and trying to push his style and techniques to another level.

Both Scotty and I really admired this in Kezlo. Initially, we'd all wanted to get into it, but we just didn't have the patience or the devotion that Kezlo had.

Prey had set him up with a couple of guest DJ spots around town, as well as in just about every house, flat, squat and empty garage where he organised his private parties. In fact, wherever he could find a place to put together a party, he tried to have Kezlo DJ-ing there. Thus he had earned himself a good reputation around town over the last couple of years.

And so back at ours, the party had continued. Kezlo and Eazy took control of the decks. The two of them began to play alternative sets between them, with each of them doing their best to out-do the other. They began to have a little fun between themselves, by trying to put a track on that was a nightmare to mix into, so that real skill was needed to keep the momentum going. Despite trying their best to mess one another's sets up, they still maintained a bouncing atmosphere in the flat.

Although it was by then early Sunday morning, the place was rocking like it was still Saturday night in some club in town. All the crew and all the estate were still enjoying the party.

'You all right, mate?' Sleeper asked.

'Yes, mate. This is all double sound, y'know.'

Just then Prey appeared. 'You ready for a second go, Chopper?'

I knew exactly what he meant, so the three of us headed off to my bedroom, locking ourselves away for the next few hours. Between the three of us we continually smoked crack. And, as odd as it sounds, and as messed up as my head already was, the drugs were bringing me back round again. This really was messy gear to be getting involved in.

'What do you reckon of this shit, Chopper?' Sleeper enquired as he passed the smouldering spliff to me.

Smiling back at him I said, 'What do you think I think, mate? It's sound, mate. It's kinda like a much purer buzz that you get from it.' As I said this, the seemingly endless stream of smoke drifted from my nostrils and mouth.

''Ere'are, Chopper. Give us some more,' Prey smirked at me.

I looked over to Sleeper again. 'Is this shit big down your way or what, mate?'

'It's starting to take off now. I got one of Eazy's yardie boys going to show me how you cook it week after next.' He was grinning at us knowingly. 'Apparently that's where the real dough is in it. Shitloads of profit.'

'What was it like piping it, Sleeper?' Prey asked, sprawled all over my bed.

'That's the mad thing. Obviously, you've all heard about it through the media, and all those stories from the States. They reckon one pop and you're hooked.'

'And… what did you think?'

'Well, to tell you the truth, Chopper, I thought that it was the most manic buzz I've ever experienced. Real pure adrenaline buzz,' he laughed as he thought back to his experience. 'I even caned the whole lot to myself, couple of grams at least. The next day I didn't give a fuck though. Didn't even think about it. Fair enough, I caned what was there, probably would have caned even more as well if it had been there… but, nah, it was all right, you know.'

'Let's pipe it then,' I announced, enjoying the buzz that was possessing my entire body.

Suddenly Prey interjected. 'No, Chopper! I told you already, this is strictly treat gear – that's all. You hear me?'

'The chief's right, Chopper.' Sleeper mirrored Prey's glare. 'Look, us lads like to have a good time, but the truth is we all got business to take care of. Nothing should start to fuck that up. The truth is, you start going getting yourself all fucked up on any sort of gear whatsoever then it'll end in tears, mate. I should know that better than anybody, mate.'

'Why's that then?'

''Cause of his brother, Chopper,' Prey told me.

'Yeah, Chopper. Pete. That was ar'kid. Older brother at that,' Sleeper sighed as his eyes glazed slightly (drugs or emotion?). 'Well, he'd been heavily into the smack business for years. Bringing it into the country – the lot. Trouble was though, he picked himself up a habit along the way. Got hooked on the shit good and proper. Fucking stupid of him really, seeing as he ran smack into the country for years without ever getting pinched for it. Used to make a fortune from it.' Sleeper looked a little sad as he relayed the story.

'What happened to him?' I enquired, although uncertain that I wanted to hear the answer.

'He OD'ed on the shit,' he told me.

'Shit,' I responded, shaking my head. 'That's fucked up, Sleeper man… I'm sorry.'

Just then Prey laughed out loud, cutting straight through the dark atmosphere. 'Yeah… but not as fucked up as the Asian kid that Pete was involved with was.'

Sleeper then began to smirk also at whatever the two of them were thinking about right there and then. 'That's the truth, brother,' he said, looking at Prey knowingly.

'All right, so who or what was that about?' Now I was confused.

Prey grinned broadly at me as he began. 'Well, Pete was involved with this Asian kid from Woking. The story went that Ramed, or whatever the fuck his name was, wanted all the action for himself. He no longer felt the need for Pete as a partner. So the little cunt spiked the gear that was used for testing, knowing that Pete would be itching to try it.'

'And?' I asked, intrigued.

Sleeper continued. 'Well, I contacted Prey once I'd heard the full story, needing some help from out of London to avenge ar'kid's death. See, you don't know this, mate, but I'm a Northerner just like you, mate. The thing is, my family moved down to London when I was still only a teenager. I'd known Prey since we were kids from the estate.'

'You what! You're from Hulme, Sleeper?' I was shocked. He was from the North – and the estate?

'Nah, Chopper; Wythenshawe, mate. Prey's nan was good friends with mine. So we knew each other from back then. I'm a lot older than Prey, but I knew even back then that he'd turn out the way he has.'

Shaking my head at this latest revelation I said, 'So go on then. What happened to the Asian kid?'

Prey laughed out again. 'What happened? What fuckin' happened? Go on, tell him, Sleeper.'

Sleeper continued. 'Well, first off we tracked him down to his gaff in Woking. He lived on this estate; place looked like little fucking Asia or something. Fucking Asians everywhere there were. Anyway, the two of us broke into his gaff and waited for him to return. He returned home at around two in the morning and we ambushed him.'

Prey was still laughing. 'Yeah, Chopper. This cat completely crapped himself, mate. Especially once we tied him to the chair and Sleeper poured petrol all over him.'

Sleeper laughed out loud at the thought. 'It all got a bit sick after that, Chopper. We tortured him for hours. He wasn't going to have it easy. Pete certainly hadn't. Anyway we began pulling out his fingernails one by one. Then we shot him up with this fucked-up smack that we'd cut with all his real screwed-up shit to really give it to him. But then the twat – if you can believe this shit – actually appeared to be enjoying it.'

Prey suddenly broke into the story. 'Yeah, mate. So then I sliced his balls clean off, Chopper.' Prey witnessed me grimacing slightly, unconsciously grabbing hold of my own balls. 'That fuckin' wiped the smile off his face, ar'kid.'

I have to admit that I found myself grinning away at the story, sick as it sounded. 'So what happened in the end?'

'Let's just say he disappeared for good after that, eh Chopper,' Sleeper said to me with an extremely broad smirk on his face.

'Yeah. Sleeper read him his final bedtime story that night, didn't you?' Prey laughed again.

They both just looked at one another, then burst into hysterics at the story they'd just relayed to me.

I finally found my way into my bed by early evening, totally knackered and still wired from all the drugs we'd smoked. By that time, the party had died down. And everybody, not only me, was pretty out of it by then, and I think that we were all in need of a little quiet time.

The thing was though, that when Donna had told me to phone her 'tomorrow', I'd obviously got confused with it being the early hours of Sunday morning when she had left. Did she mean Monday? It turned out she didn't.

'So what happened to your phone call last night, eh Chopper?' She sounded completely pissed off.

'What you on about, girl? I thought you meant tonight.'

'Yeah right… *boy*,' she snapped. Now I knew she was mad at me.

I tried to think quickly. 'What can I say, eh? Listen, we all ended up back at our gaff. No fucker left until gone six last night. Honest, Donna. That's the truth.'

Why was I explaining myself to her? I didn't have a clue why. But still, I found myself doing it all the same.

'Oh, right then. So everybody went back to yours, did they? Looks like it was a good job that *I* never came back then, eh Chopper? You carry on partying and all that...' She paused for just a second, and then, before I could even get a word in she started up again. 'So tell me, was there any girls there, eh?'

Jeez! This was worse than a police interrogation. 'No... Well, yes... Look, they weren't with me, all right.'

'You sure about that, Chopper? I heard all about you.' She sounded a little less mad now.

'Yes I'm sure. Look, I phoned you, didn't I. Now stop fuckin' about with me. You want to go out some time or not, girl?' I said, trying to play it as cool as possible with her now, although at the same time I was praying my chances hadn't been blown.

'Oh I don't know, Chopper,' she sighed down the phone. 'I hear that you've got yourself quite a bad reputation. I don't know if it would be safe for a girl like me to go getting herself involved with someone like you.'

'Nah, girl. That's just bollocks. Just stories, that's all they are,' I sighed back at her, kissing my teeth as I did. 'Look, just give me a chance, will you? You'll see for yourself.' There was that pleading sound in my voice again. Damn – I really did hate the sound of that.

'All right, you're on, Chopper. When?'

This was good. Actually thinking about it... No, it wasn't – because right then I suddenly remembered our guests. 'All right then, how about this Saturday night? I'll arrange a proper sound night out for us. Is that all right, yeah?'

That's when she started up once again. 'Saturday?' she suddenly snapped. 'I thought you wanted to see me. You know, like this week sometime, that is. Now you're making me wait until the weekend!'

She was pissed off again. Only this time it was beginning to irritate the hell out of me, though I was doing my best not to let it show in my voice.

'Listen, Donna, there is some serious shit I got to take care of this week. Y'know I want to see you and all that. But we got guests 'ere this week. People I owe a lot to. All right?' I stood my ground. Though if the truth be known, my real desire was to see her right there and then.

'All right then, Chopper, you win,' she said, a little less tersely than before. 'Give me a ring on Friday night. Let me know what time. Oh, and make sure you keep your word about sorting out a sound night for us.'

'Sweet, I'll speak with you then.'

'I'm already looking forward to it, Chopper,' she said in a much nicer tone of voice.

Bloody women, I thought. 'Me too,' I sighed, replacing the receiver and shaking my head.

ELEVEN

W e spent the entire week doing as much of town as possible. Kezlo and Eazy became practically inseparable. They'd struck up a true friendship together. Kezlo kept taking him on guided tours of the estate, showing off our old pieces from over the years and the more recent ones that he still continued to do from time to time. Eazy had loved them, saying that all three of us should definitely go back down his way to do some there. Between the two of them, they spent that week discussing, arguing, laughing and mixing.

None of us had witnessed Kezlo so gratified before. It was a good thing to witness first-hand.

The three of us took Eazy into town to meet Graham from The Spinn House record shop. Obviously the two of them hit it off straight away. They spent the entire afternoon out back, going over the business deals they could cut with one another. The two of them were reviewing, discussing and even arguing over the latest imports and white labels that had recently landed in the UK.

Finally, we had to arrange a night out just to drag him away from the store. So we headed for Courtney's Wine Bar at the back of Deansgate. This place always put a little smile upon my face. It was wall to wall with yuppie anal-types that really got my back up. We always got more than a few scowls and what they imagined to be hard stares or glares from them. Not that they ever said anything to us though. Even the management enjoyed our visiting, as they knew we'd spend good money in there when we came: a few afternoon drinks often turned into an all-day session.

Plus Scotty was always trying it on with the manageress in there. She was this nice little older woman with strawberry-blonde hair, and I'd seen what I presumed to be her husband collecting her from work with at least two kids that must have been theirs. Not that that mattered though, as she still had a great body and it was obvious that she more than looked after herself.

The thing was though, she never smiled at anything or anyone. She always looked to be in a foul mood. Scotty often joked that it was the woman's usual three weeks on and one week off. Although she seemed to have a soft spot for Scotty. When he turned on the charm, I have to say that it was about the only time that I'd see the faintest of smiles appear on her face. In fact, both Kezlo and I figured that if he carried on this way he'd be in with a chance. He reckoned she just fancied a bit of a rough toy boy to have her wicked way with. And he, of course, reckoned he was the one to oblige.

He told us he'd be a true gentleman with her. This despite him also adding that he was going to ride her long and hard all night long, laughing as he did.

So just prior to entering that night, Scotty had managed to blag himself a bunch of flowers from the market guy who was packing his gear away outside. I found myself laughing at my friend, for he really was a devious bugger at times.

He winked at all of us. 'All right then, lads. So you want to see the master at work, do you? C'mon then, let's place some bets. I reckon I'll have her in bed by the end of tonight. What do you lot say?'

'Now *this* I got to see for myself,' Eazy laughed.

Graham smiled at us. 'Is this kid for real or what?'

'You better believe it.' I was shaking my head. 'Oh, and I'd keep your dough firmly in your pocket if you've got any sense.' I began nodding at them. 'I still can't work out how the ugly twat pulls so many birds.'

So, Scotty was Scotty and turned up the charm no end – and she loved every minute of his never-ending stream of nonsense. I had to admit though, for an older woman she still had something about her. And I'll openly admit that I actually felt a slight pang of jealousy watching him work his way into her.

By 11.30 we'd left Scotty to it. And by 11:32 the dirty little sod had her over her office desk upstairs.

Oh well! It was probably better there than at our place. For both Kezlo and I knew that no one got any sleep when he was on a roll.

Prey had booked Chan Yung's restaurant in Chinatown for Wednesday night. We often ate there and Chan always loved to see us.

Prey was treated like a son by Chan. A few years back now, one of Chan's younger sons, Lee, had been on the receiving end of a very nasty beating outside some Piccadilly arcades in town. Four drunken older men were really giving it to him when Prey intervened. He put all four of them in hospital.

So since then he'd always been treated like family by Chan. Which, with the Chinese being a very tight lot to be involved with, was a bonus. Also the food at Chan's was by far the best food in town.

Chan had seated us by the windows on the second floor of the restaurant. The view was fantastic, as it overlooked the whole of Chinatown. Prey ordered way too much food, as he usually did. And God knows how much champagne he ordered. But what the hell anyway: he was picking up the bill tonight.

The thing was, he ordered so much that the waiters had to rearrange another set of tables down the middle of ours to fit all of it into place. It was, however, a great meal that they prepared for us that night.

'All right, what's next on the agenda then?' Prey enquired enthusiastically, wiping the corners of his mouth with his napkin.

'How the fuck we supposed to know; it's your manor, Prey,' Sleeper told him.

Prey just laughed. 'Who's got any suggestions then? Wednesday night: what the hell can we do?'

'What about Applejacks?' Sean suggested.

'What's that then, Sean? A club?' Lisa enquired.

'You mean that casino near the bus station, Sean?'

'That's the one, Chopper. You been there before?'

'Nah man. I ain't much of a gambler.'

'Well, it sounds all right to me,' Sleeper concluded, nodding his head.

'Sound then. Applejacks it is,' declared Prey in good spirits.

It was the usual cold, wet and windy night in Manchester and the last thing that any of us needed was to be stuck outside Applejacks arguing about whether or not the doorman was going to allow us to enter. I let out a deep sigh as I clearly saw the large, white doorman who'd shaved his head for added effect, shaking his head at us before we'd even attempted to cross his pathway.

'Not tonight, lads,' the voice sneered menacingly from his huge bulk, which blocked the entrance.

This infuriated Prey no end, who flew straight at him.

'You fuckin' what you—'

He was halted in his tracks by Sean heaving him backwards. Sensing that things were getting out of hand here, I tried my best to resolve the problem.

'Look, mate. What's the problem? We've probably got more dough on us than you make in a year.' I now realise that it probably was not the wisest thing to have said, but hey, whatever. 'So just what is the problem?' I stood before his bulk as calm as was possible under the circumstances.

'Listen, sonny,' he said, no doubt adding the 'sonny' part to try and show me he was the one in charge of things. 'There are only three girls between all of you, and none of you is dressed correctly to enter the casino.' He leaned closer towards me and smirked. 'So basically – why don't you just all fuck right off. 'Cos you see, as far as I am concerned, ain't none of you coming in 'ere tonight. That's final, you hear me?' He stood his ground with me and in a way I kind of admired him for it. Well, for about a tenth of a second, that was.

For it had to be said, he was really beginning to piss me off now. 'All right.' It was my turn to inch towards him and pull the old Manc scally blag of 'Do you know who we are?'

'Now you listen to me "sonny", as you like to put it. We respect what you're trying to tell us, but as you can see before you, there is a shitload of us. You obviously ain't got a clue just who you're dealing with, 'ave you?'

Everybody grinned, enjoying the moment, and I continued. 'And with only one of you at the door you've got to be having a laugh, haven't you? Yeah sure, you've probably got a couple more downstairs. But what the fuck anyway? We're coming in with or without your say-so, *sonny*.' I announced all of this confidently, striding straight past his huge frame.

I suddenly felt his enormous hands grab a hold of my shirt as I tried to make my way past him. But I'd been waiting for him to make his move, whereas he hadn't been waiting for mine. I moved with great speed and accuracy before he knew what was happening: he never even saw my lock-knife until its sharpened steel was pressed against his left cheek. His grip relaxed instantly.

'We got a problem 'ere or not?' I sneered at him.

I could read the fear in his eyes, so I played on it by screwing my face even more at him. 'Look, I just... wan...' Now he was blubbering like a little child. In fact it was actually quite embarrassing after the way he'd come across when we had first arrived.

I heard a trickling sound, like a slow running tap that hadn't been turned off properly. As I glanced down, I laughed out loud as I clearly witnessed that he'd begun to wet himself. Glaring up at him and smirking, I shook my head in what can only be described as pity for him. I then released my grip and, casually followed by the others, made my way downstairs.

The casino turned out to be a good choice. It was a basement club with a certain amount of class. All the croupiers were good-looking women who probably moonlighted as professional models. I found myself wondering if they offered any services beyond their job descriptions. We were all having a great time. No further problems were created, caused or addressed, and everybody enjoyed themselves.

Prey suddenly appeared, smiling at me. 'You're cold, brother, y'know that? I tell you, Chopper, I sure am glad that I've got you on my side.'

I just shrugged back at him. I never went looking to start trouble and Prey knew this. But he knew that I would never allow anybody to walk all over me, and no matter what the situation I would always stand my ground.

'How you do on roulette, Prey?' I smiled, trying to change the subject.

'Won fuck all,' he shrugged, and then added, 'But Eazy and Sleeper are doing all right though.'

Kezlo approached us both. 'Sean's doing proper all right on the poker table. He's winning pure big time over there, y'know.'

'He's got to be cheating. Little fucker. We'll have to find out what his scam is,' Prey laughed.

Just then the three girls, Lisa, Sharon and Janine, approached. 'You believe that guy at the door, Chopper?' Lisa asked.

'In't it! Fuckin' tosser,' Sharon added.

'Don't worry about it, girls,' Prey declared, grabbing my shoulder. 'We've got cold Chopper 'ere with us to protect us from all evil. Yeah, that's it, mate. Your new name: "Cold Chopper".' He announced this in a voice that resembled Grasshopper from the television series *Kung Fu* starring David Carradine.

Everybody began laughing along with him. Janine smiled at me. 'You don't take shit from nobody, do you, eh Chopper?'

It was nearly four by the time we got ready to leave Applejacks. As we all clambered back up towards the exit I was slightly ahead of everybody else. I was feeling the effects of all the champagne we'd drunk earlier that evening. Not to mention the Martell brandy that both Prey and I had consumed. It was a nice, pleasant buzz that I was feeling and I looked forward to the cocaine we had back at the flat.

I was in a very good mood and looking forward to the remainder of the night. Just as the door began to open to the main entrance, without any warning whatsoever, I suddenly found myself doubling over in pain from a blow to my stomach. What the hell…

As my ears began to ring out with the pain, the wind was knocked violently from me. Everything around me became indistinct. My arms were wrapped around my stomach over where I'd been struck so hard. As I lifted my head and tried my utmost to focus, I saw the blurred image of something large, straight and long – and whatever the hell it was it was heading for me once again.

Only this time I managed to duck. My senses came back to me momentarily and I found myself focusing on the baseball bat crashing into the wall behind me. All of this had happened in literally seconds, and I don't think anybody else had quite realised until this point that there was a problem.

Without hesitation, I grabbed onto the bat, holding it against the wall. My mind was still a little clouded and I was trying my best to buy both myself and the others some time. My attacker was struggling to break the bat free, but I kept hold of it for as long as I possibly could under the circumstances. I could feel that he was using all of his strength to release it though, and was beginning to succeed.

As he yanked it free with a surge of strength, I suddenly used it against him and pushed it back towards him with all the vigour I could manage. In one devastating, crushing motion the left side of his cheek bone and nose cartilage caved in like wet papier-mâché. He screamed out in agony as I yanked the bat free of his grip, and, climbing quickly to my feet, brought the bat straight back down onto his head with all the force that I could muster. I now saw that it was the doorman from earlier in the evening. All of these events seemed to have lasted an eternity. Yet in reality it was probably no more than a few seconds at most.

Just then, from behind the door a large group of lads he'd obviously brought down here with him came rushing past the two of us and straight through the open doorway. All of them were armed with an assortment of bats, sticks and metal poles, and I swear that I even saw the flash of a blade.

They swiftly ran down the stairway, heading straight for our crew, who by now were also charging up the stairs, having witnessed first-hand the fracas between the doorman and me. The whole place erupted into what can only be described a mass of violence, mayhem and chaos.

I turned my attention and anger back towards my attacker and swiped violently back at him with the bat once again. The second strike I'd made had split a large gash into his forehead. His face and forehead were beginning to open up severely now, as all I could think about was the relentless damage I had yet to inflict upon him.

What the hell did he think he was doing, bringing his lads down here like this? He thought he'd get his revenge on not only me but all of us, so he'd been waiting patiently in order to ambush us on the way out. I found that this enraged me even more. Glancing back down the stairs, our crew had begun fighting with all of his lads: a real battle had commenced.

Then I noticed something that would stick in my mind for a very long time as I glanced at the bedlam taking place. There was

Sleeper moving through the mass of bodies in the midst of battle. He moved with the grace of a floating spirit. He went utterly disregarded to either side. The long blade he carried appeared to have a hand-carved wooden (or was it bone?) handle. He kept momentarily flashing the blade, as each of his victims fell prey to the cold steel as he meticulously took each one of them apart like an old Samurai warrior or a Ronin might have. He no longer resembled the Sleeper that I knew. His transformation reflected what really possessed his soul: it had risen from its depths to the surface. He resembled a slaughtered soul that had returned to seek vengeance. His lethal elegance sent a cold shiver through me.

I now turned my attention back to my assailant, who still lay there trying to cover himself. I was suddenly filled with such wrath – I hadn't felt like this in a very long time. As I began stamping and batting him frantically, I felt that I was losing control. I was screaming abuse at him, but you couldn't hear me above all the noise.

He had infuriated me, and all that I wanted to do was harm him as badly as I possibly could. In fact that was the only thing that mattered to me right there and then. Kick after kick, bat after bat. I could hear his screams and cries for help, but no one else could and so no one was coming to his aid – certainly none of the lads he'd brought down here, who were on the receiving end of respective beatings down the stairs.

I'd begun to lose control of myself, not even realising what I was doing to him. I just continued beating him in unadulterated abhorrence.

I suddenly felt myself being dragged backwards. 'Chopper! Chopper! For fuck's sake… you're going to kill him!' Janine screamed at me.

I was still kicking and swiping with the bat as they continued to pull me away. 'Please, Chopper… please… stop it,' Lisa pleaded with me.

The three girls held me against the wall. My breathing was fast and unrestrained as the adrenaline raced through me. I saw the rest of the Hulme lads using all manner of weapons: blades flashing; bats swinging; even using fire extinguishers to smash skulls. Blood soared against every surface.

Just then Sharon yelled out, 'Fuckin coppers! Let's get the fuck out of 'ere now!'

This is what suddenly brought me to my senses again. I could clearly hear the impending sirens soaring through the night.

'Prey, we need to get the fuck out of 'ere now! Let's fuckin' go right now!' I yelled loudly to try to get his attention.

At that very moment everybody realised the imminent danger that was upon us. The entire crew darted from the premises as quickly as possible. We all sprinted through the dark, damp and miserable streets of Manchester, using back streets and alleys as we did so. We had to make it back to the estate. That was our only priority at this point.

Within ten minutes – give or take a couple – we had all made it safely back to Hulme. All of us were bruised but hardly battered, and it has to be said that we were all feeling good. Just who had that doorman thought he was, bringing those lads down to the club like that?

Eazy was breathing unrestrained, hard and fast, trying to catch his breath. 'Fuck me! You lads sure know how to have a lively night out… don't you!' he laughed.

Earlier that evening I'd arranged to pick up Donna from Wilmslow – where I had discovered she resided. She'd given me a hard time about just where I'd be taking her Saturday night. And in all honesty I hadn't organised anything for us yet. So being the true gentleman that I was, I took the next step and informed her that everything had been arranged for a great night out. I just figured that I would cross that bridge when I came to it.

However, tonight though was to be our guests' last night in town. They were heading back tomorrow morning. So Prey had arranged for us to all go to The Haçienda (or simply 'The Haç' as he referred to it).

The exterior of the venue looked very plain. In fact it didn't resemble anything other than one of the many disused warehouses that were scattered around Manchester. It was on the corner of Whitworth Street, its entrance curling its way around from the canal into Canal Street.

The entrance was covered by an enormous coloured guy who

we knew from Wythenshawe, called Errol. Errol always reminded me of that huge purple Muppet whose name I could never remember from *The Muppet Show*. He was enormous, but at the same time was a gentle giant. He had a great character and was always laughing. In fact, I'd never actually seen him use violence when a situation turned sore. He always used his humorous side to quell trouble, enabling him to walk his aggressors out of the front door. Although what took place away from prying eyes thereafter was anybody's guess.

Despite the plain exterior, it was truly a great place once you were inside. It consisted of two areas. There was a basement bar that played a real assortment of alternative music, although it was only small. The main area of the club, however, consisted of a large balcony that overlooked the main dance floor and stage area. I'd heard that local bands usually played there but honestly didn't know the names of any of them as I wasn't into that scene back then.

I found myself observing Eazy's reaction as we all entered the club. I think that he was as taken aback as I was with the club. In fact, it did just resemble the inside of a disused warehouse. But no matter – I really liked it. Apparently – and I'd just heard this somewhere – it had once been a boat house. Although I was not sure if there was any truth in that or not.

'Shit!' he gasped at what was before him. 'This place has got some serious potential.'

'I've never been in a club like this before. It's usually just crappy, glitzy clubs down our way,' Lisa was telling us. 'It's a simple set-up but I like it.'

Prey was smiling. I clearly witnessed a glimmer in his eye as he witnessed all of our reactions.

'And you know what? I reckon this club is going to be the club of the future,' he nodded knowingly at all of us. 'Everybody is going to be coming 'ere in the very near future, I tell you. Just wait and see,' he said enthusiastically.

'You reckon, Prey?' Scotty asked.

'Definitely, mate.'

'What's the grin for then?' Sleeper enquired.

'Look at it. It's well sound, Sleeper. And nobody has even got the place wired.' He was turning towards me. 'We'll run this club one day. That's the truth. You'd better believe it as well, Chopper,' he added, still glaring directly at me with a serious look upon his face.

'Let's hope so, mate,' I replied with a slight nod. 'Before its full potential is recognised.'

The night was turning out to be fantastic. Everybody was enjoying each others' company that evening. The music was a little mixed, but it was still all right.

Prey had just about bought out the bar of all its champagne. I remember that by closing time, he was trying his best to make a deal with the management to sell us more champagne to take with us.

They weren't having any of it though. I mean, it wasn't going to look too clever for them if there was Prey walking straight out of the front door with bottles and bottles of champagne in his arms, was it? But Errol from the door informed them who Prey was and, funnily enough, there wasn't a problem after that. They hid six more bottles of Möet in a bin liner for him to take inconspicuously.

And yes – we did continue to party back at Prey's until it was time for our three guests to finally leave. I remember thinking, as I wished everybody goodbye, that this whole experience had been like a favourite fairground ride.

And I only hoped they never stopped this ride from running, because I sure as hell didn't want to get off.

TWELVE

D onna was already waiting as I arrived at the Rex Cinema in Wilmslow on Saturday evening. It had been quite a warm day and you could clearly see from the way people were dressed they thought that summer had arrived. I always found it a little humorous the way the British grasped onto whatever little sunshine they could, almost as if they were scared that, if they didn't, the summer would pass them by unnoticed.

As I approached the cinema, I saw a group of young lads. All of them were aged between about fourteen and twenty years of age. They were all dressed the same as I did, and you could clearly see they were a really mixed bunch. Despite the fact they all wore the same style of clothes, it was clear which ones came from money and which came from outside Wilmslow, from areas such as Lacey Green or Coleshaw Farm. They were the ones out there – just as Scotty and I had been at their age – going out and doing just about whatever they had to do by any means necessary to get the clothes they wore. The others had probably quite simply had them purchased for them by their mothers and fathers.

They looked quite a bunch of characters though. And I could clearly perceive at least three of them openly smoking weed and two others in the midst of some kind of illegal transaction.

I found myself smiling as I eased my vehicle up to the curb. And that was when I saw Donna properly for the first time. 'Thank you Lord for the day of sunshine,' I muttered under my breath as I shook my head at her. She looked absolutely sensational.

She wore a short white dress that stopped just below her crotch. It hugged her amazing figure, accentuating what I perceived to be her near-perfect breasts. Along with this, she wore a pair of brown suede knee-length boots that instantly gave me the horn. She was casually tying a Levi's denim jacket around her waist as she noticed me and smiled. She held her finger out to indicate that she'd only be a moment and pulled her hair behind her head, twisting and turning as she tied it casually away from her face. God – she blew me away. It had been the first time I'd seen her since my birthday and she looked even better than she had then – if that was at all possible.

I reached over to open the passenger door for her. 'You all right, Donna?' I asked as she climbed into the car.

Then, without a single word, she kissed me both hard and passionately right there in the front seat. Her moist lips were warm and her tongue began probing for mine. I instantly felt myself becoming aroused as she moved her hand to my inner thigh and squeezed slightly. Her other hand was around my neck as her open mouth moved its way there, kissing and using her tongue perfectly..

'OK then, Chopper, what you got planned for us then?' she whispered excitedly as she continued to work her magic against my neck, causing a whole array of sensations.

She had completely caught me off guard with just about everything. I could see a few of the lads outside the cinema catching themselves an eyeful and grinning at my shocked face.

'Er… well… I hope that you like Chinese food,' I blurted out, not entirely sure what else to say.

The truth of the matter was that I still hadn't planned anything; absolutely nothing at all. So Chan's restaurant was the first thing that came to mind. I was never one for planning things like this, and in all honesty I'd never needed to before now. I honestly couldn't tell Donna that though. Especially seeing as I'd already told her previously that I'd sort out a great night out for us.

'Sounds good to start with,' she smiled. 'C'mon on then, let's get going. Which Chinese are you taking me to, Chopper?' She was gently stroking my hand on the gear stick as she did so.

Damn, this girl had one hell of a way of getting me all excited! I was doing my best to try and calm myself down, but found myself failing miserably.

'You heard of Chan's in Chinatown?' I asked, easing the car back onto the main road.

'Nope. Is it nice there?' She was still stroking the back of my hand – and it sure felt nice.

'It's proper sound there. Prey knows Chan himself, so we'll be all right. He'll make room for us,' I said, crossing my fingers. I'd never actually been there without Prey before.

'What do you mean "make room for us", Chopper? I thought you said you had this night planned.' She gave me a devious look as she said it.

I found myself laughing out loud. 'All right, girl, you got me. I planned fuck all for us.' I began smiling cheekily at her. 'But I do guarantee that I'll show you a top night out though. Just like I said I would.'

'Oh, you most certainly will now, Chopper. Bleedin' cheek of it,' she laughed.

Luckily, Chan himself was at the door, recognising me immediately. 'Ah, Chopper, my good friend. Are you and beautiful lady dining with us tonight?'

'Sweet, Chan. Is the usual table free?'

'For this beautiful girl, of course it is,' he replied, flirting in his very non-threatening manner, smiling at Donna as she blushed slightly at the attention.

Chan led us through the busy restaurant and up to the second floor, seating us in the same spot from four nights earlier.

'Your usual seat, Chopper,' he announced, easing back Donna's chair for her.

'Thanks a lot, Chan.'

'No problem. Now, drinks, Chopper. I'll send over best bottle of champagne. Obviously this beauty deserves only the best, eh Chopper?' He winked at me before scuttling away.

Donna stared hard at me. 'I hope this "usual seat" is just for you and Prey,' she pouted. Those gorgeous lips of hers.

'What's that supposed to mean then, Donna?'

'You know *exactly* what I mean, boy. I already told you that I've heard you've got one hell of a reputation for yourself.' She pouted at me again, then continued. 'I've told you before that I'm no cheap whore,'

'You sure you got the right guy?' I half laughed. 'You sure you're not on about Scotty?'

'Christ no, not Scotty,' she said, shaking her head. 'Now he's got himself a *really* bad reputation compared to you.' This time she smiled.

'That's the truth ain't it,' I laughed. 'Now *he's* a cheap whore for sure.' I was laughing at the mere thought of him.

'Yes he is. But I've heard that you're not far behind on the girl front.'

'I don't know what reputation you're on about, but it's bollocks anyway. Besides, if you have heard any stories about me, I bet they never involved restaurants, did they?' I was smirking confidently at her now.

She smiled at me, batting those gorgeous green eyes of hers. *Sweet*, I thought to myself, definitely one point to me there.

'All right then, I ain't ever heard *them* stories before.'

I observed her glancing at the menu, so I pretended to be some kind of connoisseur of Chinese cuisine. 'I recommend the banquets; they're fantastic. They just keep bringing out dishes for you,' I said, thinking that was easy enough. Well, as long as she went for it, that is.

'Sounds good to me,' she replied, smiling.

Just then, Chan returned with the bottle of champagne – Bollinger for Christ's sake. Jesus – the old man wasn't holding back.

'For the lady… only the best,' he winked knowingly at me. He popped the cork; he really knew how to play host when he wanted to.

'Oh, thank you,' responded Donna happily.

'You ready to order now?' Chan enquired.

'Just the usual, Chan.' He smiled at my order, as he knew exactly what this meant, as Prey only ever ordered one thing.

'OK, Chopper. Only the best, remember,' he chuckled, turning and leaving us both sat there.

Chan was a character that I both liked and admired. Prey had told me that the restaurant was merely a cover though. Apparently, the old man was heavily involved with other activities and was a good contact to have around. You would never think it to look at him, small, wiry old man that he was. But then again – as I was continually discovering these days – appearances could be deceptive.

'All right then, Chopper, why the interest in me?' said Donna, breaking my concentration.

'You what!' Now, I'd never had to answer questions like this before. 'Have you taken a look in the mirror recently, girl? Shit! You're gorgeous. I'm telling you, girl. And then, to top that, you're proper sound as well. What more could I ask for? However, I'm still pissed off about you not coming back to ar' flat the other night.'

'And I keep telling you. I ain't some cheap whore that you're going to use.' She did that pout again. However, there was more than just a little smile sneaking through there. I think that I'd won her over somewhat with my blatant honesty.

'I know you ain't, Donna. Look, if it makes you feel any better, girl, I ain't either, y' know? You can't go getting me into bed on the first night either.' I smiled knowingly at her.

'Oh is that right, Chopper?' Donna frowned at me, obviously not seeing the funny side of it. 'From what I hear, girls never last longer than a week with you. They're lucky if they last the night into the morning,' she said, her left eyebrow rising slightly.

'Well, there you go then, Donna,' I replied, winking at her, trying my best to humour her. 'Congratulations! You've already passed the week marker.'

We both laughed out loud at the comment and the tension that had momentarily presented itself now diminished.

The first dishes began to arrive. I tried to show Donna how to use the chopsticks, but I was on to a loser there. She couldn't get the hang of them no matter how hard we both tried. Chan eventually brought her over a knife and fork, as I don't think he could endure watching her struggle any longer. Besides which, she'd never get to eat any of the food.

'So I hear you're a great cook as well, Chopper,' she said, glancing up from her food.

'You sure seem to have a lot of information on me, girl,' I replied, looking directly at her whilst still chewing my fried chicken ball.

'Well, I like to find out as much information as possible on someone I'm attracted to.' She watched for my reaction.

'Really, eh? Attracted to?' This had put a smile on my face. I grinned joyously at her comment, liking the sound of it. 'So tell me, how come we only met last week then and you know shitloads about me already?' I was curious to discover more.

'Oh, I've seen you around,' she said, staring at me. 'Quite a lot for that matter. Karen was going with Prey... Well, whenever *he* felt like it, that is. Apparently he never stops singing your praises. Me and Chopper this, Chopper and me that. She told me that she thought that you were her competition at times.'

I had to laugh at that comment. Because Karen wasn't the first to raise the subject. Not that there was anything in it. It was just that Prey and I were close because of what we were involved with. And outsiders probably perceived it in a different light.

'Well, how come I never seen you before that?'

'Obviously you walk around with your eyes shut, don't you?' she laughed.

'Nah, serious, Donna. I ain't ever seen you around before last Saturday.'

'Ohhhh, thanks a lot, Chopper,' she said, with a hint of sarcasm in her voice.

'Hey look, what can I say? It's how it is. I'm obviously becoming so busy with all the other shit that goes on in the world that I fail to notice the important things around me.'

She smiled at that. 'Well, I knew about your party from Karen. So I basically got myself hooked onto her invitation.'

'I'm glad that you did,' I told her honestly.

'Anyway, I was determined to get your attention that night, as whenever I'd seen you out before, well, you – you never even looked in my direction. Bleedin' cheek of it,' she smiled.

'Well, it certainly worked, Donna. You got my full attention now,' I smiled warmly at her.

'I know I have,' she replied confidently.

It had been obvious what the outcome of the night was going to be as soon as we'd left the restaurant; before we'd even made it back to the car we'd been all over each other.

As we entered my flat we were immediately at each other once again. Only this time we were in private and so we found ourselves quickly grabbing, pulling, pushing, rubbing and tearing at each other's clothes as we made our way through to the bedroom.

Collapsing naked onto my bed, we began kissing and stroking each other all over, with sheer unadulterated desire and passion for discovering each other's bodies. Her hand was gently caressing my already stiffened cock. I could feel her fingers stroking the pulsating veins that ran the length of it.

I began kissing and nibbling at her hardening pink nipples. It all felt fantastic, being there with her, enjoying each other. Lowering my hand towards the moistness of her crotch, I began probing with eager fingers. Her moans of gratification were becoming louder and faster as I discovered exactly what I was searching for. Her clitoris was circling around my finger, as she moved her hips against my hand, pushing, rubbing harder and harder as between the two of us we worked her into a frenzy.

She worked herself against my hand, harder and faster, becoming moister as she did so. I continued to kiss at her nipples and she continued to stroke my cock, getting me even more worked up than I already was.

She began kissing and licking at my right nipple, breathing hard as she did so. 'Please... please, Chopper... I'm going to...' She trailed off as she seemed to spasm and shudder against me, her breathing deep and her sighs loud.

Her breath was hot, and she continued kissing and teasing my nipple, her tongue flickering seductively around it. I rolled my weight over her, positioning myself above her. I found myself staring passionately into her green eyes. Christ – this was something else. Donna pulled me closer, kissing my neck as she did so. Her hand was still caressing my throbbing cock as she directed me into her.

She gasped out loud and bit down on her lip as I pushed myself deep inside of her. As I began to ease myself in and out of her, building rhythm with each movement, we kissed each other more and more passionately as we did so. Donna's nipples were beginning to swell as I nibbled at them, blowing cool air back onto them to harden them even more. She just gasped harder and louder, holding my head and becoming more passionate.

As our bodies ground against one another, her nails were digging deeper into my back. She then eased herself up and over, so she sat astride me. She looked so good up there above me, and she was turning me on like you wouldn't believe.

She began building rhythm, riding me with such force that as she brought herself down onto me I found myself pushing upwards, faster and harder, harder and faster as we combined our rhythm in a glorified, perfect tempo.

Soon it felt as though our two bodies were in sync with one another. I don't recall just how long we were riding each other; I just recall that it felt like the best, the most passionate, sex that I had ever experienced.

Our sweat-drenched bodies slid against each other, as both of us realised that we were about to climax together. She dug her nails into my chest so hard that she began to draw blood, which only heightened my excitement; I felt as though I was about to explode. Donna began screaming out loud in sheer joy as we both suddenly spasmed, and my cock emptied itself into her as we both gripped onto each other as tightly as we could.

Donna began to slowly, yet continuously, slide up and down, tensing her muscles around my cock, sucking all of my hot come inside of her. I could feel that I was still hard inside her. God damn – it felt so good though. We stared into each other's eyes, as sweat literally streamed down our faces and bodies into the sheets.

She rolled off me to my side. We both just lay there, out of breath and staring at one another. I began to grin like the kid who just got exactly what he wanted for Christmas – and then some.

Donna looked at me, all hot and sweaty. Strands of her hair were stuck to her face. It was safe to say that she looked absolutely gorgeous at that precise moment in time. So good in fact, it was unbelievable. 'I don't know about you, Chopper… but that really felt different though.' She kissed me again.

'You kidding me or what?' I stared into those gorgeous, mesmerising eyes and smiled. 'Fuck me, Donna… I never knew that it could feel so good.'

She pushed herself up onto my chest, looking straight into my eyes. 'Do you mean that, Chopper? Or is this just the end of another week for you?' she asked, stroking my chest.

'Nah, get serious, girl. You do some serious funky shit to me.' I had to laugh out loud, as it was the truth. Nobody had ever left me feeling the way she had done. Kissing her again, I enjoyed the moment before breaking away and staring at her. 'Shit, I can't explain it at all. All that I know is that I like it a *lot* though.' I smiled at her and again kissed her passionately, before round two of the evening commenced.

We both enjoyed each again and again, only more slowly, taking our time discovering one another until the early hours of Sunday morning before finally giving in to exhaustion. We fell into a deep sleep, each of us holding the other's sweaty, sex-drenched body as close as possible.

THIRTEEN

J onah had spoken briefly with me on Wednesday night about what he'd mentioned at my birthday – he'd considered a new area of business for us to open up in. And to top that, he already claimed to have the contact for the product lined up ready for us to meet, the products being amphetamine or speed, whizz, billy, fast, to name but a few of its preferred street monikers, and LSD, acid. There were often different pictures printed on the acid blotters themselves, anything from a smiley face to a Batman sign.

Jonah reckoned that he already had a market ready and waiting for the gear. But – and this is where we came into play – it would need organising on a much greater scale than a few grams or trips here and there. He told me that the contact was talking larger quantities, but that from what he already knew price-wise, the mark-up at street level was excellent. Even at distribution level we could make a hefty profit.

To be perfectly honest, I personally knew jack about that side of business. But in order to be fair to Jonah, I had arranged the meeting for the following Wednesday afternoon at Chan's.

'All right then, Jonah. Why don't you tell me all about this top money-making scheme that you've got in mind then?' Prey said, tossing a prawn into his mouth.

'Right then. Well, Chopper has already told you the basics,' Jonah began, 'and I've been dealing personally with this older guy from out of town. He's a good punter, comes in once a week. Only buys from me. Anything up to a nine-bar at a time.' He looked around the table at us. Sean had also been brought along to the meeting.

'Where's he from then, Jonah?'

'Congleton. Wherever the fuck *that* is,' Jonah replied.

'Cheshire end. Not that far from Wilmslow,' I added.

'Whatever… Carry on, Jonah,' Prey said.

Jonah grinned boyishly at us and continued.

'So anyway, a month back now, he turns up an ounce of speed and with these trips, little flying keys on them. Asks if I can do anything with them, gives me twenty of them to see what I can do with them.' He paused, smiling at the three of us knowingly. 'I couldn't believe it... I got fivers for them from these boys from out of town.'

'*How* much?' Prey exclaimed.

'I know. But this is the best bit,' he grinned. 'If we buy them in at a thousand to a sheet they'll cost only forty-five pence a pop.'

'Really?' Prey's eyes lit up. 'You'd better tell us more.' Jonah had clearly managed to spark Prey's interest immensely.

'Yeah, what about the other thing you mentioned?' Sean asked.

'Right... Well, the speed you buy at street level can be as low as 12 per cent. This guy can supply it at 100 fuckin' per cent lads.' With this, his eyes lit up with sheer excitement at the prospect. 'That means we can bang it by five easily with this other gear that'll he'll also supply and it's still good to bang more. The return is colossal on it, Prey. You can treble or quadruple your investment.'

Prey was rubbing his chin as figures and percentages raced through his mind. 'All right, though this all sounds too good to be true, Jonah. How's this guy even getting the gear?'

Jonah laughed and held his hands out before explaining. 'This is the best bit of all. Like I said, he's a lot older than we are, probably some old hippie fucker from the sixties. Anyway, he's producing all of this shit himself. That's why he can guarantee us the gear is going to be as pure as the driven snow. Well – so to speak of course, Prey.' He watched for all our reactions again.

'You tried the shit yourself, Jonah?' Sean enquired.

'Yes, mate. The acid I tripped off for nearly two fuckin' days,' Jonah said, shaking his head in disbelief. 'But the speed – fuck me! I banged it by five with this gear he gave me. Well, it shrank my dick like a fuckin' turtle gone into hibernation for the winter.' We all laughed as he continued. 'Sharon was skitzing at first whilst I was crawling the walls. But then, jeez – once I finally did get it up with Sharon we fucked like rabbits for hours. Pure manic, finally slept after three days of it,' he said, laughing again.

'What about jackin' it though?' Prey asked.

'I don't fuck with needles, you know that. So anyway, I give it to Gus – you know, that scruffy cat always knocking about down at the shops.'

'And. What happened?' I asked him.

'It was like watching fuckin' spiderman or something,' he said, grinning at the thought of Gus. 'Because – never mind the crawling the fuckin' walls, lads – this crazy fuck, he was crawling across the ceiling right in front of my eyes.'

Sean smiled at Prey. 'You know, if this shit is as good as Jonah is saying, mate, then I know enough people both in and out of town who'll be up for buying it.'

'What's this guy's name, Jonah?' I enquired, still smiling at the story of his hibernating cock.

'Steve Griffin. He's a lot older than any of us, as I said. Maybe forty-odd. Maybe even older than that, lads. It's hard to tell, to be honest,' Jonah replied. 'Seems to know his shit though, I'll give him that.'

'All right, Jonah, this sounds sweet. In fact it sounds double sweet. But if this guy is producing the shit, what does he need with us so much?'

'Good fuckin' point, Chopper,' Prey said, smiling at me.

'Look, I don't know that bit,' said Jonah, shaking his head. 'Maybe he needs to open up his market. That's why he was going on about larger quantities rather than little bits of it. I've just brought the idea to you,' he declared, easing himself back into his chair. 'Now it's entirely up to you lads if you want me to follow up on this or not.'

'You remember when Knieldy done bird a few years back now, that Stafford Young Offenders Insti-place or whatever it was called?' Sean asked, seemingly changing the subject.

'Yeah… What the fuck has that got to do with this though?' Prey asked.

'Well, I'm sure the two kids he shared the cell with were from over that way.'

'All right, get Knieldy on it, mate. Let's see if we can check this guy out,' Prey said as Sean headed off to use the phone.

Prey then turned to Jonah. 'You've done a good job, Jonah. Let's just hope it works out for us.'

'I reckon it will. I got a good feeling about this guy. D'ya know what I mean, Prey?' he said, sipping his bottle of Budweiser.

I nodded at him and winked. 'Sound, Jonah.'

As we sat there in silence absorbing the information that Jonah had just supplied us with, Sean was already heading back towards the table. 'It's like I told you. He knows two guys that live near there. Says he'll see what he can find out for us.'

Prey was both smiling and nodding as he turned to face Jonah again. 'I tell you what, Jonah: if this shit checks out, then you and Chopper can run things on that side.' He nodded at Jonah. 'Mainly yourself of course, but Chopper will still be in charge. That's if you want to, of course.'

Jonah was smiling at him, knowing that it was a fantastic offer. It would stand him in line to become one of Prey's so-called and notorious 'lieutenants'.

'You serious, mate?' Jonah exclaimed, astounded by what Prey had just offered him.

'Yeah, mate.'

I just prayed it would turn out all right for all of us. From what Jonah had told us, we'd be fools not to get involved.

FOURTEEN

Knieldy had already arrived in Congleton by six o'clock that same evening. He'd arranged to meet up with two lads from over that way who he knew from time spent in a Young Offenders Institute where he'd spent time years before.

He'd been convicted for the wounding of one of the Gooch lads over in Moss Side when they were just a couple of teenagers. It had been over nothing really. It had been a fight that had just got out of hand and stepped to the next level. And although the lad had survived from the stabbing, he still went ahead and testified against Knieldy, then rapidly moved as far away from Manchester as he possibly could; he knew that Prey and the rest of that crew would have been out for revenge.

Robert was from a small village known as Biddulph and was slightly younger than Knieldy was. He'd served time for fraud charges brought against him. He had cleverly used the same system used for producing video membership cards to reproduce credit cards. The truth of the matter, though, was that the initial operation hadn't been down to him. He'd just taken the fall because he was being used for his computer knowledge. And as he refused to give up the names of anybody else involved in the operation, he had been sentenced to two years' imprisonment.

Dave, on the other hand, was the same age as Knieldy. He lived just outside of Congleton in a place known as Sandbach. Dave was kind of the black sheep of his family, who it had to be said weren't without money (his father was a well-renowned property developer). But despite his family's background, he wasn't anything like some spoilt rich kid living off his father's money.

He'd attended a private school, which was all well and good for the family's image, but he had been supplying drugs to his fellow pupils. And not just small amounts either. When they picked him up he was in possession of almost nine ounces of cannabis resin. And regrettably for Dave, it had already been chopped into separate deals. As he already had previous charges for possession, this time the intent-to-supply charge was going to be a definite: he was sentenced to eighteen months.

Knieldy knew he had complete trust in these two, as he'd looked out for the two of them whilst serving time with them. He had known that they weren't from the same mould as most of the inmates. So he'd made sure no one messed with them whilst he was there, and this way he had gained both their trust and loyalty. Besides which, Knieldy also knew that they were good contacts to have out of town.

He'd arranged to meet them both just outside of Congleton in a small pub known as The Farmers Arms.

As he entered the bar area he could see the two of them waiting near the back by the large, roaring open fireplace.

'Yes, lads. How you bumpkins doing then?' he laughed. (He was always jesting with them about being country bumpkins.)

'We're both all right, mate,' Robert answered, shaking Knieldy's hand.

Dave just laughed. 'So look at you then!' He was admiring the clothes Knieldy was wearing. 'You're looking good. Obviously doing something right, eh mate.'

They spent the next half hour chatting about old times and what each had been up to in the last few years.

'So what is it you need then?' Robert finally asked, as Dave was just returning with the next round of drinks. 'You were a little vague on the phone.'

'Both of your skills actually,' he said, before looking directly at Robert and saying, 'Especially yours, mate.'

'I ain't doing cards no more,' Robert declared sternly.

'That's all right then,' he said, laughing at how paranoid Robert was, ''cause that's not what I need you for,'

'What then? And why do you need me?' Dave enquired.

'It's just information, that's all. First off, do either of you know someone called Steve Griffin, by any chance?'

Robert's face drew a blank, but Dave looked to be thinking about it. 'You know… I know this young kid called Mike Griffin. Do you know if he's any relation?'

'Dunno,' Knieldy shrugged truthfully. 'How do you know this kid?'

'Weed, of course. I've bought it off him a few times now.' Dave half smiled. 'Like I said though, he's only young. Fifteen or something like that. Cocky little shit actually. Why?'

'Right then. 'Ere's what I need from you both. I need you both to find out what you can on Steve Griffin. Check whether or not it's his son.' Knieldy now stared at Robert. 'But I need you to find out everything possible on the guy himself. I know that you've done searches for others in the past, mate. So I'm sure that you can help me out 'ere, eh?'

'All right. But how soon do you need it? And what's it worth?'

'I need it like yesterday,' he said, knowing that it would probably take at least a week or so. 'All I know up to now is that this guy lives in Congleton somewhere. He appears to dabble a little with drugs, if that helps any. Also, there is a ton-fifty each for you.' Knieldy smiled at them. 'Obviously, the more you come up with the more I'll give you,' he added.

'Sounds good to me,' Dave said, returning his smile.

'No worries, mate,' Robert nodded. 'I'll have what you need by tomorrow night, good or bad.'

'So soon?' Knieldy looked shocked at his apparent confidence in the matter. 'Look, I need as much as possible, y'know.'

'Look, if I can't find anything by then, then we probably can't help... all right?' Robert said. But he knew that if this Steve Griffin had a criminal record, he'd be able to hack into the police computer system and discover the same, and it would be an easy £150 each made for simply sitting at his computer.

'All right. Sweet, lads, you got my number. I'll be waiting,' Knieldy said, rising from the table. 'It's good to see your ugly mugs again,' he smirked at them before turning to leave.

Knieldy received the call he'd been waiting for the following evening. The roads had been relatively quiet, so he had arrived back at The Farmers Arms just after eight thirty that evening. The two of them already appeared to be a more than a little drunk as he entered the pub, although both looked cheerful.

'All right, what you got for me then?' Knieldy enquired, sitting down with another round of drinks for all of them.

'What *didn't* we get,' laughed Dave with a stupid grin upon his face.

'Here you are,' said Robert, handing over a brown A4 envelope.

'Is this all on him?' Knieldy asked, feeling the thickness of the envelope, more than a little impressed.

'Yeah... Look, it turns out that was his son after all. We got chatting with him. The kid sure likes to talk. He said something that aroused our suspicions about his father's past. It was nothing really if you weren't paying attention, but it was enough for us to open up a completely new angle on him. As it turned out, it was the key we didn't even realise we'd been looking for. Let's just say that he covered his tracks really well. In fact, so well that I'd be confident in saying we know more than even the authorities know about him.'

'Really. So how good is it?' Knieldy asked, a little confused.

'Let's put it this way: you mentioned a bonus,' Robert said, staring at Knieldy. 'Well, after you've read this we'll accept a grand between us.'

'*How* fuckin' much?' Knieldy blurted out, astounded at the amount.

'Believe us, mate,' sniffed Dave confidently, 'you'll pay us for it once you've read through the contents of that envelope. So much so that we'll let you take this to your boss and let him read it. Then you can come pay us the whole amount tomorrow. Let's just say we got extremely lucky here – you'll understand later.'

'A *gee* though, lads,' he repeated, shaking his head as he did so.

'Look – we don't have to give this information to you on bail,' Robert snapped. 'We go back a long way, mate. Just take it. You'll understand after you've read it.'

'All right then... I'll take it straight back to Prey now. If it's as good as you two are making out, then I'll see you both tomorrow dinner time,' Knieldy told them, still confused as to what the hell they were both going on about.

'Yes, mate,' smiled Dave. 'See you tomorrow,' he added confidently, winking at Knieldy.

We were all waiting anxiously for Knieldy's return after receiving his phone call. Only Prey, Sean, Jonah and I were there.

'What you got then?' Prey asked as Knieldy walked into the flat.

'Don't actually know, mate. All I know is they reckon it's worth at least a grand between them,' he sighed. 'Say that we'll know why once we've read it.' He handed the envelope over to Prey.

'You already paid them?' Prey asked, surprised.

'Nah... have I fuck like.' He laughed at the thought of just how convinced the two had been. 'But they're so confident about it, they say I can go pay them tomorrow,' he added, taking a seat.

'Really... Very interesting,' said Prey as he tore open the envelope. 'Best have a look then.'

'Shit,' I exclaimed, observing the amount of paper contained in the envelope. 'You sure they got enough on him?' Prey started to distribute a few pages at a time to us all.

'Just a lot of bollocks 'ere,' Prey confirmed, looking at the top sheet. 'Been living in Congleton since early eighties. Got one son who's been nicked a few times for petty shit... Couple of speeding tickets for himself...' He informed us of all this without much interest.

We all read through the different sections, when I suddenly stopped and had to read something twice. 'Oh shit... Listen to this then,' I said, as all eyes fell upon me.

'What, Chopper? What is it?' Prey asked nonchalantly, apparently bored with what he'd just finished reading.

'Well, it looks like the reason this information is worth so much,' I said, glancing up momentarily to check that I had everybody's attention, 'and the reason why he's not mentioned before the eighties, is that ar' guy... well, he's really Paul Griffith.' I watched for their response.

'What the fuck—' began Sean.

'Yeah – listen to this bit... This guy is originally from Portsmouth. During the late sixties and early seventies he was one of the country's major smugglers,' I continued.

'What else it say?' Prey asked, smiling.

'They had two years' surveillance on him and his operation. He was running drugs in from all over back then. All kinds of shit they had on him...and not just the smuggling side of things,' I said, still glancing at the other things in the report.

'Like what?' Prey enquired enthusiastically.

'Oh shit... Get a load of this then,' Jonah suddenly exclaimed, reading from another section. 'Says that back in '73 when they finally busted him, it wasn't for only producing mass quantities of LSD and amphetamines, but also for the smuggling operation that he was running. When they picked him up they found near to a thousand keys of cannabis resin concealed in false flooring of some shipping freight that was being imported at the time.'

'*How* much?' Prey asked. 'Shit! That must have been one hell of a lot back then.'

'Fuck me... It's still a fair amount nowadays!' Sean laughed, suddenly chirping up. 'It also says that they threw in a lot of conspiracy charges as well, due to all the surveillance stuff they had on him. They sentenced him to fifteen years. Looks like they paroled him for good behaviour back in '83 though. Then he just seemed to disappear from the face of the earth after that – around the same time Mr Steve Griffin arrived in Congleton, I suspect.'

'Now why the fuck would he go and do a thing like that? Especially seeing as he'd been paroled? ' Prey asked.

'His son carries the name Griffin also,' Knieldy added. 'I don't know, but Robert and Dave mentioned that they'd just got very lucky on this guy...but that it was through something the son let drop. Maybe it's got something to do with him. Looks like the son is selling the weed he's been buying from Jonah anyway.'

'Yeah, according to this bit here it says that the son is known to the police over that way for petty shit like fighting, being drunk and disorderly, a burglary charge that they couldn't make stick... Nothing major though and no drug charges.' I told them this as I continued reading the sheets that were now being passed between us.

'So you say the son sells the weed. Why'd this guy take the risk of that?' Prey asked, looking a little confused.

'The kid's fifteen – nearly sixteen, mate. C'mon, Prey! We all did what the fuck we wanted at that age. Didn't we?' I replied.

Prey just nodded and grinned. 'Suppose so... All right, Knieldy, just how the fuck these guys find out so much?' He placed the remaining papers back onto the table.

'Mainly through Robert. He's some kind of computer geek; I'm not too sure what he does. It always baffled the fuck out of me when he told me about it. He says that the authorities haven't got a clue about any of this information 'cos he's covered his tracks so well. The guy appears to be as clean as can be on the surface. As for Dave... Well, he knows the street-level guys over that way. So I suppose between the two of them they're handy to know, eh.'

'Damn right they are. You go pay these guys tomorrow. Tell them for the grand we're paying them, this information goes no further whatsoever,' said Prey. 'Like you say, this guy seems clean as fuck on the surface. The police don't seem to know shit about him apart from his present title, and we need it to remain that way. Oh, and tell them we'll keep in touch... They've done a proper sound job 'ere,' he added, smiling.

'So when do you want me to hook up the meeting then, Prey?' asked Jonah, who by now was also smiling broadly at all of us.

FIFTEEN

Steve Griffin had accepted our invitation to talk business through Jonah the following evening. We'd set up the meeting at Chan's restaurant to keep things clear of the estate. However, I'd also arranged to meet Donna later on, so was hoping we could get through this as quickly as possible.

Prey, Sean and I were seated in the usual spot on the second floor at seven o'clock. Around ten minutes later Jonah arrived with Steve Griffin – or was that Paul Griffith? I observed cautiously as they both approached the table.

This character really stood out – or more to the point, he stood out against the likes of us. He had a weathered, hard-looking face that spoke of the myriad harsh realities of the life that he had once led. But despite that hardened glare, he had a full head of silvery grey hair that was pulled back into a sharp-looking pony tail, although his goatee beard looked like it hadn't been trimmed or seen to in a very long time, as it was sprouting all over the place.

His clothes on the other hand, compared to the rough face, were of great style and class. I didn't know the brand, but his dark charcoal suit was tailored to fit perfectly. It certainly wasn't your usual crap from Marks and Spencer's. Beneath the suit he wore a plain white shirt with gold cufflinks.

I found myself taking a liking to his style immediately; he had a certain air of authority about him, one that made you respect him instantaneously. So I was warming to Steve Griffin already and this was literally my very first encounter with him.

Jonah made the introductions. Prey merely grinned as he shook the older man's hand. 'Very pleased to make your acquaintance, Mr Paul Griffith,' he declared, not letting go of his hand.

Immediate shock took over the man's face and it's fair to say that none of us had expected Prey to be quite so direct. 'What the fuck... How do... What's goi... Fuck, you lads aren't old bill, are you? No, fuck that, no way. I can smell coppers from a fuckin' mile off. And I tell you right here and now – I ain't smelling any kind of pork today. So why don't you lads enlighten me, eh? What the fuck's going on?' he said, breaking free from Prey's hold and casually taking the vacant seat opposite him.

I have to admit that we were all surprised at the approach Prey had taken. He was continuing to grin and nod in a knowing fashion at the older man as he made himself comfortable. 'You're all right, old timer... You don't need to worry about it; we ain't 'ere to give you up to anyone.' Prey smiled at him warmly. 'But we have obviously had to find out just who it was that we're doing business with. Surely you understand that, don't you?'

Steve looked at all of us. 'I understand.' He glared at us all warily. 'Just how the fuck you find out though? This information ain't exactly floating around, you know.' He still had a look of disbelief clouding his eyes.

'We've got ar' contacts, you know. But 'ere's a little something for you though. Just for your own piece of mind, mate, the coppers over your way only know you as Griffin,' Prey smirked knowingly at Steve. 'They're none the wiser about anything else. However – your son doesn't do you any fuckin' favours though. He's been nicked for a few things now. That can't help any. Also, it was something that he let slip to one of ar' guys that put us onto your true identity.'

'Little prick... My son, that is,' Steve snapped. 'Anyway, what can I say? Full credit to you lads. You've certainly done your homework. That I can admire,' he smiled as the taut air that hung over us began dissolving slightly.

'Look, after tonight, we'll never cross this bridge again,' Prey said, staring at the older man. 'But if you ever try to fuck us in any way – and I mean any way whatsoever – then God only fuckin' knows who'll find out what we know. As it stands now, only us 'ere, plus one other of the crew, knows about this. And that, my friend, is the way it will stay. All right?'

'Fine,' he now laughed. 'Shit! It's been a long time since I heard my real name.'

'You sure did a good job of disappearing, didn't you?' I said to him.

'Last I heard is that they think I'm in South America somewhere. Think I done a Ronnie fuckin' Biggs or something.' He laughed again; he'd now fully relaxed and the hard expression he'd carried in through the door had diminished somewhat.

'Why did you stay in the country?' Sean asked.

'My kid. You see, his mother died giving birth to him. Soon after, I was sent away. He was in and out of foster homes, in and out of care. He was constantly in trouble with the authorities. He's not the brightest of lads – even I'll admit that. But I felt obliged to go take him back after my release.' He half laughed at this. 'So I disappeared, found out where he was and snatched him back. I changed his name to what it is now. It was too dodgy to leave the country back then. Besides, they're fuckin' clueless in Congleton anyway. It could be fuckin' South America for all they know,' he said, grinning at us.

'So is it the kid knocking out the weed?' Jonah asked.

'Yeah. You see, I found out what he was doing. The thing was he was buying it off this real dickhead. The sort of daft cunt that would cause trouble in the long run.' He shook his head. 'So I figured I couldn't stop him at his age, so it would be better coming through me than that cunt.'

'So, anyway, I told them about the samples, Steve,' Jonah added, eagerly changing the subject.

'Of course,' he smiled at us. 'So it's purely for my chemistry skills that you need me then.'

'Look, it sounds fuckin' top on the surface, mate. But what we need to know is exactly how your operation works,' Prey told him. 'You see, the last thing we need is any outside heat bearing down on us right now. Remember we found everything out about you, so we can't go taking risks just because the product and profit margins appear to be so good.'

'Well, that's the reason I need you lot. You see, I want rid of dumb little deals. Best to stick with large amounts or it's just not worth it,' he said, glaring straight at Prey. 'I know from the size of your weed operation – which I do believe is only one of your interests on the estate – that you're more than capable of taking care of things.'

'All right then; who are you already in business with at the moment?' Prey asked.

'No one from Manchester,' he confirmed, shaking his head as he did so. 'Just some business in Stoke, Macclesfield and Crewe.'

'Does your son know what you do?' I asked curiously.

'No fuckin' way… It stays that way as well,' he said, looking to me, then back to Prey. 'He knows what I did time for. Now he just thinks that I live from profits made back then.'

'Do you?' Sean grinned.

'Wasn't much left really, after I got out. So that's why I've set up the production side of things again. More money in producing it myself,' he smiled at us. 'Plus I got the knowledge, so I might as well use it… right?'

'Ain't that the truth,' Prey added.

'So, samples – when can we get them?' I asked, looking at my watch, impatiently thinking of Donna.

'Whenever… Tomorrow all right with you?' he enquired.

'That's fine. Early though: that way we can get the shit tested. If things work out, then it looks like we'll be in business for sure,' Prey informed him. 'We'll go over negotiations after it's tested; you'll be working with Chopper initially. Is that all right with you?'

'Sounds good to me,' he said, smiling at me. I noticed for the first time just how dark his eyes were and that they appeared to always be questioning everything.

'All right then. Tonight though, let's just eat and celebrate the new business,' Prey announced, smirking at the old man, who I think he really admired.

As I glanced at my watch for a second time and realised how long we were now going to be, my thoughts turned immediately to Donna, who I knew for certain was going to be pissed off at me.

SIXTEEN

D onna was livid at me by the time I'd arrived at The Carters Arms in Wilmslow to pick her up. I'd arranged to meet her at nine o'clock; it was near to ten thirty as I walked through the door.

'What fuckin' time is *this*?' Donna yelled at me as I held my hands up by way of an apology. All of her friends were staring from her to me.

'Ten thirty,' I answered sarcastically, glancing at my watch.

'Nine o'fuckin' clock you said.' She was enraged.

'I know – I know what I said. But I had shit to take care of, Donna – all right?' I smiled at her, trying my best to win her round. 'C'mon on now, girl. You know what I'm like. You know that this is my best time of the day anyway. You should know that by now.' I was trying to humour her as I held open my palms and shrugged.

'You're a bastard, Chopper,' she screamed at me.

'I know I am. I'd have thought that was one of my best features.' I was trying my best to amuse her. 'Besides which, we're all bastards at the end of the day, Donna. It's just that you either find yourself a bad bastard or a good bastard, eh.'

The frown dropped from her face as she shook her head at me and suddenly smiled. 'Well, it's one of your best features anyway. And as for good or bad – well, I think you have a little of both. And besides which, when it comes down to your features, Chopper, I can certainly think of a much better one.' She gave me a cheeky grin. Her friends, now bored with the entire incident, had gone back to talking among themselves.

'C'mon on then, Donna. We're off to meet Prey at The Haçienda.'

'You're joking, right? Look at the time,' she declared, looking at her watch.

'Yeah! So what? C'mon, it'll be all right,' I said, smiling at her. 'I want you to meet Prey. You already met Scotty and Kezlo this week. He's like me family, y'know.'

Without another word she kissed me. 'You're such a bastard,' she whispered.

We were back in town by eleven o'clock. We both discovered the others hidden away under the balcony area in some dark corner of the club. Steve was still there, and it looked like Prey was playing host once again. Empty bottles of Bollinger champagne lay around the tables and floor.

'Chopper. Come 'ere, ar'kid,' Prey shouted as he spotted the two of us.

I made my way over with Donna in tow. 'Yes, mate. I got someone I want you to meet,' I said, smiling proudly at him as I took Donna's arm. 'This is—'

'Donna. What you with this ugly twat for, girl?' Prey said, kissing her cheek.

She smiled at him, not at all fazed by his appearance. 'So you're the famous Prey I hear so much about then.'

'And you're the one who's got our little Chopper in a fluster this last couple of weeks, eh?'

'In a fluster, is he?' she smiled at me.

'No, I'm not…' I began to protest as Donna squeezed my side in jest.

'You must be the one, Donna. You know why?' Prey laughed.

'Why's that then, Prey?' She smiled mischievously at him.

'Well, you see, Donna, all his other birds have been so fuckin' pig ugly that he never once introduced me to one of them,' he said, roaring with laughter.

'Fuck you! That's not the reason,' I blurted out.

'Oh, right then. So you're lucky to have me then,' Donna laughed along. 'Well, I'll just have to keep you in check, won't I?'

'That's it, girl. Don't take any shit off him.' Prey slapped my shoulder, loving every minute of this. 'I like this girl, Chopper; she's all right, mate.' Prey expressed great amusement again; all this was entertaining him.

'Cheers, mate,' I added sarcastically.

'C'mon, Donna, you can help me at the bar,' he smiled, linking arms with her and heading off towards the bar.

I walked over to Steve, who was enjoying himself as he blissfully puffed away on a heavily loaded spliff. 'How's it goin', mate?'

'Fine, Chopper. Prey's been keeping me entertained... Speaks very highly of you,' he replied.

'I see he managed to keep you in town then. He loves to play the host, y'know,' I told him, as I took the spliff from him.

'I kinda got that impression about him, you know,' he laughed. 'It's all right though; I can't remember the last time I was at a club.'

'Y'know that he'll have us all up first thing in the morning for business though, right?'

'I know,' he sniggered at me. 'He's already told me that I'm to be back by ten o'clock so we can get things rolling.'

'Sounds about right.'

'He says that you should be able to do both in life. Do good time enjoying life and do good business existing in life was how he put it. Although what I think he meant was that you should do them together,' he chuckled.

'I know what you mean. I just hope things work out.'

'They will do,' Steve answered confidently. 'You've got a good crew put together... tight... I like the way you lads seem to handle yourselves. I reckon we'll have a pretty bright future together, Chopper,' he said, raising his glass.

'I got to be totally honest with you, Steve. I don't know shit about your side of business,' I responded, staring directly at him. 'Although I'm always interested in things that make money.'

'Don't worry about it, mate,' Steve shook his head at me. 'By the time we set things up, you'll have all the knowledge that you'll require. I promise you; I'll train you myself.'

'I'm looking forward to it, mate.'

'Look, Chopper, I know you'll just be involved with the initial setting up of the business, but I need to know who'll take over from you.'

'You already know him, mate,' I said, nodding at Jonah, who was stood by the dance floor. 'Like we said, we need to keep your secret safe as much as you do.'

'Jonah, you mean,' he said, smiling.

'That's all right with you, ain't it? Jonah's a top lad, and besides, if it wasn't for him we wouldn't be 'ere right now.'

'That's fine with me. Jonah's got the sort of discretion I can work with,' he replied.

'Did I hear my name or is it just my ears burning?' Jonah asked as he approached.

In the months that followed we'd built our new business steadily. I helped Jonah with the organising of the operation, the exact same way that Sean had done so with me. And within a month he had things running very smoothly.

Jonah had been promoted to 'lieutenant' within the firm. It had only been fair to do so; he still watched the street, but used Dougsy more so than before.

Steve had been true to his word, showing me every aspect of setting the business up. He taught me everything that I needed to know about his products, whilst obviously keeping certain trade secrets to himself.

I took real pleasure from working with the older man. He was a real character, with vast knowledge in so many subjects. Steve filled me with stories of his smuggling days and the risks they used to take. They were proper crazy back then, controlling the import business with pure liberties that in this day and age would be scoffed at by the authorities as impossible. No doubt their apparent impossibility was why they worked so well.

He told me how he knew that the customs and the police were on to him for such a long time, that he just kept giving them the runaround and taking the piss. He also added that it had been the reason he'd got away with it for so long.

He eventually blamed his downfall on one of his crew members who had been turned over to the dark side, as he put it, although he could find enough amusing factors about it these days and was able to laugh about it now.

It was safe to say that I really liked Steve a lot. No one from our crew had a clue who he was; nobody needed to, apart from those concerned. Besides, that side of things was already becoming larger each week, so nothing could jeopardise that position.

In general, things were good in my personal life too. Donna had taken up permanent residence at the flat. I loved having her around and everybody seemed to like her, which was really a bonus. I really loved her, but couldn't find it in me to tell her just yet.

Prey always took her away from me at every possible opportunity, informing me that, 'She's one of the good ones. Keep hold of this one.'

Truth was, I wasn't going to let her go anywhere. We never spoke about what we did business-wise. Obviously she knew what it was, but we'd agreed to never discuss it. Besides which, I didn't want to be talking business all the time.

Donna had managed to get herself a job on King Street in town, in some clothes shop. She was doing pretty well from it, being promoted from a sales assistant to supervisor very quickly, although I'd told her that she didn't need to get herself a job. But she just pouted at this and told me, 'I ain't no kept woman. What do you think I am? Somebody you can keep on a leash or something?'

I'd really admired this in her, actually. Too many women out there would have been more than pleased to just spend my money and do bugger all, all day long.

Her parents, on the other hand, had gone mental over her moving in with me. Not because they knew what I did, as they didn't. But they were a family of great wealth, something that I'd not known. I'd been totally astonished when we'd gone to collect her belongings. Their home had been huge; it took a couple of minutes just to drive up their driveway. Now I knew why Donna hadn't wanted me to pick her up from her home on our first date.

Donna's mother had been pleasant enough, trying her best to understand her daughter's decision. But her father was a different matter all together. You could see his pure hatred for me as soon as I met him. If I'd been able to read his thoughts they'd have been along the lines of *Fucking little cocksucker – take my daughter away will you, eh – I could kill you. She's my little princess...* And so on and so forth. I'm positive I sensed this in him. However, Donna told me that I was just being paranoid.

But I knew. After all, we were of the same breed.

SEVENTEEN

Just as Prey had predicted the previous year, The Haçienda entered its boom time with the new era of house music. Everybody wanted to be part of what was happening at 'The Haç', as it was more commonly known. We'd observed the club's growth from 1987 into 1988, and it would be in 1988 where everything we'd previously known would change. Every weekend leading into that year had become busier, especially Friday nights at the club, a night called Nude.

The DJs were Mike Pickering and Graeme Park, and between the two of them they played some of the most amazing sets.

Dance music was being played all over Manchester now, and some of the most dedicated DJs who had followed the music's growth were finally beginning to be heard by the mass public, who were beginning to live only for their weekends. It was good to see more and more people becoming conscious of a scene that had been bubbling under the surface for the last couple of years now. Only now was its authentic eminence becoming appreciated.

We'd monitored the music's growth from the early hip hop scene with its early imports of Chicago house, into what had now developed beyond everybody's expectations. At this moment in time it had been labelled Acid House by the media, who had very little understanding of its true roots. All that they were interested in was tarnishing it with bad press coverage of the illegal warehouse parties that were also beginning to take off, not only in Manchester but all over the country.

People just weren't contented with the night ending at two o'clock, when clubs normally shut down for the night. And so the warehouse parties were devised to fulfil the desires of people who wanted to continue dancing and generally enjoying themselves until the early hours of the morning.

Of course, Prey's prediction had been that the place would boom with both business and pleasure, as they were the two things in life he loved so much; for him, the real enjoyment was doing them both together. He'd seen the way the music industry had been changing, telling us that this time would be 'our true time… our true future'. Now it was here, so the only way to go was forward.

The music scene back then was revolutionary. It brought together so many different cultures, which previously would never have mixed. And as for all the bad press given to all the 'illegal acid house parties', as the press referred to them (or warehouse parties, as we referred to them), it would only heighten all of this. It's always the same, you see. You tell people not to go doing something, and then naturally they want to get out there and do it more. That's just life: people are naturally defiant.

National newspapers would publish stories about how the younger generation's minds were being twisted by this evil brainwashing music and the drugs associated with it. Yet the more they tried to stop it the more they enhanced people's curiosity, spreading the word further and wider.

Illegal warehouse parties were becoming massive and there was a huge amount of money to be made from them. With at least £10 a head being charged at the door, and with thousands upon thousands of people being drawn from all over the country, you can only imagine the kind of profits that were being made. The money made on the door alone was colossal, not including the trade done inside through the drugs that were sold. Large amounts were frequently consumed in order to enable people to keep dancing until the early hours of the morning.

Older generations said it was all merely hype, a new craze the kids had got themselves into; it would all soon pass. Yet nobody could have predicted that this scene would one day become an industry all of its own, run by a generation which had barely reached maturity. The simple fact was that this so-called craze could not be ignored.

The club soon evolved into a second home for us. The fact we'd hooked up with Steve the previous year had only heightened our business with the mass sale of trips (as in LSD trips) and speed. We practically ran the trade inside the club.

Along with our wholesaling the gear, the amount of money our crew was making inside the club itself was immense, as they were bringing in large sums of hard cash from the gear they were selling to the mass public. And believe me, the public at large was more than hungry for what we had on offer. Things couldn't have been better for us.

Ecstasy tablets had been around for a few years now, although we'd tried what were supposedly Es, as they were more commonly known, and hadn't been overly impressed with them. I personally hadn't really got off that much with the ones that we'd tried, thinking them to be like a good little bit of speed. Stories were floating about that 1987 had done wonders for the drug within the clubbing scene, not only heightening the level of the music, but also the whole atmosphere of the night. Once again though, I personally hadn't experienced it, or maybe we'd just had inferior pills.

There was definitely a market out there for the drug, although at the time we didn't have any contacts for the drug itself and the ones we did know of were demanding ridiculous amounts for them. Like I said, we weren't impressed enough to fork out the money those people wanted for something that wasn't, in our minds anyway, that good. This all changed one particular night.

All of us were in our usual spot for the night, breathing in the smoke-filled air of The Haç.

'All right there, lads! How's it going then?' It was Steve, which to be fair was extremely peculiar, as he never just showed up like that – especially not at the club.

'What the fuck are you doing 'ere?' Prey looked shocked to see him. 'Not that you're not welcome or anything,' he added, grabbing hold of the older man's hand and shaking it firmly.

'You all right, mate?' I nodded at him. 'Everything's still sweet, ain't it?' I enquired, a little concerned at his unannounced arrival.

'Yeah… couldn't be better, lads,' he smirked, winking at us. 'Where's Jonah?'

'Right behind you, old timer.'

'Hi'ya, Steve,' Donna smiled. She'd met him a few times

before and and, as everybody else, she'd managed to win him over.

'All right, girl,' Steve smiled at her. 'Come here and make an old man happy,' he said, opening his arms for a hug.

'All right, back to the initial question, Steve,' Prey said, laughing at the way Steve was carrying on. 'What the fuck are you doing 'ere, man?'

'I got you all a treat,' he said, letting out an excited laugh as he told us this. 'Something I reckon you're gonna like a lot that my mate from San Francisco has just brought over with him.' He opened his hand to reveal a small bag containing white pills.

'What the fuck are those things?' I asked curiously.

'These, my son, are going to change everything,' he laughed.

'How's that then, Steve?' Sean asked, who'd just returned from the bar.

Now Steve seemed really excited. In fact, I could have sworn that his eyes were shaking from his own excitable attitude. 'These are known as Ecstasy tablets,' he said, looking at all of us. 'You've heard of them, haven't you?' he asked as we all nodded. 'I tell you all now, no bullshit, I don't care if you've tried them before, because you won't have tried any as good as these little babies. These will blow your minds.'

'What the fuck we waiting for then, Steve?' I laughed. 'Give us one then. Let's find out just how good these things are.' I was eager to find out what had him so animated.

Popping the plain white pill into my mouth and swallowing, I then gave one to Donna. Prey and Steve popped theirs with Sean following suit.

Jonah scuttled off to find Sharon to give her one too. 'Right, Prey. There's another twenty-odd in there. Get someone to give them out to potential customers. Oh, and get them to give some to the real mad-heads. You know, the ones who normally want to kick the shit out of each other,' Steve said, smirking mischievously as he said it.

'Why?' Prey asked.

'A little experiment for you to all witness… watch the magic work.'

I began laughing at him; he sounded more like Merlin the way he was carrying on, going on about his magical drugs.

''Ere'are, Dougsy.'

'What's up, Chopper?' he asked as he came over to where we were all standing. I explained what he needed to do with the Es and he then scuttled away.

'You talking real crazy tonight, old man,' Prey informed Steve, who hadn't stopped smiling since he'd first come into the club.

'Maybe, maybe not though,' he laughed wildly at us, shaking his head. 'C'mon on, Donna... Come help me with the drinks, will you,' he said, linking her arm.

Prey turned to me. 'You any idea what the fuck he's going on about, Chopper?'

'Not a fuckin' clue, mate,' I replied, laughing at the mental picture of the crazy old man.

'Sure seems happy about something though,' Sean said.

'Ain't that the truth,' Jonah laughed, returning with Sharon in tow.

Steve and Donna returned with the drinks. 'All right, every-body,' Steve said cheerfully. Damn, he sure was in a good mood tonight.

About half an hour had passed since we'd all dropped the pills and I still couldn't feel the effects of whatever it was that I was supposed to be feeling. 'Just wait and see,' was all that Steve kept saying to us. His face now looked illuminated with bubbling titillation.

Just then I could feel Donna rubbing against my side. Glanc-ing at her, you could see her eyes beginning to roll. 'You all right?' I asked, a little concerned, as she never usually did any drugs.

'Oh yes,' she purred seductively as it suddenly started to hit me.

A whole fusion of different sensations – extremely horny, hot then cold, sexy, hot again, rushes, dizziness – it all seemed to be coming at me from a thousand different angles – and all of it at once. I began shuddering as the Ecstasy began to take control of my body. Shit... it sure felt good though. And it wasn't like anything that I'd come up on before. Although I couldn't explain it properly, all I knew was that I liked it a lot.

'These are *good*, aren't they, Chopper?' Donna said, dancing sexily next to me.

The pill was becoming stronger and more intense. I could feel the grin across my face as I found myself moving along unwittingly to the bass of the tunes flowing from the sound system. I gazed over at Prey and Steve… Now these must be *extremely* good – Prey was actually dancing. I'd never really seen Prey dance before now; well, at least not as enthusiastically as he was doing right now. 'Damn these are colossal… aren't they?' I mumbled, kissing Donna, which sure felt good too.

'I'm so hot,' Donna whispered.

I glanced over to Jonah and Sharon and they were all over each other. Sean was just grinning away and dancing like a madman. His arms seemed to be almost controlling themselves and it looked as though at that precise moment he didn't care for anything else but to dance the night away.

Just then a massive judder shot through me; my body was rippling from the effects of the drug. 'Fuck me!' I said, shaking my head in disbelief at what I was experiencing. So this is what Ecstasy was supposed to feel like… I'd never felt anything so good before.

Holding within me a feeling of being at one with everything around me. Overcome with the sensuous feeling of euphoria.

'These are fantastic, Prey!' I smiled, grabbing hold of him. Then, for no reason except that I felt like it, I began hugging him, unsure as to why! All I knew is that it felt good to be doing so. Before realising it, we were all dancing and hugging each other.

'I told you so… I told you,' Steve laughed, watching the effects of the pills he'd transferred as they took control of all of us.

'I feel well sound,' Prey laughed at me; his face was perspicuous with joy. 'I haven't felt anything like this before.'

'No way… Look at them go,' I said, pointing into the crowd where Dougsy had distributed the pills. You had lads who were normally scowling at each other genuinely hugging each other without a single care in the world. 'Shit, check that out, Prey. Ain't that Paddy and Chris?' I was nodding towards the edge of the dance floor where we could clearly see the two of them.

'Fuck,' laughed Prey. 'Would you fuckin' believe that shit, Chopper? If I didn't know better you'd have thought the two of them were gay.'

It was true. The two of them were hugging and kissing everybody around them. We knew that it was only the effects of the pills they had been given – but it really was a sight to behold. 'I think that Paddy is freaking some of the Salford lads out, Prey.'

'In't it, Chopper,' smiled Prey, shaking his head. 'If only we had a camera right now. What a picture that would make, eh. I don't think that anybody would believe us if we told them we saw Paddy hugging people.'

'Yeah,' I laughed. 'They'd be like "I know Paddy. Always hurting people".' We were both laughing at the sight of this. It honestly had to be seen to be believed.

'No way!' Jonah pointed to the stage area, breaking through our laughter. 'Check Sean out,' he laughed. Sean was jumping up and down, grabbing everybody; he was enjoying himself to so much. He wanted to meet everyone who was also dancing around him. Even they seemed to enjoy themselves more at the way he was carrying on. What a night this was.

Dougsy came over. 'What the fuck are these things you've give me? They feel proper sound. Have you seen everybody I give 'em to? They're going mad out there. They all keep thanking and hugging me. Even that fuckin nutter Paddy has hugged me. It's well fuckin' mad… It really is,' he announced, laughing.

As the night came to a close at The Haç, we all returned back to our flat. Kezlo started up on the decks. Scotty had been missing the last couple of days so had missed out on the experience of that evening. He'd been doing this more and more lately. Not that it concerned us, as he was usually off with some girl somewhere.

Steve had another bag full of Es, and so we all enjoyed each others' company until the early hours of the morning.

They were good times. Ecstasy – proper Es – had arrived. It felt like we tasted the future that night.

EIGHTEEN

Prey was still talking incessantly about the Es on Monday afternoon; he hadn't stopped going on about how great they were all weekend. We'd arranged to meet Steve that afternoon at Chan's to discuss purchasing terms required for them. As yet, the only people who we knew definitely were interested would be those who sampled them on Friday night, although we didn't consider this to be a problem after we'd experienced them ourselves.

'I still can't get my head round it, lads,' Prey smirked at Sean. 'Especially you, Sean, bouncing up and down like a crazy fool up there on the stage,' he laughed.

Sean laughed, also thinking back on the experience. 'I know, mate; I just don't know what possessed me. I had no control of my body dancing.' He shook his head in disbelief. 'I was hugging lads from Salford that I fuckin' hate. Well – apart from that prick Chris. Oh, and not forgetting that other prick – Paddy.'

'You see 'em though?' I asked.

'I know,' laughed Prey. 'These fuckin' pills certainly have more than one plus side to them if they can calm Paddy down.'

'In't it,' smirked Sean. 'All I know is that at the time I loved just about everybody and everything.'

'I reckon if we can get a good price on them we'll clean up, y'know,' Prey declared, smiling as he did.

'I know what you're saying, Prey. I've spoken to some of the lads on Saturday that we gave them to,' Jonah informed us. 'I reckon we can pull at least twenties back on them inside the clubs. Just think about the parties too. It's going to be double sweet,' he added.

I began smiling at them all. 'Y'know that Steve planned this, don't you?'

'What you goin' on about, Chopper?' Prey asked.

'Just think about it, mate. He's a crafty bastard when you think about it. He used his noodle, mate.' I was tapping my forehead, smiling at the three of them sat there, not understanding what I was going on about. 'That's for sure,' I added, at the thought of what he'd done.

'I'm not following you,' Sean said, as the other two were also shaking their heads.

'Well, look,' I began, 'he turns up out of the blue... Jonah had already seen him that day and if he merely wanted us to sample them he would have just given him the bag of samples for us to try. But he wanted to see our reactions to this new product of his,' I said, laughing out loud. 'I mean, think about it – sure we've been quoted prices to buy Es before, but not like these ones. Don't you think it's odd that we ain't had a price yet?'

'So what you're saying is this guy from the States doesn't exist?' Sean asked.

'No, not at all,' I told him. 'In fact, I imagine he's very real. But his mate's turned up with them, right? Knows that you can get a good buzz off them; knows that there must be a market for these so-called Ecstasy tablets that apparently every fucker is going mad for. He knows that Steve should be able to do something with them... But don't you understand yet?' I was smirking knowingly at them as they sat there absorbing everything that I was telling them.

'Spit it out will you, Chopper,' Prey said, a little irritated.

All eyes were on me. 'I've just said it – the price of course!' I sighed deeply and kissed my teeth. 'They ain't got a clue how much to charge for them! We played right into his hands. He's seen for himself first-hand how much everybody liked them. Now he'll charge us the earth for them...y'know it.'

'Sly bastard,' Prey chuckled.

'You got respect him for it though,' I added.

'In'it... How much you reckon he'll ask for them at whole-sale?' Jonah asked.

'Don't tell the cunt how much we reckon we'll get for them,' Sean added, laughing at just how the old man had played us.

'I reckon it just depends how many this guy has brought with him,' I responded, shaking my head. 'Hopefully it's a shitload, but in the long run it won't help us,' I said, looking directly at Prey.

'Why's that?' Jonah asked.

'Because they'll run out, obviously,' Prey stated.

'That's right, but we all know Steve,' I said, smiling at the thought of him. 'The way I see it, he'll be trying to manufacture them himself before long. Just depends what he needs for the recipe.'

Steve suddenly appeared without any of us noticing him. 'Recipe for what?' he asked, smirking at us. He wasn't stupid.

'Nowt, mate… Just some new dish I want to try,' I quickly responded, not even convincing myself.

He just grinned at me as he sat down. 'Whatever. You lads all all right?' he smiled at the four of us. 'What do think then, after Friday night?' he asked, looking over to Chan.

'You lads ready to order food now?' Chan enquired.

'Just the usual, Chan,' Prey said, before any of us had time to even consider ordering anything different. Chan scuttled away. 'All right then, Steve. How much for the pills?' Prey asked bluntly.

'First things first.' He paused and looked at us one by one. 'I got to tell you there aren't a lot of these pills, so the price is high.' He waited for our reaction.

'Just how fuckin' high, Steve?' I enquired.

'Well, let's say tens on five hundred at a time.' He looked to Prey.

'You having a laugh or what?' Sean asked, diverting his attention. 'Five grand for—'

'You don't see me laughing, do you?' Steve replied sternly.

'Why only five hundred at a time?' I asked him.

'My guy has brought ten thousand with him. If you flood the market with them, then there'll be none left.'

'That's where you'll come in, I suppose?' Prey asked.

He smiled. 'Look, they'll take some doing to manufacture,' he winked. 'I reckon it'll take at least two months to set up properly – once I've got together the initial funds to do so, that is. The main ingredient is MDMA.'

'What the fuck is MDMA?' Jonah asked.

'Can't remember to save my life, Jonah,' he laughed. 'All I

know is that it's what gave you all that feeling you had the other night. That's why those ones that you tried were as good as they were. I don't know whether or not you've tried any in the last couple of years, but if you have done I bet they were fuck all like those ones. The last time this country saw the kind of pills you lot had the other night would have been years back now – and they wouldn't have been used for going out to clubs on back then.'

'So can your guy get the gear?' Prey asked. 'This MD-whatever shit.'

'That's the dodgy bit, you see. I know him from my smuggling days,' he said, shaking his head. 'The one thing that we both know is that shipping gear in from the States is dodgy as fuck,' he added, lighting a Benson and Hedges cigarette. 'But it could be done. Only it's going to cost big time.'

'So what you saying is that we're all right for four to five months tops – that's it?' Sean asked.

'All right, here's the deal. Your crew gets the exclusive on these ones. I won't let any other fucker touch them. You pay tens on them; that way, my mate and me can get the money back required to set things up properly,' he said, blowing out smoke.

'Why does your guy not just do them over there?' I asked, a little curious as to why he'd brought them over to England in the first place.

''Cause no fucker wants them,' Steve laughed. 'They're all fucked-up crack and ice heads over there. This gear isn't strong enough for them. Besides, they ain't got the clubbing scene like you lads have.'

'All right, old man, you got a deal,' said Prey, who'd been sat there quietly, thinking things over. 'But when you got things running properly, our price drops – understood?' he added, sipping his drink.

'All right – you lads got a deal then,' Steve confirmed, smiling now that he'd got exactly what he'd set out for.

NINETEEN

After the first batch of our Es hit the streets, we knew that it was an absolute 100 per cent necessity for the continuation of the sale of Ecstasy. People were going mad for these pills and just about willing to pay whatever price we were commanding for them. Although we knew that it was inevitable that we'd have to move into the wholesale side of things before someone else managed to get it wired.

Steve's mate had begun to do the runs from the States with the required MDMA. But it was almost three months after the original batch was depleted before Steve managed to get the Ecstasy tablets right, so there were some dodgy batches along the way. Some were too strong, some not strong enough. Eventually he got the formula right, but saying that, they were never as good as the first batch that hit Manchester.

What was important though was the increased demand for them as the year went by. We were still paying over the odds for them; Steve still wouldn't drop the price. Besides, he knew we weren't going to stop buying them from him. After all, business was business and no other supplier even came close, quality-wise, to the ones that Steve was producing for us.

So for us to wholesale them was hard, as everybody wanted in on them. We were already purchasing over a thousand a week, but to wholesale them meant charging daft money. Although it's fair to say that we were still making excellent money from them inside the clubs.

It was around this time that all the really dodgy Es hit the open market. They were mainly capsules filled with a combination of speed and trips. Not only that – you also had pills that did nothing at all to you. You found the likes of Paddy's crew knocking these out, as he knew nobody was going to confront him over it. But in a way, they probably did us more good than harm, as it kept custom regular for the good ones.

Although it wasn't long before we began to run into troubles. You see, Steve was insistent that he couldn't find MDMA anywhere in the UK. He'd told me in the beginning that our downfall through them would come from having to have the gear smuggled into the country from America. Apart from our crew, he was selling around another thousand out of town, so he claimed that the risks involved in bringing the gear into the UK were becoming increasingly higher. Prey, on the other hand, thought Steve was just pushing up the price on us, and so a meeting was arranged.

'So what you're saying is the guy in the States isn't prepared to bring it in no more?' Prey said through mouthfuls of duck noodle soup.

'Smuggling from there is dodgy,' Steve replied.

'He's only done a couple of runs up to now and we haven't even been up and running that long for him to start getting cold feet,' Sean added.

'I know he has,' Steve sighed. 'But he's starting to get paranoid as fuck about it all now.'

'So what's the price you're asking now?' Prey asked, looking up.

'It's not that, mate.' He shook his head. 'Look, I'm trying to keep my word on bringing the price down, so I ain't going to go putting it up on you, am I now?' Steve said, looking offended.

Prey smiled. 'Well, that's one thing at least. I thought you were just pushing for more bees,' he laughed. 'All right, old man. What are our options, if there are any for that matter?'

'I suppose I could try making some other ones. But they just won't be the same,'

'So what would they be then?' I asked.

'A cocktail of speed and trips. Not in capsule form – they'd be pills,' he told me, watching me tut at the prospect of having to do that.

'Anything else?' Prey enquired, also pulling his face at the first option.

'One other thing, which I'd have to find a source for – Keta-mine,' Steve said.

'What the fuck is that?' Sean enquired.

Steve laughed before answering. 'Horse fuckin' tranquilliser.'

'You're kidding, right,' I blurted out, spitting my rice out at the mere thought of it.

'No. My mate used to use it years back,' he laughed. 'He says it's a top buzz you get from it. Turned up once whilst I was inside, completely off his tits.' Steve laughed and so did we.

'Fuck that one… Well, for now anyway,' Prey laughed.

'How much shit we got left?' I asked.

'With what's already made and the MDMA left, I reckon about two months tops.'

'So what then? Too much money and enjoyment is involved 'ere,' Prey said, still grinning about the Ketamine.

'It's the amount really,' Steve said, shaking his head again. 'You see, I have to cut him in on what I make. It just ain't worth it.'

'Well, we just can't stop,' Sean said.

'Look, I've got an idea,' I told them.

'What's that then, Chopper?' Prey asked, rubbing his chin.

'All right, what if we increase the amount of pills we buy from you?' I said, looking at Steve.

'You not listening or what, Chopper?' Steve sighed, lighting himself another cigarette and leaning back.

'Well, look: what if we guarantee the purchase of ten thousand a week from you? That way it's more than worth it,' I said, smiling at all of them.

I knew that Prey would understand, as Sleeper was also driving him insane with his incessant demands for them in London. He smiled. 'That way your guy will be making so much more he can get someone else to bring it in.'

'Exactly. Everybody will be happy,' I grinned.

'You can guarantee that amount, can you?' Steve asked, contemplating the deal.

'Definitely – look what we've got going in town. My guy in London is itching to get in on the action for sure,' Prey said, smiling at me.

'It could work, you know. I'll have to check with my guy, obviously,' Steve said, smiling at us. 'But it does make sense as he can just be involved with the purchasing side of things. The only thing is I'll need to bring in someone to help with the increased production,' he continued, drawing thoughtfully on his cigarette.

'Will that be a problem?' I asked.

'Yes and no. I've got someone in mind… I'll have to think about that one though,' Steve replied.

'So we got a deal or not?' Prey grinned.

Steve smirked back. 'As good as. Let's leave it at that.' Then he winked at us.

TWENTY

Manchester was the one place in the country that everybody was talking about. The year had been fantastic. Some of the best parties organised were growing into bigger and better things all the time. Our weekends were filled purely with clubbing and the best parties.

Before anybody knew it, one year had flowed into another and Manchester had become known in the press as 'Madchester', mainly because of bands like the Stone Roses, Happy Mondays, The Charlatans and 808 State, to name only a handful who were constantly in the press for one reason or another. It was mad business-wise too. We'd stepped up to a new level with the ever-increasing sales surrounding Es and an assortment of other drugs that were now in demand.

All the hype was down to the media constantly plugging Manchester, but to us it was still town: it was the place we'd grown up in. We thought the 'Madchester' hype was for the tourists.

Also around this time though, gun culture had crept in, with the increased sale of crack-cocaine, or 'rocks' as it was referred to. On the estates like Moss Side and along with ongoing disputes over the smack, business had furthered the use of guns.

But despite our other successful areas of business, smack was still one of Prey's best money-makers. As dirty a business as it was, it was the one drug that they came back for time and time again.

No matter what is done to try and stop heroin use, it will always be here. So with all the wars going on around town, especially behind us with Moss Side fighting constantly, either with themselves (the estate was split into different areas) or with Cheetham Hill, Prey had us arm ourselves.

He'd used some contacts through Chan to make sure the guns were clean. And I have to admit, I loved the feeling of power I got when handling my piece. The crew chose an assortment of different handguns. Personally, I went for an Italian model that was light in weight and didn't have anywhere near the same recoil that Prey's Austrian Glock did. Although the Glock was a lot lighter in weight than my Beretta 9mm model 92, as it was made from polymer, I thought the kickback on the Glock was more lethal than the Beretta.

It had also caused one hell of a row with Donna, as I'd left my pistol on the bedside table, which wasn't the brightest of places to leave it, I know. She'd gone mental over what I needed a gun for. Then she'd burst into tears when I'd explained I needed it for protection. She'd sobbed for hours about how she couldn't bear losing me.

Another issue at hand was the ever-increasing demand for crack-cocaine on the estate. A lot of the smackheads were mixing it on foil to make it run longer when they were chasing it.

Prey had asked Sean and me to meet him round at his flat to see what our thoughts were on getting into the business ourselves. 'So what do you reckon then?' he enquired, after we'd sat there debating whether or not we thought that we should enter into that side of things.

'We'd be dumb not to, Prey,' I simply said.

'We're already knocking out the charlie, Prey, so what difference will it make?' Sean added, toking on a spliff.

'I know. Sleeper's cleaning up with it down there.' He shook his head. 'And he said that we're losing pure bees by not doing it.' Prey was now pacing the living room.

'So what's the problem?' I asked.

'It's too fuckin' nice – that's the problem.' He came to a standstill.

'Ain't that the truth, brother,' Sean laughed.

'Look, it's just another commodity to sell,' I replied, staring at the two of them. 'Fuck it. We've got fuck all to lose,' I said, taking the spliff from Sean.

'Chopper's right, y'know. The coppers still ain't close to us, Prey; we've got the estate wired,' Sean told him. 'All they've picked up is foot soldiers and that's never on anything major. So a few are doing bird – that's just business. It's the business we're involved in.'

'At the end of the day, if the old bill nicks us for smack then it might just as well be rocks,' I said. 'I mean, to them it's merely class fuckin' A or B, in't it mate.'

'I know… but I just worry some of the lads will get fucked up on the rocks. D'ya know what I mean like?' Prey said, sitting down.

'Look, Prey, just keep it involved on the smack side,' I told him. 'Don't let any of the younger kids knocking out the weed in on it. All it needs is setting up properly.'

'You're both right. In fact, there is one other thing that we need to go over, but I need all the crew there for it,' Prey announced, rising to the phone.

'Who you calling?' Sean asked.

'Chan. I want a table for all the crew on Wednesday night,' he said, dialling the number.

'All of them?' I exclaimed, astounded.

'Yes, Chan. It's Prey, mate. I need a table after hours, mate.' I looked at Sean, baffled; he returned the same look and shrugged.

'That's right, after hours, mate… About forty-five or fifty or so,' Prey said.

'What's he going on about?' Sean asked me.

'Yeah, mate. I thought you wouldn't mind once you knew the amount… All right then, mate, see you then,' Prey said, replacing the receiver.

'What's that all about, Prey?' I asked him.

'We need to hold a meeting then,' he smiled, 'so as not to fuck business up. C'mon, Chopper, surely you thought of that.'

'Yeah, so what if I did… Just looking out for your interests.'

'So what's with the meeting then?' Sean enquired curiously.

'You'll both have to wait and see like the rest, won't you?' he grinned at the two of us.

The restaurant's second floor was packed. Everybody was joking and laughing and having a good time. It was one hell of sight to bear witness to. It made me suddenly realise the extent to which things had increased in the last few years when I saw all of Prey's crew together like this.

'All right, Chopper?' Kezlo asked, sitting next to me, Scotty just behind him.

'You got any idea what this is about?' Scotty asked.

'All right, lads… Nah, mate,' I answered. 'Haven't got a clue. How's business been this week?' I asked, changing the subject.

'Sound, mate,' Scotty smiled at me. 'Me and Kezlo had to sort out this kid this week though.'

'What for?'

'Went missing for a few weeks, didn't he,' Kezlo said.

'Who?'

'Little Louie… Decided he needed new clothes before paying his bill. Little bastard,' Scotty said, laughing as he did so.

'All sorted now though?'

'Yeah, mate,' Kezlo chuckled. 'Funny how a shooter stuck in someone's face changes the situation.'

I laughed; it was good to see the two of them. I'd moved out of the flat recently, getting another place on the estate with Donna. Living there with all that business just wasn't fair to her, although she never said anything.

The three of us still remained close, but some things had changed. Basically we'd grown up a lot. The scores had been knocked on the head for a long time now; it wasn't that we didn't enjoy doing them – we did. But our other activities were the main concern, and things had to run smoothly. Nothing could get in the way of that nowadays.

I observed Prey conversing with Chan by the kitchen doors, both smiling and joking. I noticed Prey pass a large padded envelope to Chan. The small, wiry old man shook Prey's hand firmly.

Just then Sean appeared and sat down. 'All right, lads… how's it going?'

'Still don't know why the fuck we're all 'ere then?' I said, shaking his hand.

'I know what you mean, Chopper.'

He looked at all of the crew, along with the street grafters and smiled. 'Must be important though. I ain't ever seen all the crew together like this before.'

Prey came and sat between the two of us, grinning as he did so. 'Well, that's the scran taken care of.'

'So are you going to tell us what the fuck this is all about?' I asked eagerly.

He laughed. 'Patience, ar'kid. Remember, patience is a virtue.' He smiled at me, and then rose from his seat, banging his fork against the bottle of Möet.

The crowd fell silent as everybody took their seats. 'All right then. I know that you're all wondering why I asked you all 'ere tonight. Well, the thing is, we've got ourselves a decent crew together, a tight crew that's been built up over the years.' He yelled the last bit and everybody cheered.

'You all do good for yourselves, right? You're looked after, right – am I right?' Prey soaked up the resultant applause.

'So I'd like to thank each and every one of you for your help in building our small, but strong, business.' Another frenzy of cheers.

'This is one hell of a way to just say thank you,' I whispered to Scotty and Kezlo.

'In't it, mate,' Kezlo replied.

Prey began banging the bottle once again to calm everything down. 'So the truth of the matter is this. Like I said, you've all helped to build what we've got. Some have been with this crew longer than others; some have helped more than others.' He stared around the tables as everyone waited for his next words. 'We've lost good men to prison, which isn't so good, but it is business, and that's the business you've all chosen to be involved in. This isn't fuckin' kids' stuff you're playing with. But the police have not got near the heart of our operation, and that's the way it has to stay. Are you all agreed?' He looked around the room for everybody's reactions.

We still had no idea where all of this was leading. Everybody knew what he was telling them. Although it was a little odd to give the crew a message that they were already aware of.

'We're considering new areas of business to enter into, business which we can't ignore. Something that if you're not careful, could hurt both yourselves and the crew – and I won't allow anything whatsoever to jeopardise what has taken so long to build up. Are you all in agreement that this is a necessity to going forward?' Everybody nodded.

'The police will try anything to break us, so the only way forward is to become stronger,' he said, arms straight, palms flat against the table.

All I kept thinking was that this was all a bit over the top. I accepted that the crew needed this sort of information, but it could easily be passed down to street level through the older heads. No, it wasn't making much sense. My thoughts began wandering to my stomach. I was starving, so I was hoping he'd get a move on so that we could just eat.

'So then – for us to make the crew stronger I've made certain decisions. Important decisions.' He smiled. 'Changes are to be made from within. A whole reshuffle. Some of you will be put into new positions, and some won't. But I believe that good work deserves rewards and those people are going to receive those rewards. Do you all like the sound of that, eh?' He screamed the last words, and everybody began cheering once again. I began wondering what positions people were going to be put into.

He began his banging of the fork once again. 'But tonight we're here for something else. Something that will make our crew stronger and more powerful. You will all hear of your new roles this week – that is if you've been appointed one. But two of you will hear your new roles now.' As he said this he took both Sean and me by our arms, raising us to our feet. Now I was really confused.

'What the—' I began to say, whilst Sean just looked as confused as me.

'These are to be your new bosses. They are my true brothers, without who I would not be where I am today.' He smiled at our bemused faces. 'These are to become full partners and are to work alongside me in their roles as your newly appointed bosses. Are you all happy with that?' he roared, as the whole place went berserk.

Prey began hugging the two of us. 'You serious, Prey?' I asked, astounded at what he'd just announced.

'Why, you not interested, Chopper?' he asked, smirking at me.

'I… don't know what to… what can…' Even Sean was lost for words.

'What's wrong with you both?' he laughed. 'You're both the obvious choice, lads. You both deserve it. I need you both now more than ever.'

Staring at everyone standing, clapping and cheering, both Kezlo and Jonah were shaking my hand, and it all seemed so unreal.

'I can't get my head round this,' I said, to no one in particular.

TWENTY-ONE

'Times are double sweet, ain't they,' Prey said, as he sat in his La-z-boy chair enjoying a smoke. He was referring to our ever-expanding business.

After both Sean and I had deposited our investment money, enabling us to become equal partners with Prey, we'd enjoyed watching our investment money multiply dramatically. Of course with the extra cash now available, we'd been able to successfully expand the business to even greater heights. Don't get me wrong: the money that I was previously making had been more than substantial. But this... This was astonishing as we were dividing profits between the three of us. Of course Prey was still making as much as he used to. Because of our expansion, the profit margin was increased substantially, especially with our investment in crack-cocaine, which was making colossal amounts of cash for us.

Once Sleeper had shown us the way forward with the actual cooking of the rocks from the powder, the profits were amazing. So much so, that we didn't know just how we'd managed to trade so successfully without them before now.

Being made an equal partner had never crossed my mind before that night at Chan's. Apart from anything else there were Prey's so-called lieutenants there before I'd even been involved. I remember worrying about how they were going to react to the fact that I'd been promoted to full partner and it had bothered me immensely. The last thing that I had wanted was to step on anybody else's toes within the crew. I'd always run my side of things without becoming involved with their side of things. Although I realised that it had been pretty much down to both Jonah and I – the development of Steve's side of the business – I kept wondering whether this was the reason Prey had given me the opportunity.

Prey had explained afterwards that, apart from deserving it, it was a necessity for the business, telling me that he had spoken with the others afterwards to make sure that there wasn't any ill feeling. He told me that it had been quite the opposite, saying that they all respected just what I'd done for the rest of them over the years. Prey also said that he'd observed the way I'd matured and that I'd become so successful with the work that I carried out that he felt he needed these skills to help the crew grow to greater heights. Although I still felt a little uneasy at first.

We'd spent the first week reshuffling everybody. Scotty was now handling the weed side of things. Kezlo had hooked up with Jonah for the increased sales of Steve's products, although he never had any contact with Steve himself. We still kept Steve out of the picture as much as we possibly could so as not to arouse suspicions too much. Ever since we increased our distribution of Es, things had become so much greater. The money being brought in from the Es was more than immense; it was beyond all of our expectations.

Knieldy controlled the other lieutenants, quickly becoming chief lieutenant, the position previously held by Sean. Diamond and Parksey took control of the rocks, although Parksey was involved mainly with the cooking side of things. He was the only one who could be completely trusted, as all Parksey ever did was smoke weed and drink like a fish of course. No one could drink him under the table.

Security was our main concern, being reviewed on a weekly basis. Our business had grown so extensive that voids constantly had to be searched for. Up until now, the police had only ever managed to pick up the street grafters, who never gave anything up to them. They all knew that they would be looked after, both inside and out, and more importantly were fully aware of the consequences their betrayal of the crew would bring.

Sean answered Prey. 'Fuckin' too right, mate. You know the rocks are outselling the smack already.' He smiled at the two of us.

'I told you so,' I said, giving them a smug little smile. 'I knew we'd have been fools not to have got ar'selves involved with them.'

'Have any of the grafters fucked up yet?' Prey enquired, all serious.

'Just one of the new kids... what's-is-name... Keith,' Sean told him.

'Why? What the fuck happened?' he asked.

'Just disappeared at the end of last week. He owed a fair wedge for the rocks he'd bailed that week. Kezlo and Jonah clocked him though, going into some squat at the back of the park. They fucked him up good and proper, put him in hospital,' I told him.

Prey shook his head. 'What about ar' bees though?'

'No worries, mate,' Sean said. 'Diamond went to pay him a little visit in the hospital, whilst the kid's old man was there.'

'And?' Prey asked.

'And,' I laughed, 'he stuck a shooter under the sheets against the kid's cock. The kid almost passed out right there and then.'

'The old man paid up that night. Diamond warned him as well.' Sean shook his head at the thought of Diamond at the hospital. 'He said that we had more than enough shit on the kid to put him in it as a major player if he said shit to the police. So we won't get any comeback.'

'These fuckin' kids, eh?' Prey laughed.

'I know,' I smiled. 'No fuckin' morals these days, have they?' I added, laughing out loud, as did the other two.

'Anyway... after the story got out,' Sean told him, 'I reckon it's done us no harm whatsoever. I don't think anyone else will fuck up. I hope not anyway.'

'They're all at it though, y'know that,' I told them both. 'The thing is that they're making the bees, so they got no reason not to pay for them. The thing is we can't stop them. After all, we like to do it now and then ar'selves.'

'I bet they're fuckin' piping it though, ain't they?' Prey said.

'You know it, mate,' Sean said, lighting the spliff he had just finished rolling.

'What about you two?' Prey grinned. 'Have you tried piping it?'

'Nah, man,' I told him. 'Been pure tempted to though, to be totally honest about it, Prey.'

'I take it from the grin, mate,' Sean said, 'that you've done it before.'

Prey rose to the phone, grinning. He dialled Diamond's mobile phone number. 'Diamond? Yes, mate... your daughter... sweet, mate,' was all he said before replacing the receiver. We both knew exactly what the reference 'your daughter' had meant: somebody's daughter referred to a quarter of any amount of anything that you were requiring.

Mobile phones. Everybody had them these days. I personally hated the things as they were so big and bulky, although they were a great asset to the business. All the street grafters used them between drop-offs. The police had been unsuccessful recently in trying to pick up anyone who actually had gear on them.

Sean smiled at Prey. 'I take it that was for what I think it was for?'

'Yes, mate,' Prey answered, wandering off to the kitchen.

We sat there smiling, knowing exactly what Prey had just ordered, especially as he was returning from the kitchen with an empty water bottle.

'So what's it like then?' Sean asked curiously.

Prey began to pull apart a Bic biro pen for the pipe. 'Just wait and see,' he grinned at the two of us. 'The thing is though... It's like before, remember?'

'Just a treat,' I laughed. 'We know, mate.'

Prey had burnt a hole into the side of the bottle, sticking the empty plastic cartridge into it. 'I'm double serious, lads... You both know how nice this gear is in a spliff alone.' He then began folding the tinfoil over the top of the bottle.

'That's all right, mate,' Sean said. 'Is it really colossal though?'

Prey was now piercing tiny pinholes in the foil. 'Yes,' he answered abruptly.

Diamond arrived about fifteen minutes later with seven grams of crack-cocaine. 'You lads having a party?' he laughed as he tossed the bag to Prey.

'We are – and you ain't invited to it,' Prey smiled at him as he began to empty the contents of the bag onto the table.

'That's right, Diamond, get back to work,' Sean laughed.

'Cheers, lads,' Diamond shrugged, smiling, seeing the funny side of it.

Prey placed cigarette ash over the holes that he'd pierced. The ash acted as a filter to the rock, as it turned to liquid as you burnt it. It was the only other way possible if you didn't have a glass pipe. 'Right, 'ere we go then,' Prey announced as he took the glowing flame to the pieces of rock.

Crackling away as the flame went to work, Prey sucked eagerly at the thick stream of smoke that flowed through the pipe. He continued to suck on the pipe like some old Indian chief sat there with a peace pipe. His eyes began to roll as he placed the bottle down onto the table before him. Endless streams of smoke drifted from his nostrils and a mouth stuck in a permanent grin.

'You all right, mate?' I asked, as Sean began to repeat the process.

He just continued to smile mischievously. 'Sweet, mate... Couldn't be better.'

I took the pipe from Sean, filling the top with fresh ash and small broken pieces of rock. Sean held a reflected look of Prey.

'Why not, eh? Donna's at her old dear's anyway,' I said, lighting the flame.

The rock crackled before my eyes as it devolved into smoke through the pipe. There it was again, that taste... God knows where I thought I knew it from. As the smoke filled my lungs, I continued to suck eagerly on the pipe. As I tried to place the smouldering bottle down onto the table, I was suddenly knocked back into my seat.

My whole body rushed, my vision blurred momentarily as the rock took control of both my mind and my body. The feeling was one of complete power... power that I'd never engaged with before. Breathing in, feeling the power, was amazing. I felt at that precise moment like twenty men all put together as one. Gazing at the other two I found myself smiling.

'Fuck me... that was truly amazing. It's well top gear,' I declared, falling back into the comfort of the settee.

'Let's just cane this gear that's 'ere,' Prey told us. 'That's it though... Like Sleeper told us, we got to keep our shit together.'

'Yes, mate,' Sean managed half-heartedly.

We stayed rocked out of our minds until the early hours, before eventually caning the entire lot. Both Sean and I left Prey's flat around three o'clock in the morning, going our separate ways, each of us with mirror-image grins.

Donna was waiting as I entered the flat. I definitely could have done without that, that was for sure. 'Where the fuck have you been? I phoned Prey's; it's been engaged all night,' she said, hands placed firmly on her hips.

I'd forgotten that Prey had taken the receiver off the hook, although, saying that, I didn't feel like I could give a shit right then.

I could feel myself rocking back and forth. 'C'mon, girl... don't give me a hard time,' I responded, smirking cheekily at her, the drug still rushing through me.

She pouted those lips at me. 'Just look at the state of you, will you,' she shook her head at me. 'What the fuck have you been up to, Chopper?' She looked me straight in the eye. 'You look messed up, boy.'

I tried to think quickly. 'Just some new batch of skunk weed we got,' I said, smiling as best I could. 'Prey, Sean and me have been testing it.'

Donna glared at me. 'You sure about that?'

'Come 'ere, Donna,' I said, grinning, grabbing her waist. Then without realising it, I suddenly said. 'You know I love you so much.'

I'd told her. I couldn't believe it. I'd actually told her for the first time.

'Now I know you're fucked up,' she smiled. 'You ain't ever told me *that* before.'

'Well, I mean it,' I said, pulling her closer. The buzz still felt fantastic.

'I love you too, Chopper,' she said, kissing me. 'Just don't go messing yourself up... all right?' She kissed me again, and this time it really began to arouse me.

'C'mon, Donna,' I said, feeling extremely horny, 'let's go to bed.' I kissed her passionately.

'I really do love you,' she said as I picked her up. Her legs were wrapped around me as I carried her to the bedroom.

TWENTY-TWO

K onspiracy's club was over by Victoria train station in Shudehill. It was by far the craziest club I'd ever been to. The club itself was a basement club, divided into all these separate rooms. Each room played a different style of music.

I had to admit, though, that not only was it the craziest club I had ever been to, it was by far the shadiest club I'd ever been to. Some areas were so dark you couldn't see shit for trying. But despite all this, the music and atmosphere was kicking. On Saturday nights it was a great venue to go to, as The Haçienda's main night in those days was Friday.

As far as business was concerned, I honestly believed that you would never know who the hell you were doing business with in there, which is probably the reason we never worked it.

Besides which, we didn't need it, not with the money we'd been making from wholesaling the Es lately. Plus it was mainly our gear being knocked out in there, whether they knew it or not.

It was Kezlo's birthday this particular Saturday night. We'd celebrated the previous night as well, but today was his actual birthday, so all the crew were out for it. Konspiracy's wasn't your champagne sort of club, so the brandy and cokes had been flowing steadily all night, and everybody was in good spirits, if you'll pardon the pun. The Es that had been dropped helped too.

The club was bouncing. The ceiling was literally sweating with the intense heat. You actually felt as though you were breathing in the heat itself.

I was enjoying myself with Donna as we danced away with each other. It was just then that I noticed something happening – Jonah arguing with this older black lad, although nobody seemed to have noticed the argument. I continued to dance, but I made sure that they were still in view.

Donna noticed that my mind was elsewhere. 'Chopper? Chopper, what's wrong?'

Smiling at her, I kept my eyes on them. 'Nothing... Don't worry yourself,' I shouted over the music.

That's when it suddenly happened, so suddenly in fact, that even Jonah didn't see the bottle slicing through the air as the lad smashed it full force into the right side of Jonah's head. As the bottle shattered, both beer and blood sprayed into the crowd of dancers. Screams rang out as Jonah collapsed to the floor.

The crowd screamed in horror. I pushed Donna out of the way. 'Get back... Stay away,' I yelled at her.

As I turned, I witnessed the flash of a blade striking down at Jonah as he lay helplessly half-conscious on the floor.

A mass of confusion hit the club as people sensed the imminent danger and began to scatter, making it difficult for me to move swiftly. Nobody but me seemed sure what, who or even where the trouble was coming from. The assailant's blade sliced swiftly and cleanly through Jonah's shirt, blood seeping into the cloth, which was soon awash with deep crimson shadings, spreading dramatically as the kid continued to slice away with deadly accuracy.

Jonah's assailant was about to plunge the lethal blade forward once again just as a space opened up before me. Without a moment's hesitation I ran straight at him, grabbing an empty bottle from the floor as I did so. Just after he struck the blade lethally into Jonah's chest, the lad suddenly turned towards me, sensing threat. All I saw was the whites of his eyes, filled with a mixture of fear and panic as I swung the bottle into his skull, shattering the glass. The blade fell from his grip as he stumbled backwards to the sound of cries and screams from the onlookers.

Suddenly our crew realised where the trouble was coming from. They had spotted me as I had gone after the lad. I suddenly felt myself being dragged backwards, wild punches striking my head blindly. It was his friends – punching and kicking at me with all the force they could muster. I managed to break free by falling to the floor and I kept rolling away so as to avoid the oncoming onslaught. Help had to be on the way.

The club erupted in a mass of violence; all our crew rushed into the crowd. I'd managed to break free – I'd leapt to my feet as our crew had rushed into the group. The problem was, they hadn't realised Jonah was in danger. I began looking for Jonah's attacker, my eyes scanning the mass of chaos erupting around us. People, innocent bystanders, were all rushing to break away from the onslaught. Then I saw him, crawling across the floor, his eyes darting one way then the other as he searched for his fallen blade. The blood streamed from an open wound on the right side of his head.

Looking around for Jonah, I saw Donna holding onto his bloodied body. She was trying her best to apply pressure to his chest to stem the flow of blood that appeared to be coming from everywhere. There on the ground, blood seeping from both his head and stomach, he was barely conscious.

Jonah's attacker was fumbling around on the floor, still searching blindly. He now found exactly what he was searching for – the blade he had attacked Jonah with. As he went to grab it from the floor, he didn't see my foot striking out towards him. He was soon falling backwards into a crowd that was frantically trying to get away from the scene.

Then all my control dissipated, leaving me in a state of unrestrained rage. Grabbing the blade that had been knocked from his grip as he crashed to the floor, I flew straight at him, first striking at his face, tearing through the flesh around his left eye, slashing away in a frenzy to the right... then the left... his face tearing open with each slice, his screams for help drowned out by the music that continued to pump out from the sound system and the sound of the crowd.

The remaining crowd had formed a circle, and were watching and apparently enjoying the fight. 'Chopper – Chopper – C'mon, Chop,' Prey screamed out loudly.

I was now punching the lad beneath me. 'Get Jonah the fuck out of 'ere, Prey,' I yelled back at him.

I then turned my attention back on the one who had started all of this trouble. I watched menacingly as his eyes filled with terror, blood oozing from the open gashes upon his face. I then plunged the knife deep into his stomach, driving the blade further in, stabbing him again and again, not wanting to stop.

Donna was screaming my name, but it was too late: I'd gone beyond the line of sanity.

I tossed aside the blade, and I saw Sean pick it up from the floor. He stared into my eyes questioningly as I took the Beretta 9mm pistol from the back of my jeans. The lad was barely conscious as I smashed it into his mouth, shoving the steel of the gun into its depths as he gagged for air.

More screams could now be heard. 'Fuck with us, will you? Not got anything to say eh, you fuckin…' I began to squeeze back the trigger filled with absolute wrath. The whole place was echoing with screams, although to me it seemed like there was only the two of us there.

Just then, without any warning whatsoever, Sean struck out with his foot, sending the lad toppling backwards away from me and the gun. As I began to spin round towards him, he grabbed hold of me.

'Chopper… Listen, ar'kid… We need to get the fuck out of 'ere – now, mate!' He screamed the final words at me, pulling my body away from the lad, who now lay unconscious, blood seeping out onto the dance floor around him. Taking hold of my shooter he broke it free from my tight grip. 'This ain't the time, brother… c'mon. Sharon… get these the fuck out of 'ere. I'm taking Chopper through the fire exit.' He passed her the shooter and the bloodied blade as discreetly as possible.

'What happened? Where's Jonah?' she asked, shaking as she did. She'd been in one of the other rooms when all the trouble had started.

'Go now, find Kezlo. He'll know what to do,' he instructed her, pulling me in the opposite direction.

You could see my bloodied victim, people starting to crowd round his body. My head dropped as Sean guided me away from the chaos.

Sean wouldn't let me anywhere near the hospital, instead taking me back to his sister's flat out of the way. Luckily she was awake when we arrived. Sean sent her to bed with no questions asked.

'We've just got to wait,' Sean told me sternly. 'I spoke with

Kezlo. He says he dropped Sharon at the hospital. He told me that Prey told him not to hang around and that they'd phone us as soon as they knew anything.'

'Did he say how bad Jonah was?'

'Says they took him straight into surgery. Apparently the slice to the stomach was deep. And the stab wound to the chest was obviously serious. They're worried it might have damaged internal organs.'

'I should have killed that fucker,' I said, spitting the words out. 'I don't even know what it was over.'

Sean passed the spliff to me. 'Ere'are, mate… Look, Chopper man, I didn't even know it had gone off until it did do, y'know. Jonah's lucky that you spotted him,' he said, rubbing the back of his head.

'You know who those lads were, Sean?'

'Seen them around town, that's about it,' he replied, shaking his head at the night's events. 'Listen, Chopper, I respect you for what you done tonight, but the truth is, we need to find out what's happened to the kid…' He paused and looked at me. 'You know… we just got to hope he pulls through.'

'Fuck him! What about Jonah, for fuc—'

'Jonah too of course. All I'm saying, Chopper, is that you fucked that lad up good and proper. If I hadn't stopped you, then…' He trailed off.

'I know, mate. Look, Sean, sorry I snapped, mate. I'm just more concerned about Jonah right now…'

Just then the phone rang.

Sean answered it immediately. 'Yes, Prey… how's Jonah?' he asked, as I waited as patiently as I could.

'He's doing all right. Luckily for him the blade missed anything major. It looked worse than it was,' Prey told Sean. 'How's Chopper doing, Sean? You saw it in his eyes tonight, didn't you, mate?'

Sean nodded at me to let me know Jonah was all right. 'I know what you're saying, Prey. It's just a good job he's on ar' side, ain't it?' Sean replied, winking at me.

'Just one other thing,' Prey said. 'They brought the other kid in tonight… He's still unconscious and in surgery. It doesn't look good, y'know.'

'Shit,' Sean sighed deeply. 'I thought so, y'know. The kid almost pulled the fuckin' trigger. That's after he'd done that to him.'

'Fuck. All right, I'll keep you po—' Prey stopped what he was saying. 'Looks like the coppers have just turned up. I'll be in touch. Tell Chopper to take it easy.'

Sean replaced the receiver. 'Looks like Jonah should be sweet.' He stopped and stared at me.

'But?' I asked, knowing something was wrong.

'The other kid's in a bad way. They don't know if he'll make it,' he said, shaking his head. 'Plus the coppers just showed up as well.'

'Phone Steve,' I said. 'He should know. Him and Jonah are close.'

Steve arrived at St Mary's within the hour, informing the receptionist that he was Jonah's father. 'How is he?' Steve asked, running up the corridor towards the others.

'How the fuck...? Prey began, startled. 'I take it Chopper let you know.'

'You girls all right?' Steve asked, kissing their wet cheeks, both of them nodding and trying their best to smile.

Donna's clothes were still soaked in Jonah's blood. 'Doctors say he's stable at the moment. They'll know more tomorrow though,' she said, comforting Sharon.

'Steve, the police were 'ere earlier,' Prey said, 'asking all sorts of questions. Donna and me give false names. We just told them we brought him 'ere... that we just found him in the street.'

'You'd better tell me everything,' Steve said. 'C'mon, I need a snout anyway.' He turned, heading for the exit.

Prey relayed the whole the story to Steve, including the fact the kid was also in the hospital and how it wasn't looking too good at all.

'All right, go get Donna. The two of you go wait in the car,' Steve told him. 'I'll take Chopper over to my gaff until we hear more. Guaranteed you'll have the serious crime squad detectives down here over this soon enough, sticking their fuckin' noses in.'

'I sure hope this turns out all right. You know, Chopper really is a...' Prey stopped himself as Steve nodded his understanding. 'Won't let shit happen to any of his mates. You don't find too many around like him, y'know. What if this all turns pear-shaped?'

'We'll cross that bridge only if we need to. For now we just need to get him out of the area. God knows what kind of witnesses they've got,' Steve was saying as he shook his head. 'Hopefully this kid will come around. Let's just keep our fingers crossed.'

'All right, mate. I'll wait in the car. Send Donna out.'

'I'm going in to see Jonah,' Steve announced. 'Just want to make sure he's stable before we set off.'

TWENTY-THREE

We'd heard that Jonah was doing well, all things considered. He'd kept telling Sharon to thank me, although she'd been told over the phone to tell him it wasn't necessary, as he would have done the same thing if the situation had been reversed.

As for the other guy though, Leroy Benning, from what we'd been informed he was still critical. He'd been in a coma since Saturday night and today was Wednesday.

We'd also heard that the whole argument had stemmed from this Leroy character claiming that Jonah had sold a snide batch of Es to his younger brother. Jonah knew it to be complete nonsense and had rightly told Leroy so. So in all fairness, it looked like he was just itching to cause trouble with somebody on the night in question.

Prey had been told that it would be Detective Inspector Stevenson that was to head the investigation. Even though none of us had ever had any contact with him, this guy we'd all heard of before.

Stevenson had brought down some serious lads over the years, not only from Manchester but also the surrounding areas. He was a determined son of a bitch; we had to give him that much. He knew Jonah was part of Prey's Hulme crew. He knew that somehow this whole incident was related and he was all over this case.

Therefore it was inevitable that he would go to the hospital.

'Just stop fucking with me, Jones, or is it Jonah?' Stevenson had snapped as he stood there besides Jonah's bedside. 'I know how you all like your nicknames.'

'Hasn't the doctor told you?' Jonah smirked back at him. 'I'm a sick lad. They said you shouldn't be questioning me if I don't feel up to it.'

Stevenson shook his head. 'I don't give a toss what they say. Look, son – Jonah – I know that you weren't the one who put the kid into a coma; at least I don't *think* that you were the one who put him in it. Anyway, just tell me who it was, and get yourself off the hook.'

'I passed out,' Jonah sighed. 'I already told you that, Stevenson.'

Sharon squeezed Jonah's hand. 'What's your fuckin' problem, eh Stevenson? Can't you see that it was all down to this other guy?' She spat the words venomously.

'I've got one of the doormen saying that you were dragged into a taxi,' Stevenson said, looking around. 'By two unknown people. But that the fighting was still happening inside the club. Plus, those – unknowns – according to the hospital cameras, look a lot like O'fucking Prey. A very good friend of yours – or is it boss of yours, Jonah?'

'What the fuck you...' Jonah spat, before stopping himself. 'Anyway, what have any of the witnesses told you?' he'd then enquired out of genuine curiosity.

'Fuck all,' he snarled. 'They'd let every bastard out of there before we got there.'

Jonah laughed at him. 'So you know shit then, Inspector.'

'Not exactly,' he said, laughing a little. 'We received an anonymous phone call. They said it was Billy Chorlton. You know him, don't you? He's one of your good mates – Chopper, ain't it?' He smirked as he said this.

'Fuck you, Stevenson!' Jonah snarled the words back. 'Chopper wasn't even out Saturday night.'

'Have it your way. But wait until we check the cameras from the club this afternoon.' He smirked again, as if scoring a point for himself. 'I'm sure they'll shine some light on the whole matter.'

Sharon hadn't been able to control herself and burst out laughing. 'The what?'

'Cameras...' Stevenson looked a little unsure about himself.

'Check away. You wonder why you've not received them yet, Stevenson,' Jonah grinned. 'Way I hear it, those things are just empty boxes stuck to the wall to try and scare dealers off. Not that it does any fuckin' good, as just about everybody knows. Well, just about everybody, eh Stevenson?'

'Yeah well… we'll see, won't we?' he told them both, a little less sure of himself now. Jonah could see Stevenson was contemplating whether or not there was any truth to Sharon's information.

'Will there be anything else, orifice,' Jonah laughed. 'Sorry – officer,' he added, undermining Stevenson, who was already becoming more enraged.

'Look, we know that Chopper's skipped town. We've already checked,' he answered back angrily. 'You better tell him though, we're on to him. If the kid in there bites the bullet, we'll find him. He's going down for this one. And it'll be for murder in the fir—'

'Yeah, whatever you say, Stevenson,' said Jonah, cutting him off. 'Fuck you very much.' Jonah laughed once again at him as both he and Sharon watched him turn and leave the room without another word.

Leroy had come out of his coma by Friday evening. And by Saturday morning Stevenson was back at the hospital.

'All right, Leroy. How you feeling?' he'd asked the lad, trying his best to appear sympathetic to Leroy's stitched, swollen face.

'Like shit,' Leroy had responded angrily, whilst grabbing his wounded stomach as he did. 'How the fuck do you think I feel?'

'No need to be like that, son,' Stevenson smiled. I'm just here to try and help you. We want to find who did this to you as much as you do.'

'Oh yeah? And how the fuck you going to do that then?' Leroy snarled back at him. 'It's been a week. From what I hear, you boys ain't got shit.' Leroy grimaced with pain.

'What can you tell us?' asked Stevenson, trying the smile again. 'We've got a good idea who done this… but why don't you tell us?'

'Fuck you! I haven't got a fuckin' clue who done it… It was dark in there,' Leroy said, looking away from the detective.

'Don't give me that shit,' Stevenson sighed, becoming irritated. 'Just fucking tell me who the fuck done this to you.'

'Go fuck yourself, copper – I ain't no fuckin' grass!' Leroy screamed at Stevenson, his face pulled taut with the pain that came from straining to scream at him like that.

'So you're not going to take this further. Is that what you're saying?' Stevenson enquired. In truth he'd hoped the kid would have died so he could go after Chorlton on a murder charge. Now though, it was beginning to turn sour for him and he knew it. In truth, he knew he didn't have a solid case against Chorlton.

'You got it… I don't know who done it. Even if I did do, you'd be the last person I'd tell,' Leroy said, looking away from the detective again.

'You what? This is fucking nonsense, son. Just fuc—'

'What the hell is going on here?' the doctor said, who'd entered the room.

'He's harassing me,' said Leroy. 'I've told him I can't and won't help him. I keep telling him to leave me alone, but he won't.' He put on the saddest look he could muster. Although with his current appearance, that wasn't so hard.

'Right you – Inspector or not – I want you out of my hospital right this minute. You hear me?' the doctor shouted.

'This isn't on, you hear me?' Stevenson said, reluctantly heading for the door.

'And don't bother coming back. You fuckin' hear me, you…' Leroy broke off, wincing with the pain.

The whole episode had enraged Stevenson, who'd stormed his way out of the hospital. He'd been trying to build a case against Prey and his lads for a long time, yet he just couldn't find a way through to them. He realised, stood there on the steps of the hospital, that what he needed was to bring in some extra help – and right there and then, he realised he knew just the man for the job.

TWENTY-FOUR

'What's wrong with you, Mike?' asked the bemused Detective Inspector Walsh as Stevenson had come crashing into his office, obviously upset.

'Those little bastards from Hulme,' Stevenson spat. 'Look, Martin, sorry to crash in like this. I just needed someone from the old school to talk to.'

The two had known each other for a number of years now. Although they'd never worked with one another, they both respected each other's achievements in bringing to justice – well their kind of justice at least – some of Manchester's most notorious criminals.

'That's all right, mate,' Walsh said. 'Who is it this time? Fucking O'Prey, I'm betting?'

Stevenson sat on the empty desk opposite his friend's, nodding his response. 'You know what: I reckon it's all of them this time, you know. You heard about the major fracas down at that club last Saturday night?'

'Yeah, just what was in the newspapers though, as they've got me working some other crap at the moment,' Walsh replied, sipping his coffee.

'There's this black kid in hospital,' Stevenson was saying, lighting a Silk Cut cigarette, throwing the pack to Walsh. 'Just come out of a coma on bleedin' Friday... Well, you know that Paul Jones from Hulme? Got quite the rep for leaving anybody who he gets into a fight with in hospital? He's been on our radar for a while now.'

'Yeah,' Walsh said smiling. 'But I don't want to state the obvious, Mike: he's white.'

'I know he fucking is, you daft twat!' Stevenson grinned at his friend's sense of humour. 'Anyway, Jones got himself knifed in there last weekend. At first it looks like he came off worse and is the one in hospital this time round, but says the usual: can't remember shit. The thing is, shortly afterwards this Leroy Benning is brought into the same hospital. I mean in a bad fucking way, half-dead and from the same fucking club. So obviously we're getting a call.' He shook his head as he thought about the state of Benning's scarred face, not to mention the stabbing he'd received.

'Face shredded to bits... stabbed several times. Now he's saying he doesn't know who the fuck put him there. Absolute bollocks, I can tell you.' Stevenson had stopped drawing on his cigarette, letting the smoke drift aimlessly above his head.

'So who done it then? Jonah?'

'No witnesses. They let every fucker go before our lot turned up,' Stevenson said, tutting. 'But Jonah had already been taken out by O'Prey and some young girl, who I couldn't get a good look at from the CCTV. One of our snitches says that this time round it wasn't Jonah who put the kid in hospital – but that everybody knows it was Billy Chorlton. Apparently, after they got Jones out of there, this Chorlton character lost it big time. He fucked this kid up with everybody stood around watching him without a care in the fucking world. Completely lost it from what I hear. Really went to town on him and then some. After seriously doing some damage to the lad, he then shoves a fucking pistol into the kid's mouth, and that was after he'd half fucking killed him in the first place.'

'Chorlton... Billy Chorlton,' Walsh said, lighting up. 'You mean Chopper, right?'

'I thought you might know the son of a bitch, Martin,' Stevenson said, smiling knowingly at his friend. 'That's why I came to you.'

'You know what, Mike,' Walsh began, 'years back now, we nicked a load of them Hulme lads over in Salford whilst I was stationed over that way. Anyway, this big fight with Patrick McNally's lot had gone off. You know – Paddy. It was real messy... but guess who we nicked over there at the time?'

'Chorlton,' Stevenson said, blowing out smoke.

Walsh nodded in acknowledgement. 'But check this out then... You see, it's O'Prey's lot fighting with McNally's lot.

Now little Chorlton has only got to be twelve or thirteen at the time. The reason I've always remembered Chorlton so much is that he was the cockiest little bastard I'd ever met.'

'Why's that then?'

'You know what he did all the way through his interview? Now you got remember he's only a kid at the time.' Walsh was getting worked up just talking about it. 'No fucking comment all the way. The little bastard, eh? He kinda stuck in my mind after that.'

'There is another reason I've come to see you, Martin,' Stevenson said, sighing deeply. 'The reason I checked into this fight last week is because of Jonah and who he's involved with. You see, Kieran O'Prey, Sean Macreedy and that fuck-head Billy Chorlton are running that estate nowadays. Now I'm going to bring them down. We've been onto them for some time now. They've got their paws into everything, including this fucking Ecstasy shit that's hit town in a big way. Apparently they're the ones supplying Manchester with it. The problem I've got is we just can't seem to break through though. They're a tight lot. In fact, they are one of the tightest I've worked on yet. The team I've put together isn't old school like you and me, and I think that we're gonna have to bend a few of the rules here to bring this crew down. That's why I'm here. I need some fresh help. Some new ideas and objectives, Martin, from the old school way of thinking. You interested or what, mate?'

'You're asking me to come in with you on this?' Walsh asked, smiling, thinking of the current piece of nonsense they had him working on.

'I need your help. The investigation will be down to mainly the two of us. I've already had the Chief give his approval for you to jump on board. So it's down to you, Martin – are you in or out?'

Walsh just grinned, feeling elevated. 'You don't have to ask twice, mate,' he replied, smiling at the mere thought of bringing in the kid that had sat there in front of him so many years ago and made a mockery of not only him but the entire police force. He was the one he'd never been able to forget, even after all this time.

Stevenson returned his smile. 'We'll break 'em, Martin. I promise you that. One way or another we'll bring all of them down.'

TWENTY-FIVE

D erby days in Manchester were always mad. Throughout the
eighties, football violence had blossomed. So when
Manchester United played Manchester City, it was only natural
in this day and age there'd be trouble.

I personally enjoyed watching Man United at Old Trafford or
on television. But all this mindless violence associated with it just
wasn't me at all. Don't get me wrong: I'm not suddenly painting
myself as some kind of angel, but the fact of the matter is that
violence in the world in which I existed was a necessity – it wasn't
mindless.

Fighting over football teams just seemed screwed up to me,
especially in town, as the lads battling with one another would more
than likely have been enjoying a pint together the previous evening.

So I always avoided town centre on these days. Only on this
particular Derby day, there was the Save-the-Rave protest outside
the town hall. A bill was to be passed through Parliament that
week to put a stop to the illegal warehouse parties.

For months now, Blackburn had been the centre of these huge
warehouse parties. The venues were huge, like nothing we'd ever
seen before, and they were always full. Thousands upon thousands would travel the length and breadth of the country to
attend. Only now, due to all the bad publicity surrounding them
– not only the Blackburn ones – the Government had finally
decided it was time to intervene.

Prior to this, they had been unsure who they should actually
prosecute for the parties, or even what the actual charges were.
Besides, the police rarely knew who the organisers were, so
everyone was here today in protest at the proposal of such a
shoddily constructed bill.

However, I was not holding out any hope. I mean, it was the
Government we were talking about. 'Fuckin' pointless this,' I

stated. 'Y'know it is, Prey. What the fuck are we even going for?'

We were heading out of the G-Mex car park towards the town hall.

'I know it is, mate,' Prey laughed. 'It's just for the crack.'

'You really think they'll stop the parties, Chopper?' Donna asked, linking my arm.

'Shit,' I laughed at the question, 'of course they will.'

'They can't stand anybody having a good time, can they, Prey?' giggled Kathy.

Kathy was Prey's new 'sex kitten', as he referred to her. She was too: a very attractive girl indeed. Even if she was a more than a bit dizzy at times.

Prey had told me that all he had to do was throw a couple of Es down her neck and then she wouldn't leave his cock alone for the entire night. I'd laughed, pointing out the fact that he was now drugging girls to get laid.

'That's right, ain't it girl. Can't stop our fun though, can they?' Prey grinned as he pinched her arse, making her giggle some more.

'C'mon, we'll be late. It's due to start soon,' Donna said, tugging at my arm.

'Fuck!' I exclaimed, observing the mass on the opposite side of the road. 'You seen this, Prey?'

Prey smirked. 'Ah fuck... I forgot it's Derby day, ain't it,' he said, watching the huge crowd of around fifty, possibly sixty or so, Man City fans marching in the direction of Oxford Road.

'What's Derby day?' Kathy giggled. 'Are they here for the protest?'

Like I said, not the sharpest tool in the shed.

'One kind of a protest,' I laughed. 'Just not the same one as ar's though.'

'What do you mean?' she asked. 'What are they protesting about?'

'It's football, Kathy,' Donna said, shaking her head. 'You know... Man United are playing Man City today.'

'Oh yeah, right,' she replied, absolutely clueless as to what the hell we were going on about.

'Chopper... look.' Prey nodded ahead of us at the opposite side of Oxford Road. 'Clock that lot.'

At the actual crossing of Oxford Road were riot police everywhere, all fully kitted out. They had dogs on standby, along with at least four riot vans from what we could see. All of them were waiting for the inevitable distress ahead. Just beyond them was a massive crowd of opposing Man United fans, all chanting and shouting abuse at the police, who stood their ground.

'Shit!' I said, shaking my head. 'Could have done the fuck without this lot.'

'It's nothing to do with us, Chopper,' Donna said, scolding me for no reason and pouting. 'Just stay out of it.'

'You too, Prey,' Kathy added.

Prey laughed at the two of them. 'Why the fuck would we start up with this lot?'

'I just know what you two are like,' Donna said firmly.

'Don't be stupid,' I told them. 'This is why I hate coming near town on this day. C'mon, let's get out of 'ere before it goes off.'

Just then the chants erupted into screams of abuse. Suddenly all of the Man City fans across from us charged towards Oxford Road. Simultaneously, Man United fans rushed forward towards them. The police were still standing back, observing.

The two rival groups of fans stopped head to head with each other in the centre of the road. All were screaming. All were waiting for the first moves to be made. All the traffic had screeched to a halt... A mass of noise was all that could be heard.

Suddenly, a metal bin was hurled through the air at the Man City fans, crashing into them. There went the first move.

The whole crowd erupted in a mass of mindless violence before our very eyes. You could hear Prey laughing wildly, enjoying the view as we spectated from the sidelines, so to speak. This had nothing to do with us.

'Dumb fucks,' I said, shaking my head. 'Scrapping over fuckin' football.'

The police were running everywhere trying to arrest someone – anyone, for that matter – doing their best to resolve the situation at hand. But the fact of the matter was that they were doing a piss poor job of it. They looked like headless chickens running around in circles as the thugs ran in every direction.

The next thing we all knew was this one officer was charging towards *us*. I mean, he was actually charging at me, screaming like a wild animal as he did so. This idiot thought that we were involved. Either that or we were just an easy target for him.

I could hear Prey from behind me now. 'C'mon, girls, move away.' I heard him say this just as the police officer was almost upon me, his riot stick swinging extravagantly in all directions.

'You little bastard – come here you little…' he screamed at me. As everything was happening so quickly, I was frozen to the spot, trying to assess the situation. I mean, I didn't want to get arrested for smacking a police officer – and, like I said, this had nothing at all to do with us.

His stick swished through the air towards me. I stood there, unable to move. Donna suddenly screamed, and it's a good job that she did, for it instantly brought me round, leaving me fearing not for myself but for her. I quickly sidestepped the stick as the officer swung it at me. I watched him lose balance from over-swinging. He fell sprawling to the floor.

'You twat,' I screamed, kicking out at him as he tried to stand up. I hit him full force and, riot gear or no riot gear, he toppled backwards to the floor once again.

I began stamping on his perspex visor as he wriggled around on the floor. 'You fucking tosser – we weren't even with…' I was at a loss for words as I continued to stamp onto his head. Although I probably wasn't causing too much damage to him, not with all that gear he had on.

Just then Prey grabbed me, laughing out loud as he did. 'C'mon, Chopper, let's get out of 'ere…' He was still laughing as we took off back towards the G-Mex car park, after the girls.

'Fuckin' pig!' I screamed after the police officer, who was still lying on the ground.

Prey was doubled over with laughter as we arrived back at his new Mercedes Benz. 'You're crazy, Chopper, y'know that?' He couldn't stop his laughter.

'You all right, Chopper?' Donna asked, putting her arm around me.

'He started it,' I protested, unable to see the funny side of it. 'It wasn't my fault.'

'Ah, my little Chop-Hopper,' Prey chuckled as we all piled into the car.

I suddenly began to laugh along with them. 'Well, he shouldn't have tried picking on us.'

'So are we still going to the protest?' Kathy asked, as if oblivious to what had just taken place.

'Tell you what,' Prey said. 'We'll swing the car by, and if it looks shite we'll just head for Dry Bar... all right?' He was smiling as he looked at me.

'Dry Bar sounds sweet to me, mate,' I said, grinning back at him. 'I said the protest would be pointless anyway.'

TWENTY-SIX

'C hopper. It's Steve, mate.' There was real urgency in his voice; he didn't even give me a chance to say hello. 'I need to see you lads today.' Something was wrong.

'What the fuck's up?' I enquired, concerned now.

'I can't find Prey. His mobile is off and he's not home,' he snapped. 'I need to see the three of you.'

'I know where he is,' I said. 'What time can you be in town for?'

'What time is it now?' he asked, and I could sense he was getting himself worked up – really agitated. 'My head's all over the place, Chopper.'

'Calm the fuck down,' I told him. 'It's nearly five o'clock. What time can you get yourself over here for?'

'Right… I'll see you at the usual place at seven. Traffic's going to be a nightmare,' he sighed.

'All right then,' I replied. 'See you then. Just stay calm, all right, mate?' I told him, replacing the receiver and wondering what the hell that was all about.

'What's wrong?' Donna enquired, staring at me.

Donna lay on the bed behind me. We had been there all day as it was her day off and we'd been out last night. 'To be honest, I ain't too sure, y'know.' I was shaking my head. 'Look… I've got to get off. Something I've got to sort out. I need to find Prey.'

Donna pouted. 'You fuckin' what, Chopper?,' she suddenly screamed at me. 'You promised me that you were going to take me out for that meal tonight.'

'Fuck that!' I told her, irritated at her attitude. 'And just who the hell do you think you're screaming at?'

'For fuck's sake, Chopper,' she said, scowling at me. 'Always fuckin' business… ain't it?'

She was pissed off at me, but I was already irritable as I didn't have clue what the problem with Steve was. All I knew was that something was wrong and the three of us had just made a large investment money-wise.

'Well,' she yelled again, 'maybe you'd like it if I went out and—'

She was irritating the hell out of me now. 'Just what the fuck has got into you, girl? Just chill the fuck out and get the fuck out of my face,' I screamed back at her. I was never usually this way with her, but something wasn't right I could feel it as I pulled my jeans on.

'What did you just tell me to do, you fu—'

'Chill the fuck out, Donna,' I calmly told her. 'Life doesn't just revolve around you.'

Donna flew at me with her nails. 'You're such a fuckin' bastard, Chopper! After everything that I...' She was clawing, scratching and even punching me. I just took the abuse, laughing at the way that she was carrying on.

I finally grabbed her arms and she couldn't do anything to me. For a moment I saw fear in her eyes and she suddenly started shaking. I was sneering at her, something that I had never done to her before. I threw her to the bed before exiting the bedroom.

I could hear her smashing things as I left the flat. I hated leaving things like this – but there were more important issues at hand right now. I'd deal with Donna and me later, I told myself as I walked out of our front door.

Prey was breathing heavily as I spoke to him down the phone at Kathy's. 'He said it's important.'

'For fuck's sake, Chopper,' he grunted, trying to catch his breath. 'I'm in the middle of a nosh 'ere mate.'

'He sounded serious, Prey,' I told him. 'Just remember what we've got in there from last week.'

'Fuck it!' he exclaimed, coming round. 'You reckon it's that, Chopper?' He gasped, as he was obviously on the verge of coming. Prey always made me laugh; this is one guy who could never get enough sex.

'I don't know. All I do know is it sounded important,' I said firmly. 'Me and Sean are heading down there now.'

'All right… all right,' he gasped again. 'The old man better have something important though. Reckon I'll still have enough time to finish up here though… all righ… late… arhh!' he cried out as the line went dead.

I found myself laughing as I replaced the receiver.

'Where's Prey?' Steve asked, beads of sweat clinging to his face as he rushed into Chan's. 'Where the fuck is he?' he snapped.

'Calm the fuck down,' I told him. 'He'll be 'ere soon. Now, what the fuck's happened?'

'Yeah, Steve, is our investment safe?' Sean added.

Steve lit a cigarette, drawing deeply before exhaling the smoke. 'There he is now,' Steve said, pointing out of the window.

Prey was crawling out of Kathy's Ford Fiesta, tucking his shirt in as he looked up at us, giving us a mischievous wink.

Steve was wiping his forehead with a napkin as Prey approached the table. 'Right then, old man… what the fuck's up?' Prey asked as he sat down. 'You realise just how busy I was then.'

'Our operation has turned sore in the States,' Steve said, watching for our reactions.

'You fuckin' *what*?' I exclaimed. 'You realise what you've just said?' I had had an inkling that this is what the problem was going to be, but actually hearing it confirmed hit me full on.

'We got fifty gees invested in the last shipment that's due next week,' Prey said, staring at the older man.

'That's why I called you,' Steve said, drawing heavily on his cigarette, shaking his head at us.

'So what are you saying?' Sean snapped. 'That's it? It's just bye-bye to our fuckin' dough? Are you sure about that, Steve?'

It had only been the second time that we'd invested money in the operation, prior to the Es being produced. The thing was, Steve hadn't been able to cope with our increased demand each week, so we'd put the money up to cover the extra shipments.

'So tell us what happened,' Prey asked sternly, not taking his eyes from Steve's.

'My guy's missus phoned this morning,' Steve told us. 'She says they busted both of them yesterday morning. She posted bail though. However, he wasn't so lucky. They're asking a fortune for *his* bail.'

'Where's our dough?' I enquired without much hope.

'She says he was up to all sorts over there apparently – our gear was just the tip of the iceberg. They busted him big time; our gear was just a small part of his stock.'

'You reckon this is kosher?' Prey asked.

'What do you mean?' Steve asked, gulping his whisky straight.

'That he's been nicked, of course,' Prey added.

'Definitely, lads,' Steve told us. 'Look, me and this guy go back too far. I know it's a shitty business we're in, but this guy is like a brother to me. Just like you three are to one another.'

'You know if they got anything on you, Steve?' I asked.

Steve shook his head. 'It's unlikely. We never used the line at his place. We always used a secure outside line. The DEA has been on to him for the past six months,' he informed us. 'If they're on to his operation over here, they ain't going to waste time coming over for the amount of gear he was sending.'

'*They* might not,' Sean said, 'but what if they've put customs on to it 'ere though?'

'That's right, Steve,' Prey added. 'And what about our dough? You're not insured against loss of money.'

Steve nodded sombrely at us. 'I know. Look, I'll sort the dough out somehow.' He sighed deeply at the thought of the money loss, but more for the loss of his friend to the authorities. 'It may take a little while, but I'll sort it out.'

'All right, Steve,' I said. 'But you ain't going to achieve it through our original set-up. You're going to need the Es to get you back on your feet.'

'What are suggesting, Chopper?' he asked, lighting yet another cigarette.

Prey butted in. 'Chopper's right. We got way too much going with them to lose it. Can you get out of the country?'

'You what?' Steve exclaimed, confused.

'America,' Prey stated. 'Can you get to the States? Check this lot out and see whether or not you can set something else up.'

'Fuck…' Steve half laughed at the mere suggestion. 'Not a chance, man. You need visas – the lot. They'll check me out too much. Especially if the customs guys are on to me in any way. But maybe…'

'Maybe what?' I asked, watching as he sat there deep in thought.

'Maybe Europe,' he said, smiling at us. 'I could easily travel Europe, no problem. I've done it before.'

'What use is that?' Sean asked irritably.

'Hear the man out,' Prey told him. 'What you got in mind, Steve?'

'I got a friend over in Amsterdam. Maybe, just maybe, he might be able to help.'

'So call him,' I said, shrugging.

'No can do,' he laughed. 'I'll have to find him first. It's been a long time, you know.'

'What the fuck are you going to do, Steve?' Sean said, tutting as he did. 'Wander the fuckin' streets of Amsterdam calling his name out loud?'

'Look, I still know heads over there,' Steve declared, glaring at us. 'Put it this way: if I don't find him within a week, then there will be no chance of finding him.'

'All right then, Steve.' Prey was scratching his face with the back of his hand. 'Let's say you find this guy. What makes you think that he'll be able to help?'

'He used to supply me with the gear I needed for the trips and the speed back in the sixties,' he informed us. 'Last I heard was that he was still active. That was a couple of years back now,' Steve said with a grin, possibly brought on by old memories.

'Sweet, then,' Prey said. ''Ere's what I suggest then. Jonah can shoot back over to your gaff tonight with you. Send him back in the morning with at least two weeks' worth of gear, just in case there's any kind of problems. Then you get on the first possible flight.'

'You sure your passport will be all right?' I asked, concerned. The last thing we needed was to lose Steve altogether. Besides which, I really liked the guy.

'I travelled to Portugal with Michael a few years ago to see an old mate of mine. You know, just to see if the passports would work,' he laughed. 'No problems.'

'All right then, mate. That's that then. Ain't fuck all we can do about it now, eh.' Prey said nonchalantly. 'So let's fuckin' eat then, 'cause I'm fuckin' starving.' He signalled for one of the waiters.

TWENTY-SEVEN

'You lads want the good news or the bad news first?' asked Steve. He'd been three weeks in Amsterdam.

'Where the fuck you been?' Prey enquired, already in a foul mood with Steve. In fact, we'd all started to panic somewhat, having not heard from him. 'One week you said. Not fuckin' nearly three! Why haven't you phoned us?' he snapped.

'Take it easy, lads... I just got kinda caught up,' he smirked. 'You know how the 'Dam gets sometimes, all those cafes and women.' He laughed out loud.

'That's nice for you,' I told him sarcastically, agitated by his attitude.

'So you find this guy or not?' Sean enquired.

'No, I didn't,' Steve simply said. Then he smiled. 'But that's the bad news.'

'So what's the good news then, old man?' Prey asked, obviously more than a little irritated.

'The good news is I met someone else out there.'

'Who can get the MDMA, you mean?' I asked eagerly.

'Not exactly,' Steve shook his head. 'But he has a chemist out there. He can supply this other gear – very, very similar to it.'

'How good is it though?' Prey stared at Steve. 'Last fuckin' thing we need is some fucked up shite.'

'Look, the samples he gave me are very good,' Steve smiled. 'Maybe not quite as pure as what we had before, but all the same, it's definitely better than all the other shit knocking about out there.'

'So are we back in business or what?' Sean asked, not looking at all certain about what he was hearing from Steve.

'Well, you see, that's where we come into another slight problem,' Steve said, looking at all of us and sighing as he did. 'This guy's not interested in shipping the gear at all.'

'So what you saying then?' I asked. 'You've got to ship it in yourself?'

'No… *we've* got to ship it ourselves,' he said, shaking his head again. 'Now, you lads know my past, so I can't go getting involved on that side of things. Way, way too risky for me.'

'So what you got in mind then?' Prey asked. 'If we've got to ship it in, then the cost is going to get all fucked up. Besides which, we don't really know fuck all about the smuggling side of things, Steve.'

'It doesn't have to fuck things up,' he grinned at us, winking. 'I can help with the organising of the shipping side. But a little renegotiating needs doing though.'

'So what are you saying then? Stop talking in fuckin' riddles and just come the fuck out with it, will you?' I said, both agitated and curious to know what he had in mind.

'Well, first off,' Steve said, 'I really don't have to tell you lot this bit, but here goes anyway. This new gear is half the price of the other gear.' He watched for our reactions.

'Seriously?' Prey asked, surprised.

'Yeah… So here's the deal.' Steve paused. 'You lads bring the gear into the country. I'll help set it up, like I told you. You'll need a couple of birds for the job – good girls who we can trust 100 per cent. We'll need to pay them well – really well in order to keep them sweet.'

'What your angle 'ere though, Steve?' I asked, knowing that he was leaving something out.

'Ninety per cent of my business goes to you lads already,' he declared. 'So what I'm suggesting is a partnership between us.' He watched once again for our reactions. 'Now, I know what you're thinking. I know that you've got other interests, other activities. Well, I don't want in on that side of things – you can keep that between the three of you. I only want in on my side of things.' He sat back into his chair, awaiting our response.

I could see Prey contemplating this. 'So apart from the half price shipment, what else have you got on offer?'

'Look, I owe you lads a lot. And I don't just mean dough,' Steve said. 'You've been good to me in the past. So apart from the wages to my guys for producing the gear, which is a mere cost from what can be made initially, we'll then split all the profits between the four of us. Just think about it. You'll get the gear at cost, not wholesale. To be totally honest with you, lads, it'll help me with paying off the debt also. So what do you think then?'

'Sounds all right on the surface,' I told him.

'Look, I'm not stupid,' he continued. 'I know how much you're bringing in off the gear I supply to you. All I'm asking is that I be brought in on it too.' He smiled knowingly at us.

You could see Prey's brain working overtime. 'All right, old timer, why don't you go get yourself a drink at the bar?' Without a single word Steve rose and disappeared to the bar.

'What do you reckon then?' Prey asked. 'You reckon it's kosher or what?'

'I reckon so,' I nodded. 'I've just worked out some rough figures in my head and definitely think that this could pay off big time.'

'Chopper's right, Prey,' Sean added. 'I've just done the same thing. Obviously Steve will have to be more specific on the price of things, but I say yeah.'

'What about the shipping side of things?' Prey asked the both of us. 'We ain't been involved with that side before.'

'What about Sharon and Janine?' I suggested.

'Sounds all right. You reckon they'll go for it?' Prey enquired. 'It's risky.'

'We'll just have to make it worth their while,' Sean added. 'Besides, if the gear is going to cost a lot less, then we gonna have more dough to play about with, ain't we?'

'True, very fuckin' true,' Prey said, smiling at us. 'So we all agreed then?' Both Sean and I smiled in assent.

'Good,' Prey laughed. 'I really like the old bastard anyway.'

'Just one other thing,' I said. 'With Steve's past history, I say we keep this partnership between the four of us only. None of the others should acknowledge him as a partner whatsoever. Let's just keep things the way they are. Nobody apart from Jonah and Knieldy know who the fuck he is anyway.'

'You're right, Chopper,' Prey smiled. 'Like you say, only Jonah and Knieldy know his past. None of the crew apart from Kezlo knows where the gear comes from. They might suspect it, but they certainly don't fuckin' know it, that's for sure.'

'I know that,' I declared. 'It's just now we're going into new areas once again, we've got to keep control of security surrounding our business.'

'Agreed… fully,' Sean added. 'So then, it's settled – yes?'

Prey signalled to Chan to come over. He whispered into his ear, Chan scuttled away and Prey shouted Steve over.

As Steve made his way back over to us, Chan reappeared behind him with a bottle of Bollinger, popping its cork open. The froth flowed frenziedly.

'I take it,' Steve said joyously, 'that we've got ourselves a deal then, lads.'

TWENTY-EIGHT

'What time did Chopper say he'd meet us, Scotty?' Kezlo enquired casually as he returned from the bar and passed a bottle of Budweiser to his friend.

'Fuck knows,' Scotty snapped in response. 'Do we ever know what the fuck he's up to nowadays,' he added, gulping his beer back hungrily.

Kezlo kept quiet for a moment, observing the sour man before him. Kezlo knew it was best to leave him be when he was in one of these moods. He knew that Scotty was pissed off at Chopper, and had been ever since Chopper was promoted into a full partner. He hadn't even congratulated Chopper at Chan's that evening, but merely shook his hand and walked away. As kids they'd always done everything together. Kezlo had supposed Scotty – possibly even Chopper back when they were kids – had assumed that it was always going to be that way.

But it hadn't bothered Kezlo at all. In fact, Kezlo was very proud of Chopper being put in such a position. Besides which, Chopper had continually looked after them, had always given them their rewards. So what if they didn't see each other every day? So what if they didn't pull down scores any more? So what if they didn't bomb the estate any more? That was all part of life, moving on, growing up… which was exactly what they'd done.

Scotty just had to realise these things. After all, he played a major role with the crew. Chopper had given him the weed business to take control of. It had been Chopper's old position and now it was his.

Kezlo sat thinking about his current role in the business, working with Jonah.

Chopper had always run things so that no one knew anything whatsoever about what the other was really doing. As far as Kezlo knew, prior to meeting Steve, he'd always just considered him to be one of Prey's older friends from the past. But how wrong he'd been! This guy was one of the major players in the field. Although he hadn't had direct contact with Steve, he knew exactly what role he played within the crew. This, Kezlo respected immensely.

Scotty just had to remember that Chopper was like their true brother, always would be. No matter what happened.

Suddenly Scotty broke Kezlo's thoughts. 'What time is it now?'

Kezlo glanced at his watch. 'Just gone seven thirty, mate.'

'He said seven o'clock,' Scotty snapped back at him. 'Who the fuck does he think he is, keeping us waiting like this? D'ya know what I mean, Kezlo?'

'Calm the fuck down, will you,' Kezlo tried. 'What the fuck are you in a hurry for? Business is taken care of for tonight. This is just lads' night out, y'know. Old mates out on the piss.'

'What the fuck you know about old mates?' Scotty scowled back at him. 'Me and Chopper grew up together. We're proper old mates.'

'Well, fuckin' act like it then, you dick!' Kezlo had heard enough. 'What the fuck's got into you? You think 'cause I ain't known either of you two since little kids that we're not close? Well, fuck you, Scotty. You two will always be my brothers.'

Scotty dropped his head, ashamed at his outburst. 'I'm sorry, mate, I really am. I'm just wishing it was like it always was before.'

'Times change, Scotty,' said Kezlo. 'We're doing top business with the crew. Shit! We're making top bees! I ain't got any complaints and neither should you. Chopper's always looked out for us; he always will.'

'Why'd he get made top boy though?'

'He deserved it,' Kezlo said, sipping his beer. 'I'm glad it was him. If it hadn't been then we'd not be where we are today.'

'I suppose so,' Scotty sighed. 'When he lived with us though, it was different. Now that he's got Donna, I don't know, mate: it's just different…'

'Chopper!' I heard Kezlo suddenly yell out as I walked into the Dry Bar. I could clearly see as I walked in that they appeared to be in some kind of argument, but thought no more of it as I made way through the crowded bar.

'Over 'ere, mate. Right, knock it on the head, you hear me, Scotty,' Kezlo forewarned his friend.

Scotty watched Chopper making his way through the crowd, almost everyone greeting him, stopping him to chat a little. 'There you are, look, Kezlo,' Scotty snapped again. 'He thinks he's some kind of fuckin' Don.'

'Just leave it the fuck alone, will you?' Kezlo snarled back, staring hard at Scotty.

I approached, smiling. 'Yes lads, how's it going? Good to see you both,' I said, pulling back a chair.

'All right, mate. You're looking good, Chopper. That a new jacket?' Kezlo enquired, shaking my hand.

'Yes, mate. Donna got it me from someone she knows in the buying department at her shop. It's all right, ain't it,' I said, admiring my new three-quarter-length black leather Armani jacket.

'All right,' Scotty managed sombrely.

'You all right, mate?' I enquired. 'Shit, Scotty, you've lost some weight, lad. What's wrong? You missing my cooking?' I said, joking with him.

'What the fuck is it to you?' Scotty sneered back at me. 'What do you give a shit for, if I've lost weight or not.'

'Easy, ar'kid,' I added, still smiling. 'Calm the fuck down. Why don't you chill a little?' I stared at my oldest friend and for the first time noticed something seemed different, but I couldn't quite put my finger on what.

'Get off my back then, why don't you?' he snapped, viciously this time.

'You got something on your mind, Scotty?' I enquired, trying my best to calm the situation. 'You need to talk, mate?'

'Nothing's wrong, is it, Scotty!' Kezlo said firmly, glaring hard at Scotty.

'All right then. What you lads drinking?' I asked, a little confused at the situation in hand.

'Sweet, mate. How about some Jacks?' Kezlo suggested.

'All right… That sweet with you, Scotty?' I asked him, his head dropped in a sulk. He nodded his approval as I left for the bar.

As I made my way to the bar I sensed something was wrong and turned back to observe my two closest friends. I could see Kezlo talking to Scotty, but they were out of earshot so I couldn't really hear what was being said.

Kezlo turned on Scotty. 'Calm the fuck down, will you?' He shot him a filthy look. 'What's up with you tonight? In fact, whilst we're on the subject, what the fuck's been up with you recently? You've been like this now for a while.'

'Nothing's up. All right, Kezlo?' Scotty sneered.

They had then sat there in silence whilst they waited for their friend to return from the bar with the drinks.

''Ere' are, lads: drinks,' I'd announced, placing down the three JD and Cokes as I returned from the bar, still a little confused as to what the problem was here.

'Cheers, mate,' Scotty said, sounding almost normal, and momentarily making me feel a little better.

'It's all right, mate. Now don't blow your fuckin' top with me, but are you all right?' I was truly concerned.

'Just tired, mate…y'know. Late night last night. That's all it was,' he replied, flashing his familiar grin at me, bringing back old memories.

'How's Donna, mate?' Kezlo asked, sipping his drink, changing the subject.

'She's sound, mate,' I said, smiling at the mere thought of her. 'Had a massive row the other week though. But we're double sweet now though.'

'That's birds for you though, mate. But I bet she wanted it her own way,' Kezlo laughed.

'Ain't that the truth,' I said, also laughing. 'Who's your new one then, Scotty? C'mon, mate, there must be at least one or two of 'em out there.'

'No!' Scotty snapped abruptly back at me.

'All right, we'll get off the bird subject then,' I tried, staring at him in confusion. 'Things still running smoothly, mate?'

'Why the fuck wouldn't they be!' he snarled back at me once again.

'For fuck's sake… I've had enough of this shite,' I said, glaring hard at Scotty. 'Just what's got into you, eh? You banging fuckin' gear or what? You fuckin' schizo.'

'Fuck you!' Scotty suddenly screamed at me. All heads turned in our direction. 'How long have I known you, and you're asking if I'm a fuckin' skag head? Fuck you, Chopper!' He was spitting the words out at me.

'Easy, Scotty… just sit down,' Kezlo said, watching all the other people staring at us.

'Calm yourself down, Scotty. Now!' I demanded sternly. 'Either sit the fuck down, or get the fuck out. Every fucker is staring at you.'

'Fuck all of you! You bunch of fucking wasters!' he yelled at everybody, including Kezlo and me. He then shot out of his chair and steamed out of the door.

I sat there bemused, completely baffled by the whole thing. 'What the fuck was that all about?' I asked Kezlo, as everybody returned to his or her own conversations.

'I don't know, mate,' Kezlo said, taking Scotty's abandoned drink. 'He's been agitated for the last couple of months now.'

'Yeah, but come on, mate. I ain't ever seen him like that before.'

'Reckon he just misses you not being around all the time,' Kezlo told me, sipping Scotty's drink now.

'I'm just busy. Y'know how it is.'

Kezlo grinned at me. 'Shit, *I* know that, Chopper. I appreciate everything you done for us, mate.'

'I want the truth, Kezlo,' I told him. 'Is he on gear or what?'

'Not smack anyway,' Kezlo confirmed, looking at me. 'Does a few rocks. No more than anyone else though. All the lads are doing it, Chopper. Y'know that.'

'I know they are,' I replied. 'What I want to know though, is how bad is Scotty on it?'

'Nah, you got it all wrong.' Kezlo paused momentarily. 'He's not that bad. Not from what I know anyway. He only ever does a little bit when I'm around. I can't say that it's out of hand.'

'Is he still disappearing all the time?'

'Yeah,' Kezlo answered.

'He say where he goes to?'

'Just out shagging birds,' shrugged Kezlo.

'And busin—'

'C'mon, Chopper. You know that he takes care of business. You ain't got any complaints, have you?'

'That's true. Ah, fuck it,' I sighed. 'He'll be all right, won't he?' I said smiling, though still a little concerned. 'Just let him calm the fuck down eh?'

'Like I said, mate, you've been more than fair with us lads. You deserve everything you've got.' He grinned at me. 'So tonight, let's just get mashed up big time.'

'Sounds good to me, Kezlo.'

'Come to daddy, c'mon now… I know you want me to smoke you… Oh how I do love you sooo much,' Scotty announced, placing the plastic tube between his lips whilst hidden away behind the locked doors of his bedroom engulfed in total darkness – hidden from the likes of Chopper and Kezlo, who couldn't discover his dark secret. Scotty still got that small rush just before igniting the pipe, burning that pure heaven in the form of crack-cocaine lying there peacefully among the ash, before turning itself into the monster that it really was.

As the rock began to take control of Scotty's mind and body, his eyes began to flutter. 'Oh yes… oh yes… that's the one… that's the one.'

Scotty sat there semi-naked with his jeans around his ankles, playing with his flaccid cock whilst he smoked the drug of his choice. Scotty was sore and swollen from the incessant masturbating whilst smoking the potent rocks.

Some poor quality hardcore porn movie that Scotty had borrowed was playing on the television in the background, but he had no interest in porn at that moment in time. No one had realised that Scotty had been smoking crack for years now, even well before the Hulme crew had begun dealing it.

In fact, Scotty had been smoking crack surreptitiously for so long now that even he hadn't known just how bad his habit had become. In fact, ever since the lads over in Moss Side began selling it, Scotty had become a regular punter.

It wasn't smack though – was it? And Scotty knew that it was more of a mental addiction rather than a physical one. At least that's what he'd kept on telling himself.

Everybody was smoking it these days. It was just that some were controlling it better than others were.

'What... what you say? Oh, only if you insist,' Scotty muttered to himself as he reloaded the pipe.

'What the fu... nan... who...not like th...' Scotty was completely out of his mind as the drug took control. He'd been sat there constantly reloading that pipe for the last three hours.

'No, it's not that much... I know it's not... go away will you... haaa... haaaa... haaaaa...' Scotty was totally lost as he'd reloaded once again.

'Fuck it... What Chopper don't know won't hurt him,' he announced, obviously to no one but himself once again, rolling about, laughing hysterically. He was so smashed that he hadn't even realised that he'd been talking to himself and had been for quite some time now.

TWENTY-NINE

'I s that you, Chopper?' Donna called out as I fell drunkenly through the front door.

'Yeah,' I slurred in response. The drink had taken effect big time. Kezlo and I were both completely smashed by the time we had left Dry Bar.

'All right, Donna,' I said, staggering into the living room. 'I got us some scran from Sampson's.' I was rocking back and forth from all the alcohol that had been consumed.

'Good. I'm starving,' she giggled. 'Just look at the state of you! You look boozed out of your head. I take it you and the lads had a good night then?'

'Me and Kezlo did anyway,' I slurred, as she took the bag from me and I collapsed into the chair.

'Where was Scotty?' she shouted through from the kitchen.

'He's fuc—' I belched and I shook my head. 'Fucked.'

A few moments later Donna returned with two plates of food. 'What was that? You were all fucked?' She handed me my plate.

'No… Yes… I don't know. What was the question?' I asked, tearing into the goat curry, rice and peas. Given my state, I think goat's arse would probably have tasted just as good.

'I asked if you were all messed up,' she laughed.

'Scotty is. He's a weird bastard.'

'What's up with Scotty?'

'I don't know. Something, nothing… I don't know.'

'You're hammered, Chopper,' said Donna, smiling. 'You're not making any fuckin' sense at all.' She laughed again, hitting me in my ribs playfully.

'I know I'm not,' I slurred once again, not sure what I was exactly going on about. 'Damn, this food tastes good though.'

'Ahh fuck… My head's banging,' I declared, sitting up in bed. 'We got any pain killers or Pepto?' I asked Donna as I climbed out of bed.

'In the bathroom, Chopper… What time is it?'

'Just gone twelve,' I informed her, heading for the bathroom. 'I've got to meet Prey and Sean at one,' I added, disappearing into the bathroom, relieving myself of an apparently never-ending stream of hot piss. 'My head's *killing* me!' I declared to the bathroom wall.

'So it should do,' Donna laughed. 'I've not seen you that hammered for a long time.'

'I know, me and Kezlo downed untold amounts of Jack last night.' I was chuckling to myself, thinking back to the previous evening and the state the two of us had been in.

'Chopper,' Donna called out just I was returning to the bedroom swigging from bottle of Pepto Bismol that I swore tasted like some funky cream my old dear used to put on my cuts and grazes as a kid. 'Is Scotty all right?'

'Why do you ask?' I said, a little concerned.

'When you got in last night you seemed proper upset with him. Not that you were making much sense. But in the night you woke me. You sat up in bed shouting his name. But it wasn't in anger, more like concern.'

'He's all right… He was just boozed when I got there, and he just got off early,' I lied.

Though I *was* worried about him. I'd never seen him like he'd been last night; maybe it was nothing. Surely Kezlo would have said something if anything had been wrong.

'Right, I need a cold shower before I get off,' I told Donna, kissing her.

'That stuff really stinks like Germolene, you know,' Donna said, pulling her face at the smell of the Pepto Bismol I'd just consumed.

'I knew that I knew that taste and smell from somewhere,' I said. 'But it works wonders for my stomach,' I added, laughing, and returning to the bathroom.

We'd arranged to meet Scotty along with whoever his latest flavour of the month was. I'd felt pretty bad about the way we'd parted the last time we'd hooked up, so I thought we'd try a different approach to the night out, with a meal at Chan's. As

Donna and I entered Chan's we spotted Scotty already seated with a very attractive (albeit very skinny) mixed-race girl.

'Hi'ya, Scotty. It's been a while,' Donna said, kissing his cheek. There was, however, mild shock written all over her face; she obviously couldn't believe the extent of his weight loss, although she said nothing.

'I know, Donna. Sorry about that,' he said, holding her hand warmly. 'Shit, sorry you guys. This is Jackie.'

'All right, Jackie,' I said, nodding my head. 'This is Donna.' The two greeted each other and began to chat.

'Sorry again about last week,' Scotty said, half smiling at me as I took the seat next to him.

'Stop apologising, will you?' I replied. 'I already told you, it don't matter none. You're looking better tonight; that's all that matters.'

'It seems like ages since we been to Chan's together,' he smirked. 'It's good, y'know, to see the two of you.'

'You know where we live,' I laughed.

'I know… I'll have to make more effort,' he added, still smiling.

'Makes two of us then,' I said, grinning back at him. 'Tell you what: next Wednesday night you and Jackie come round and I'll sort that Indian dish out for you, the one you like so much.' Although the invite was more out of concern for his weight loss.

'Sound, mate, I'll look forward to it.'

The rest of that evening turned out to be great. We'd all been in good spirits and enjoyed each others' company immensely. It was like old times with Scotty, who was on top form that night, cracking jokes and making us all laugh. As midnight approached we all headed our separate ways.

'Jackie, pass that pipe will you,' Scotty told his new girlfriend. As he lit yet another pipe he felt Jackie rubbing his crotch area, getting him aroused. He really liked this girl – and as an added bonus she loved to smoke rocks as much as he did and would literally do anything to him or for him as long as he kept her rocked up through their drug-crazed sex sessions.

'I really like Chopper and Donna,' she said, unzipping Scotty's jeans and removing his now hardened cock and caressing it slowly.

'We grew up together. He's like my brother,' he said, smiling at the thought. 'Nothing will ever change that,' he declared proudly, passing Jackie the pipe as he watched her greedily suck away at the smoke that was aimlessly drifting around the empty water bottle.

'This is top gear, y'know,' Jackie announced as she fell back against the back of the settee, allowing Scotty to unbutton her blouse, a trail of smoke drifting from her nostrils. She was enjoying the rush as it hit her system.

Scotty grinned at her. 'Let me take your clothes off, eh.' The rocks were making him horny again. Yet another thing he cherished about them.

'I'll go one better than that, Scotty,' she said, smiling and dropping to her knees between Scotty's legs. 'Load the pipe again and I'll show you a little trick that I think you're gonna like a lot, Scotty.'

He quickly did as he was told as Jackie stroked his cock expertly. Just as he eagerly put the pipe to his lips, he cracked a small smile as he realised what Jackie's little trick was. Her mouth engulfed his manhood and she went enthusiastically to work on his pipe – just as she had keenly done on the other.

THIRTY

We arrived in the 1990s with some great memories of the latter half of the 1980s. Prey, Sean and I had observed the growth of the clubbing industry, alongside our ever-expanding success within the drug trade.

The drugs side of the scene alone had developed into a revolution that nobody – including ourselves for that matter – had ever expected, with the introduction of everybody's favourite so-called 'love drug', as it had recently been dubbed by the media. They were constantly working against us. But it had to be said that the more bad press Ecstasy and other drugs associated with scene and the business got, the more our profit margins increased beyond belief.

The new revolution that we witnessed first-hand was opening drug use up to a much wider audience, so to speak. And over the last couple of years, it was a market in which we were certainly reaping benefits.

'C'mon, Chopper, it'll be a proper sound day out,' Prey informed me, as we all sat around the benches outside The Spinners Pub. We had been there all Sunday morning as they'd opened early for us – or maybe they hadn't closed since the previous evening. Everybody was waiting impatiently for me to make a decision as to whether or not I was going to join them for their planned day out. 'Every fucker's gonna be there for it. It's goin' to be a massive day out,' Prey continued.

They were all trying their best to get me to come along to see the Stone Roses at Spike Island in Widnes later that afternoon.

'Who says everybody's going?' I sighed, as I really did not want to go. 'Look, I ain't even heard the band before. Y'know it ain't even my kind of music, Prey,' I declared.

What I said was true. I'd never even listened to anything the band had done before. It was all part of the indie scene that was growing strong again within Manchester, with a lot of the most popular bands in the country hailing from the estates within the city and the surrounding boroughs.

'You do know who the fuck they are though, right?' Sean said. 'They're well sound, Chopper. You seen all the kids in town wearing their t-shirts, haven't you? Why the hell do you think we've got all these baggy-as-fuck kids running about out there with their outrageous flares?'

'It don't make 'em good though, does it?' I grinned at Sean, who shook his head at me.

'You're getting too old for a good day out, are you, Chopper?' Donna smiled at me. 'I reckon you just can't keep up with us young 'uns these days.'

'That'll be the day,' I replied, laughing at her.

'See… even your missus is coming with us,' Sean added.

Prey stared at me. 'It's been sold out now since the beginning. I got us all tickets from Batty over in Wythenshawe, who was screwing with me 'cos he knows he'll get pure bees for them down there today.'

The truth was that I couldn't really be bothered, as we'd spent the entire weekend out clubbing it in both Manchester and Warrington at some new club called Legends, which appeared to hold great potential for a Saturday-night takeover. And besides which, I wasn't at all interested in a band I'd never listened to before.

It just wasn't my taste in music. Although I suppose I was being wilfully ignorant of the fact that there was a lot of other good music out there besides hip hop or dance music. It's just that that was about all we'd ever seemed to listen to whilst growing up.

'Just look at the weather as well,' Donna announced. 'It's been chucking it down all week – now look at it.' She gazed at the clear blue sky.

'That's right, Chopper,' laughed Kathy. 'The sun's come out just for you. You really are a miserable bastard at times.'

'Chopper just likes the rain. Don't you, kid?' added Helen, who was Sean's girlfriend of almost a year now. She had a full head of brown curly hair and wore some of the craziest outfits that I'd seen. But despite that, she was a really nice girl who I'd taken a liking to almost immediately. 'What you going to do if you don't come, eh Chopper? Sit around on your jack all day?'

I smirked back at her, then shook my head in defeat. 'All right... all right,' I sighed, finally giving way to them. 'If it keeps you lot off my fuckin' back, let's go to Widnes then. Wherever the fuck that might be, eh.'

They all just smiled at me, knowing they'd won me over despite my great reluctance and pointless protests.

'Fuck me,' I gasped, totally astonished at the amount of people wandering around this huge open field. At the far end was probably the biggest stage I'd ever set my eyes on. 'Are all these 'ere for this band?' I enquired, still looking around in utter disbelief.

'There'll be almost 30,000 from what I hear, Chopper,' Sean confirmed enthusiastically.

'You really like this sort of music?' I stared at him, shaking my head slightly. 'I mean seriously?'

'Their album is proper sound, Chopper,' he replied. 'Nothing like you'd expect. You'll be surprised, mate.'

'What about you, Prey?'

'I ain't heard shit by 'em, mate,' he laughed in response. 'Sean just wanted to come and see 'em, so I told him we'd all come.'

'Bastard,' I joked with him, punching him lightly in his ribs. 'I thought you'd heard them.'

Donna returned from the bar with Kathy and Helen. 'There are loads of people here. Have you seen everybody from town?'

'This is going to be well top,' Kathy smiled. She'd lasted longer than most of Prey's girls, and all I could think is that she really must be a true sex kitten as he still referred to them. I grinned to myself at the thought.

'Guaranteed, Chopper – you'll have a great day,' Helen told me, linking arms with Sean and smiling as she did so.

'Whatever,' I laughed, taking hold of Donna's hand.

I had to admit though, that the day was turning out to be all right. In fact, it was safe to say that it was good day all round. I was feeling really chilled out, lounging around the grassy areas with the others, enjoying some of the new batch of skunk weed that we had picked up that week, and the warm-up bands and MCs were keeping us entertained. They'd even brought over New York DJ Frankie Bones, who was playing some awesome sets. Everything just seemed to go with the flow and the ambience of the day.

'C'mon, Chopper,' Sean nodded, as he took the smouldering spliff from me. 'Let's go get some more drinks in.'

'Sweet, mate,' I replied lazily, breaking free from Donna's embrace. 'Same again?' I smirked at Prey, who winked his answer back at me as the two of us took off towards the bar areas to purchase more warm beer, served in those God-awful plastic cups.

'It's all right, in't it, mate? You're having a good time, ain't you, Chopper?' asked Sean, as we made our way through the masses of people who all appeared to be as chilled out as we were.

'Yes, mate,' I agreed, smiling back at him. 'Y'know what, Sean – and this'll piss you off after the way I carried on earlier – but I'm having a proper sound time. I'm really glad you all talked me into it now.'

'Told you, Chop.' He suddenly stopped and looked around. 'Have you seen all the heads from around town that are 'ere?'

'Shit yeah… I tell you, mate, I was well shocked by it,' I said honestly. 'I never knew the Stone Roses were that big. I read some shit about them in *The Face* and all the hype they're creating around town. But y'know how it is, mate: I'm pure into another type of music scene.'

'Just wait till you hear them, Chopper,' he smiled confidently at me. 'You'll be well shocked, mate.

'We'll see,' I said, laughing once again at his enthusiasm for this band.

We struggled through the hordes of customers that were all queuing for the same pints of warm piss that we were. Not that we were going to let that spoil our day.

Sean then whistled out loud to try and get some attention from the bar staff. ''Ere'are, mate,' he shouted over the crowded bar, trying his best to get noticed. 'Oi – can we get some service down this end of the bar, mate? Will someone take some notice of the fact that there are punters down this end!'

I felt a sudden uneasy presence surrounding us. I looked to my right-hand side where a group of lads had just arrived at the bar. Just then, one of the group turned in our direction.

'All right, Macreedy?' asked Paddy of Salford fame. He was stood there smirking broadly, his entourage beside him. Now this was the kind of attention we definitely hadn't requested.

'Everything's sound, Paddy,' Sean told him calmly, nodding and smiling. I automatically sensed that Paddy appeared to already be on edge. And that was the kind of thing that you wanted to stay clear of. Not only that, but there were only two of us. 'Just 'ere having a good time, y'know, Paddy. No trouble, right?'

Paddy was glaring at the two of us. I swore that his eyes constantly looked wired, and they twitched unnervingly. There were at least six lads behind him, possibly more. And one of them was Chris Walker. He was real sight to look at these days, after the punishment that he'd suffered at the hands of Sean and that baseball bat some years earlier. He had grown his mousy hair quite long to try and hide the scars that had been left behind. In fact, looking at him now he kind of reminded me of an uglier version of the Hunchback of Notre Dame, were that possible.

'Just the two of you little pricks is it?' Chris smirked, although he was still keeping his distance behind Paddy, hopping from one foot to the next as if on hot coals.

'Y'what?' I smiled at him. 'Y'think we need more than two for the likes of you, Walker?' I laughed at him.

This was not my first face-to-face encounter with them. Obviously, being in the position that we held around town, I'd come into contact with the two of them several times before today. I knew that I should show Paddy more respect than I did, with him being one of the older heads – but I just couldn't bring myself to do so. I had no time for either of them. And the thing I hated about Paddy was the way he used the fear to control people around town.

We had an unspoken agreement to stay the hell out of each other's way. And that's the way it had always kind of stayed. He'd never really got in my face, and for whatever reason had kept his distance. But with Sean, it was a whole different story, stemming back to that one time when Paddy's crew had tried to have over Prey and Sean back in the early eighties.

'How's it goin', Chopper? See you're still nothing but the scally little fucker that you've always been, eh? Suppose some things will never change, eh?' Paddy sneered menacingly at me.

'Yeah whatever, Paddy,' I sighed, already bored with him.

'Seriously, kid,' Paddy said right back at me. 'Just who the fuck do you think you are?'

'I think that y'know who the fuck I am, Paddy,' I replied. 'And we're not fuckin' kids any more.'

'You what, you litt—'

'Seriously, Paddy,' I snapped back before he could finish. 'What do you think? That the entire world is afraid of you? Well, I'm sorry to inform you – *Patrick* – but that just isn't th—'

'Do you realise just who the fuck you're talking to, Chopper?' snapped Chris, cutting me off.

'Well it wasn't you – was it, Walker,' I replied, smiling at him.

'You—'

'We done here?' I asked Sean, who nodded.

'You don't go fuckin' anywhere until I fuckin' say so,' sneered Paddy, moving right into my space and pressing his face up against mine.

'Oh yeah, Pad—' I began to say, as I pressed my forehead against his.

But before I could even finish his name, Sean had pulled me back, keeping a hold of me so I couldn't get near to him. 'Easy, Chopper… There's way too many of them.'

Paddy stood there grinning at me. 'I see that you've still got that fiery temper of yours that I keep hearing so much about, eh?' he said, smirking at me confidently. 'You're nothing but a little scally twat. And that, my son, is all you're ever gonna be.' He was laughing, provoking me.

'So you want a shot at the title, boy?' asked Chris, stepping forward.

'What?' I laughed. 'With you, little girl?'

'With *me*,' added Paddy, stepping towards me.

I could see that all of the lads who were with him were becoming agitated. They stood there, knowing that there was violence brewing. It was written all over their faces as they began to move in on the two of us.

By this point I honestly didn't care how many of them there were. I'd had enough of this bullshit. This is the reason why Paddy was allowed to get away with so many mindless acts: people were always backing down from him because of the fear he inspired. Well – enough was enough. I think Sean sensed I felt this and gripped my arm tighter.

'OK, fuck it!' I was enraged. 'Let's do this shit, Paddy,' I said. Sean clung to me, trying his best to reason with me.

'There's too many, Chopper,' Sean told me. 'Let it go for another time,'.

'It's all right, Chopper,' Paddy said, winking at me. 'It's your boyfriend 'ere that we've been waiting to see, not you. I think we've got us some unfinished business, Macreedy.' Chris was nodding in agreement behind Paddy.

'That was a long time ago now, Paddy,' Sean stated, slightly taken aback by Paddy's reference. As a result, his grip on me began to weaken. 'Besides which, Paddy, it was down to your spar there anyway.' Sean pointed accusingly at Chris.

By now a large crowd had gathered, drawn by the sound of our raised and angered voices, all of them eager to see what was going to happen.

'Fuck you, Macreedy,' Paddy yelled back at Sean. 'Chris's one of mine. You should know by now. And y'know what else you should know? You never fuck with one of mine.'

'This is outrageous, Paddy,' sighed Sean. 'This is well old news. Christ – why the fuck are you bringing it up now?'

'Chris was hospitalised for over a year after you batted him round the fuckin' head.'

What Paddy was saying was all true. Chris had been in hospital a long while. But it had been over business and was past history now. I mean, I was only a kid myself when all that had gone down. So why was he bringing it up now after all these years? Whatever the reason, it was clear that Paddy was more than a little disconcerted.

'You're bringing up the past, Paddy,' Sean informed him. 'What was done is done. This is out of order.'

Sean had completely loosened his grip on me now, so I decided that a different course of action was needed here.

Stepping away slightly from Sean, I carefully observed the scene before me. I knew that Paddy was unpredictable. Therefore I knew that to catch him off guard I would have to play him at his own game. As all the focus was on Sean, I silently flipped open my lock knife without anyone seeing.

'Well, fuck you… I never forget things. I've been waiting to catch up with you and your girlfriend, the one I left with the belated birth mark on his face.' He sneered the last of the words, screwing up his face as he did so. 'Yet another prick. Just who the fuck do you lot think you are anyway? I reckon you've all got way too big for yourselves. Don't want to share any business with any of the others from town, eh? Is that it eh, Macreedy?' Paddy said.

It was all beginning to make more sense now. He was merely using the incident from years ago to create this problem. Well, that was all right then, because I was about to *give* him a problem. No one saw me make a move, but I'd heard enough of this nonsense and by now my adrenaline had picked up and was racing. The way I figured it, there couldn't be a moment's hesitation here. I shot silently, swiftly and smoothly past Sean, flying straight at Paddy's face with the open blade. Paddy seemed to be the only one who was aware of it, quickly trying to move away.

He was fast, but I was faster. My blade sliced through the air, the sunlight bouncing off it, momentarily dazzling Paddy.

'You prick!' I screamed, as the blade sliced cleanly through the flesh below his left eye. Blood sprayed wildly into the now frenzied crowd.

'You little twa—' His cry trailed off, as my left fist followed through and crashed into the side of his face, knocking him to the ground.

I immediately descended upon him again to finish the job. All that could be heard at that moment were the screams that were attracting unwanted attention from security guards in the vicinity.

I was inches from Paddy as Sean suddenly yanked me back before I could reach him. I could clearly see the rage in his eyes as he leapt to his feet. Chris and the rest of his lads were helping Paddy up just as security guards came bursting onto the scene.

'It was them lot there – all of those lot right there,' yelled a barman who'd observed the entire thing. He was only pointing in the direction of Paddy's lot, however.

Just then, all of the security guards rushed at Paddy, Chris and the rest of the lads with them. As they grabbed them, all hell broke loose as they all began fighting viciously with one another. But as we broke free from the boundaries of the enlarging crowd, I could see more guards were arriving on the scene as they fought their way through the mass of people in order to bring sanity to the chaos taking place. I was grinning like the kid who'd found the key to the candy store as Sean continued to pull me away.

'It's sweet, mate. Sean, it's all right, mate. Look!' I was saying, as I pointed at the fight between Paddy's crew and the security, not to mention the arrival of more guards, who now rushed at them.

Sean stopped and turned so that he could also observe the guards and Paddy's lot as they all battled with one another. 'Sound, Chopper,' he laughed. 'At least they'll kick them the fuck out of 'ere now, eh.' We both smiled as we headed off in the direction of one of the other packed bars.

'Fuck the drinks, Sean,' I announced, as I observed more security arriving. 'We'll send some of the girls to sort it out. I think it may be best if we lose ar'selves in the crowd back out front, mate.'

'In'it,' agreed Sean as we changed direction.

'Y'know, Sean – I fuckin' hate that Paddy,' I said as the two of us made our way back to the others empty handed. 'Always 'ave… ever since that day that I seen him slice Prey's face open all that time ago.'

'I know what you're saying, mate. He really is a prick. But y'know, he still puts the fear in me. I honestly think that Prey's the only one who Paddy is actually scared of. Well, maybe even you a little now, eh, Chop?' He suddenly stopped walking and stared at me. 'Listen, Chopper, I just want to say th—'

'Ah, fuck it Sean. You always looked out for me whilst I was growing up,' I smiled at him. 'I know you always will as well. Likewise, y'know.'

Once we both returned to the others, Prey just laughed when we relayed the story to him about what had happened. 'You're like a tiger boy,' he laughed at me. 'We're going to have to cage your arse soon.'

'You sure you're all right, Chopper?' Donna asked, kissing me.

'Of course I am, girl.'

'You always seem to find trouble, don't you?' she pouted at me.

'No – that's not true!' I said defensively. 'It just seems to always find me.'

With dusk approaching there was now an almighty cheer as DJ Frankie Bones spun his last house tune and the deep throb of voodoo howlings from a backing track had everybody up on their feet. The whole place began to erupt into a frenzy with everybody rising finally to greet the Stone Roses. As the band appeared on stage, I can remember thinking that they had real presence.

Ian Brown, the lead singer, came bouncing onto stage with his arms spread wide as Reni, the drummer, started up a manic bouncing beat, and the crowd became even more enthused for them. Just then, Mani, who was the band's bassist, kicked in with a huge bassline that sent a shudder through all of us. And then John Squire, their main songwriter and lead guitarist, unleashed his immense talent onto the now enthralled audience.

By now I was determined that I was going to have a great night, and honestly wasn't bothered if the band was good or not. I had to also admit that I'd enjoyed cutting Paddy. Even if it wasn't a major slice, it had still marked him, and deep down I'd had a desire to one day confront him, one to one, to show him that not everybody was afraid of him.

'This is "I Wanna Be Adored",' Sean informed me as Ian Brown began to sing and the 28,000-strong crowd began cheering and singing along. I had to admit that it was a fantastic atmosphere.

As they continued through their set, I received a running commentary about the tracks from an over-enthused Sean, who was soaking up every moment of what he kept informing me was the greatest night of his life. And the more he buzzed the more I enjoyed myself.

There were these ever-changing projections behind the band that were apparently John Squire's painting and collages.

As the evening progressed I was enjoying the band more and

more, and just then they cut in with a wild wah-wah funky tune that the crowd went wild for. 'This you're gonna like, Chopper,' said Sean.

'What is it?'

'"Fools Gold", mate,' he replied, smiling at me.

That's when it suddenly hit me. Sean was so was right. I mean, I know that I'd protested earlier, but these lads from Manchester really had something. Something different. Something that was almost inspiring. "Fools Gold" was amazing. They'd got me – I was hooked. They shattered all my previous assumptions about such music (although I was trying my best not to show it after all my objections). But I was transfixed by their music. How wrong I'd been.

I glanced at Prey, who I realised was also enjoying the band, and who in turn smiled and nodded with me. Sean watched the two of us and started laughing out loud. 'I told you both… didn't I?' he said, smiling and looking like he was having the time of his life as he wrapped his arms around Helen's waist. 'I said that they were proper sound. Didn't I?'

'Yes, mate, you did,' I said, smiling at his exuberance.

Donna reached up and kissed me. 'See? Now wouldn't you have been pissed off if you hadn't come?'

'Definitely,' I replied, kissing her back, thinking what a fool I'd have been to not have come along today.

The band played for almost two hours, keeping us transfixed by their music. As the concert came to a close, it ended with a massive fireworks display, bringing the evening to perfect closure.

'Where the cars parked, Sean?' I asked, as we'd driven to Widnes in both his Audi and Prey's Mercedes Benz.

'I'm not exactly sure,' he replied. 'This way I think. The place is mayhem.'

He was right. It was pure chaos outside of the grounds, people wandering the streets aimlessly, searching their transport home for the night. We must have been drifting the streets for almost half an hour before Prey finally gave a sigh of relief.

'There… Look over there.' Prey pointed to their cars parked up ahead.

As we all made our way over to the parked vehicles, we hadn't had even noticed the black Ford Escort trailing behind us, slowly following as we headed towards our destination. Everybody was still in good spirits after the day we'd had.

''Ere we go then,' Sean announced brightly as he began to unlock his Audi.

Suddenly, with no warning whatsoever, the screeching of tyres pierced the stillness of night and we all heard the unmistakable sound of gun shots; the night turned into a mass of unrestrained pandemonium.

Instinctively we all ducked, taking cover behind the cars, as gun shots were far from uncommon on the Manchester estates. The only thing was, this wasn't Manchester – this was Widnes, for Christ's sake. The girls instantly became hysterical, screaming and yelling out, shock controlling them.

The shots continued exploding and suddenly my mind filled up with memories of the one time I'd resorted to killing. I looked around me, taking in my surroundings with the panic of the hunter hunted. It seemed like an eternity, though it could only have been a couple of seconds that had passed, if that.

I could see that Prey had all of the girls covered. His head was bobbing back and forth and up and down cautiously as he tried to get a better view of the situation at hand. All that could be heard were screams, along with the screeching of tyres and yet more shots tearing through the night.

I honestly don't know how I was missed, but I suddenly witnessed Sean's body jerk sharply one way, then wrench the other way from the force of the bullets entering him with ferocity.

'Nooooo! Sean!' I screamed out loud in both fear and panic – more for him than myself. I was caught between feeling that I was stuck in a nightmare, yet knowing very much that it was reality. Without a moment's hesitation, I leapt from the ground towards Sean.

More shots rang out as I grabbed his flailing body. I clearly saw the white flashes of ferocious fire from the gun that was pointed out of the rear of the black Ford Escort as it sped by. Another bullet had made contact with Sean's back; the sheer force threw the two of us to the hard surface of the pavement.

At the same time I felt a fierce, sharp, burning sensation from within my own chest as we both crashed helplessly to the ground. However, that was not my concern. My only worry was with Sean.

Two more shots rang out and the Audi's windows shattered with the force.

As the girls crouched and screamed, Prey suddenly leapt over the bonnet of the Audi, his gun already pulled. 'C'mon, you motherfuckers!' He screamed the words with a rage I hadn't witnessed in him for a long time, emptying his Glock 9mm pistol at the Escort, which was already fleeing into the night.

As reality suddenly kicked in I found myself helplessly holding Sean's limp body in my arms. I also realised that the burning sensation I'd felt was where the bullet had exited through Sean's chest and struck me. My breathing was hard and painful, but all I could think of was Sean lying there in my arms. Blood continued to seep unrestrained; there was just no preventing it. 'Sean... Sean... no... no, no this can't be... Please no... no... no...Noooo!' I was yelling out loud, holding his limp, bloodied body tighter.

'Sean – Sean – oh my God... Nooo, please no... Sean,' It was Helen, standing there in shock. Donna and Kathy still lay on the floor, crying. Both were in complete shock.

'Chopper! Chopper – we got to get the fuck out of 'ere. C'mon, Chop, get yourself together, kid... *Chopper!*' screamed Prey, now stood over me, immense anguish in his eyes as he glared down at us both, shaking his head in utter disbelief.

He bent down, tearing at my shirt with panic in his eyes. 'You're hit. I don't know how badly. We need to get you home right now, kid. Can you make it, Chopper?' Although I could see his mouth move, his words were falling on deaf ears.

'Oh my God... Chopper.' Donna was now standing there, holding her face. 'You've been shot.' She was bending towards me, tears filling her eyes at the sight of both Sean and me.

Prey grabbed hold of me, pulling me up. 'You've got to get out of 'ere... *We've* got to get of 'ere, Chopper... before the police get 'ere. C'mon, ar'kid,' he said, pulling me away from Sean's blood-drenched body.

'Not Sean – nooo!' I was screaming loudly, as the pain from my chest suddenly brought me round. 'AAARRRGGGHHH.'

'Exactly… C'mon now!' Prey demanded. 'We can't do anything 'ere… Not now.'

'Chopper… Chopper, are you all right?' Donna was stood before me; I could feel the warmth of her hands on my cheeks as she held my bloodied face.

'Donna, get Kathy in the car… *Now*,' Prey shouted at her.

'What about Helen? Just look at her,' Donna said turning to where Helen lay holding Sean's body, sobbing hysterically.

'You're right, Donna. We can't take her anywhere yet,' he sighed. 'Are you gonna be all right 'ere, Donna? I mean, to stay 'ere with her? I'll take Chopper and get him some help. But listen, Donna – just tell them that it was just the three of you 'ere tonight. You got that, girl?' He opened the car door, pushing me into the rear.

Suddenly, just like that, Donna ceased crying and almost immediately became totally calm. 'You're right, Prey. Just go and get Chopper some help. Make sure he's all right. Promise me that, Prey. Please.'

Prey was dragging a paralysed Kathy from the floor, heaping her into the passenger seat. 'Don't worry: Chopper will be all right. I can't believe Sean…' Prey looked at his friend lying there; he knew it was too late for him.

'Go now,' Donna instructed us firmly as the tears began to return.

THIRTY-ONE

'What's his name, love?' the ambulance medic asked. 'His name, love... I know it's hard, but if you could, please.' He stopped and looked directly at Donna.

'Sean Macreedy,' she answered him.

Of course Donna had known immediately that it had been too late. By the time the police and the ambulance had arrived at the scene, Sean had already passed away. She knew this as she lay on the floor holding onto his limp, blood-soaked body.

'Where are you lot from?' the uniformed officer now stood there asked gruffly.

'Manchester,' Donna answered, still comforting Helen. Donna saw that look on the officer's face as she told him where they were from. He tried to hide it from her as he turned to speak into his radio, but Donna had already seen it.

'I just... can't... beli... believe that he's gone... he's dead... They just shot him... dead,' Helen continued to sob into Donna's shoulder.

'I know, Helen... I know,' Donna answered, tears tumbling down her face too. Sean was dead, and her thoughts now turned to her boyfriend Chopper, who had also been shot. Oh God, she just prayed that he was going to be all right. Such a great day had ended so badly. It was beyond belief. In fact, it had turned into their worst possible nightmare.

'Mike, it's me. Macreedy's dead,' Walsh simply announced to Stevenson over the phone.

Stevenson glanced at his watch and realised it was just gone one o'clock in the morning. 'Where and how?'

'He was shot in Widnes about an hour, hour and a half ago. Sounds like some kind of drive-by shooting. I haven't got all the details yet.'

'What the fuck was he doing in Widnes?'

'Some big concert, the copper told me,' Walsh stated. 'He says it's mayhem down there. They've not even been able to stop any cars. He says by the time they arrived on the scene that Macreedy was already dead. When they checked his name, they called it in over here. Desk sergeant called me straight away.'

'Any witnesses, Martin?' he asked, not holding out much hope.

'Two. Macreedy's girlfriend and – wait for this – Chorlton's.' He paused, waiting for a response on the other end of the line. 'That's right: Miss Donna Hayes,' he added.

'Yes. This could be just what we're looking for. Pick me up straight away, Martin,' said Stevenson. 'We'll head straight over there now.' He replaced the receiver and smiled to himself.

Donna and Helen had been seated in an empty interview room since arriving at the police station. It was now the early hours of Monday morning. Stevenson had telephoned ahead and had given strict orders that no one spoke to either of them until he and Walsh arrived.

'Who's at the scene now?' Stevenson asked as they made their way through the small police station in Widnes.

'Forensics is still there. They cut the area off straight away. I tell you though: this Macreedy was well messed up. He must have pissed the wrong people off rotten. The holes in him were massive, like he'd been hit with cannonballs or something,' answered Detective Shaw as he led them towards the interview room.

'Why'd you phone us in?' Walsh asked.

'When the girlfriend said Manchester and the fact he'd been shot…' He sighed, trailing off. 'Well, I figured he must have been heavily involved somewhere. Once his details came up on the computer I figured your lot would be interested.'

'Good work,' Stevenson smiled at the detective. 'Bloody good work.'

'Time to speak to the girls,' Shaw commented before pausing outside the interview room. 'You do realise that it's our case?'

'We understand fully,' Stevenson nodded. 'We've been after

this lot for a while now, and, to be honest, this could be the break we need.'

'Well, I figured if you knew them,' Shaw said, smiling at the two of them knowingly, 'then it would probably be more help to us in the long run if you spoke with them first.'

'Say absolutely nothing, Helen,' Donna instructed her friend as the detectives entered the room. 'I'll do the talking, you hear me? Just remember that there was only the three of us there tonight – all right?'

'I still can't believe he's gone,' Helen sobbed, tears running down her face.

'Hello there, I'm DI Stevenson; this is DI Walsh. We're from Manchester. Oh, forgive me, this is Detective Shaw from right here in Widnes. Are you girls OK? Can we get you anything?' Stevenson asked in a soft, considerate voice.

'No thank you. We'd like to just go home please,' Donna replied, her arm still around Helen.

Shaw loaded a tape into the machine, giving the time, date and who was present in the room. 'We need to tape this, girls, OK?' he said as he finished setting the tape up.

'Long way from home, aren't we?' Donna said, eyeing Stevenson suspiciously.

'Friendly faces for you,' he replied, giving a flawless smile. 'Macreedy was from our way, so they called us in. Now tell me Donna, what happened tonight?' Stevenson enquired.

'Well, the three of us had come to the concert. We'd been inside all day. We were heading for Sean's car when all of a sudden shots rang out. I could see flashes coming from a car speeding past...' Donna stopped, looking at them.

'Please tell us what else happened. We know this is hard, but we need to know everything about what happened. How about you, Helen?' asked Walsh.

Donna ignored him. 'The car windows shattered. Then it was horrible... just terrible.' She began to cry. 'Then Sean just fell to the ground. There was blood, lots of blood everywhere.'

'We realise it's hard, but we need more details,' Stevenson said.

'That's all we know!' Donna suddenly screamed back at him.

'Do you have any idea why this happened?' asked Walsh.

'No, we do not,' Donna snapped back at him irritably.

'You sure just the three of you were there?' Stevenson added.

'Yes. Why?' Donna asked calmly.

'You sure that boyfriend of yours wasn't there, Donna?' Stevenson said casually. 'Chopper, ain't it?'

Donna obviously knew that Chopper had always been in and out of trouble, and the kind of reputation that he had back in Manchester. She'd even known that the cops knew of him. But why bring him up now?

'No, Mr Stevenson, Billy wasn't there. It's really not his kind of thing.'

Stevenson hadn't expected this kind of response. 'Don't go pissing up our legs now, Donna. We know all about your boyfriend and his mates, you hear me?'

'What the hell has this got to do with Sean being killed?' Donna asked calmly.

Walsh intervened. 'Come on, Helen. You're very quiet. Why don't you tell us what actually happened?'

'He's dead. Dead. Shot…killed.' She began sobbing hysterically again.

'OK, sorry love… calm down,' Shaw intervened. He wasn't over-keen on the way the other two were going about any of this. In fact he was beginning to wish he'd never called them.

'You're both bastards,' Donna stated firmly. 'Just look at the state of her, will you! Her boyfriend got killed in front of her tonight and you're grilling her like she's the one who done it!'

'Look, Macreedy was up to his eyeballs in all kinds of shit,' Stevenson said sternly. 'He got what he des—'

'That's enough!' Shaw snapped firmly, staring hard at Stevenson.

'Can we go now, please?' Donna asked Shaw, as he seemed to be the reasonable one.

'No, you can't!' Walsh yelled, taking them all by surprise.

Just then the door flew open and the police doctor waltzed in, looking extremely pissed off.

'I can't believe you've not had these two girls checked out, for

Christ's sake,' he declared sternly, throwing filthy looks around the room at the others. 'Jesus H Christ – are you insane? Are you two all right?' he enquired kindly of the two girls. 'Come on, you're both coming with me,' he then announced, completely ignoring the police detectives standing there, as he took Helen's hand.

'What do you think you're doing?' Stevenson interjected.

'Just look at this poor girl, will you?' The doctor stared at Stevenson, then at Helen. 'She is in a state of complete shock. I'm taking both of them to the hospital, where they should have been taken in the first place.' The doctor then led the two girls out of the interview room.

'We'll be in touch, girls,' Walsh called after them.

Donna then turned back to them.

'I'm sure you will be.'

She shook her head, putting her arm around Helen once again.

Donna had tried to get hold of Chopper from the hospital. She was worried sick about him. Not only because of the gunshot wound that he had suffered, but also because of the fact that Chopper was notorious for his temper. She knew from what had happened earlier that day that they would be blaming Paddy for the shooting, whether he was responsible or not. She began crying as the phone just continued to ring.

'You OK, love?' asked the nurse who'd just come from Helen.

'I'm just so tired… I can't find my boyfriend,' she sniffled.

The nurse put her arm around her. 'I heard what happened tonight. I'm really very sorry, you know,' she said, with genuine sympathy in her voice.

'How's Helen?'

'We've given her something to calm her down a little,' the nurse smiled warmly. 'She was in a complete state of shock. I still can't believe they didn't bring you straight here first.'

'Will she be all right?'

'She'll be shook up for a while, but she'll pull through,' the nurse replied. 'We've phoned her parents and they're coming to collect her. Would you like us to phone yours?'

'No thank you… it'll be all right,' Donna replied, wondering what the hell her parents would think if they knew what had happened.

'OK, give me a shout if you need anything,' the nurse said, walking away.

'Thanks again,' Donna said, picking up the receiver once more. Only this time, she dialled Prey's number.

Prey answered at the first ring. 'Donna?'

'How's Chopper?' She almost snapped the words at him impatiently.

'Doctor Hassid is with him now. The bullet only really broke through the surface of his skin. It had lodged itself against a rib bone, just slightly fractured from what the doc can tell. Luckily for Chopper...' He paused. 'Sean?'

'Died almost instantly, Prey,' she told him, as she felt the tears begin to well again. The line was completely silent for almost a minute. Prey had known his friend had died immediately, but hearing the words out loud, confirming it, had left him feeling empty. As the minute dragged by, Prey's thoughts drifted to all the times they'd spent together, from being little kids roaming the estate to present day, and he let his tears flow freely. Eventually, he shook his head to try and clear it and asked, 'How are you two?'

'Helen's in a really bad way shock-wise. But I don't think it's fully hit me yet, Prey,' she told him.

'I know what you mean,' he answered very quietly, collecting his thoughts. 'It all seems like a bad dream, doesn't it? Y'know, Sean and me, well... we were...' He was not able to find the words.

'I know, Prey... I know,' Donna said.

'You need someone to come pick you up, Donna?'

'No. Helen's parents are on their way over,' she answered. 'Can I talk to Chopper?'

'Not at the moment, Donna,' Prey told her with no emotion. 'He hasn't said a word since it happened, y'know. He'll be all right though. I just think that it's hit him pretty hard.'

'Look after him, Prey,' she replied. 'At least until I get there, please.'

'Of course,' he replied. 'Kathy's in bed. She's still crying.

Look, I'm sorry, Donna, but, well… Donna, I need to as—'

'They brought two in from Manchester, Prey,' Donna said, cutting him off, knowing what he'd wanted to know.

'Who?'

'A Stevenson… he seemed like he was in charge. Oh, and someone called Walsh, I think.'

'Walshy, eh?' Prey knew him from years ago, and although he had heard of Stevenson he'd had no contact with him.

'You know him?' she enquired. 'They seem to know all of you lot.'

'What they bring them in for?' he asked, thinking aloud. 'It ain't their patch.'

'I've no idea, Prey,' she sighed deeply, thinking back to the two detectives. 'But like I said, they definitely knew Chopper. And they kept going on about Sean, so no doubt they know you too.'

'Probably,' he replied, not caring. 'Forget about it for now, eh Donna,' he added, shaking his head at the information he'd just received and wondering what it meant for the future.

'I'm scared, Prey,' she told him. 'I don't want to lose any more of you – in any kind of way.' As she said this, the tears began flowing uncontrollably.

'Don't you worry about a thing, Donna,' he told her reassuringly. 'You just get yourself home to Chopper.'

'I will,' she sobbed. 'Just make sure he's—'

'No worries,' Prey interjected. 'We'll both see you soon Donna.' He replaced the receiver.

What the hell were two Manchester detectives doing over in Widnes, he thought to himself. They must be looking into him and the rest of the lads; they had to be. Prey sat down in his chair as his mind raced in a thousand directions. Memories of his lost brother. Thoughts of what was to take place now. Police involvement in the entire matter. He could feel yet another tear escaping. He just let it roll down his face.

'Prey… he should be OK,' said Doctor Hassid as he now appeared in the doorway to the living room. 'I've treated the area around the wound and removed the remains of what was left of the bullet. You don't know just how lucky he was, Prey. The fracture was only minor. He'll be in a lot of pain for a while though. I don't know how it didn't cause further damage,' he added, tossing the discharged bullet to Prey.

'Thanks, doc,' Prey told him, staring at the bullet that had injured Chopper and taken the life of his friend, his partner, his true brother. ''Ere's your money.' He handed an envelope to him.

'Thank you, Prey,' the doctor smiled, not easy under the circumstances.

'Now just remember,' began Prey, 'no matter what y'hear or what y'know, it goes no further than these four walls.'

'Of course, Prey,' Hassid said, tutting as he did so, a little irritated. 'How long have we known each other?' He then smiled, shaking Prey's hand. Prey knew that Hassid had a point. After all, it hadn't been the first time he'd used him.

'Thanks,' he said.

'Oh, I'll be back again in a couple of days, just to check on Chopper.'

'Thanks again,' said Prey as he saw the doctor to the front door.

Sighing deeply as he shut the door, Prey then turned and made his way up the stairs to see how Chopper was doing. He stood in the doorway for some time, silently observing his friend sat there on the bed with his back against the wall.

'You all right, ar'kid?' Prey asked as he now entered the bedroom. I nodded my response slowly to him.

'Sean's dead, isn't he?' I asked, already knowing the answer as Prey nodded, then shook his head.

'Almost instantly, Chopper,' he sighed, sitting down on the bed next to me. 'How's the stomach?'

'Hurts like hell,' I replied. 'How are Donna and Helen?'

'Helen's in bad way,' he sighed, putting his hand on my shoulder and squeezing it slightly. 'But Donna's a good kid, mate, stronger than we give her credit for. She sends her love, mate. I told her you'd be all right.'

'We both know who did this, Prey,' I declared, glaring directly at him.

'I know we do. We just got to use ar' noodle 'ere, mate,' he told me, tapping his forehead, still shaking his head in disbelief.

'They had two Manc detectives over there tonight. Donna says they knew all about us.'

'Of course they know,' I replied, trying to sit up and instantly doubling over with the pain. 'But they can't prove shit on us,' I wheezed.

'I know that,' Prey replied with a sigh. 'All I'm saying is that if we take Paddy out straight away, well, then they'll be expecting it.'

'How the fuck will they know it was Paddy?'

'Look, Chopper,' Prey said, glaring at me, 'anything that takes place – and I mean anything, Chopper – then they'll try relating it to this. We've got to play this one right. Remember, kid: me and Sean went back a long, long way.' He stopped and looked at me with utter sadness on his face. 'I ain't going to let it drop – am I now, Chopper?'

'Y'know something, mate…' I said, standing up and trying my best to ignore the pain that shot through me like a thousand daggers. I trailed off and began pacing back and forth before suddenly stopping and glaring right at Prey as he simply nodded in response, knowing exactly what I was thinking.

'There is only one certainty from this day forward in life, Prey. And that is that Paddy is a dead man walking.'

ACKNOWLEDGEMENTS

T his novel was inspired by all the good times and all of the bad times spent in Manchester and its surrounding boroughs back in the 1980s and 90s. The author will always be grateful to the people of Manchester and Salford, with whom those times were spent.

No matter what's happened, the past is the past. What can I say? Everything grew beyond any of our beliefs. And when this happened, the dark side associated within the industry we were involved in, and everything related to it, somehow managed to eclipse all of the good times.

Though the events and characters, including Chopper, are fictitious and wholly of the author's imagination, this story could not have been written without the contribution of memories from times spent back then.

I wish to thank Ar'kid, Graham, Jamie and Ren, for all their help and support (especially through those dark, lost months of 2006 when I wasn't quite sure where the hell I was). I really lost the plot for a while and without you guys I wouldn't be here now.

I owe a debt of gratitude to Toby, Thiago, Junior and Rildor for all the tremendous help and support with the work you've done since I discovered *Ar' Back Yard* was to be published (and don't forget, we've still got a lot more work ahead of us, lads).

I wish to thank and give much appreciation to Audra, who introduced Maxim from The Prodigy to *Ar' Back Yard* and who very generously allowed me to use some of his music for the website.

I'd like to thank Sandy Diaz and the crew at TCI, through whom *Ar' Back Yard* has found a greater audience.

Last but by no means least I thank the staff at Athena Press for giving me the opportunity to finally, after many, many years, get this story into print.

GLOSSARY

Ar' Back Yard	Where we live
Ar'kid	Sister or brother or someone who's close enough that you consider them to be
Bailed	Taken on credit where you'll pay for the drugs after they have been sold
Bang	To have sex or to inject drugs
Bees	Money
Bird	A girl
Bombin'	Graffiti art
Breakin'	Break dancing
Brief	Lawyer/solicitor
Brown	Heroin
Bundle	A load
Charlie	Cocaine
Clock	Look at
Crew	Organised gang or group of people
Dodge	Area
Doing Bird	Caged like a bird, as in doing jail time
Double	Twice as much
Dough	Money
Es	Ecstasy
Evo	Evo Stick glue
Gaff	Where someone resides
Gear	Drugs or stolen goods
Heat	The police

Jacks	Jack Daniels
Joint	Hand-rolled marijuana or cannabis cigarette
Keys	Kilos
Nicked	Arrested
Nine Bar	9 ounces of weed/cannabis
Noodle	Using your brain
Nosh	Oral sex
Old Dear	Mother
On Your Jack	By yourself
Pear-shaped	Gone wrong
Pills	Ecstasy
Pinched	Arrested
Pulled	Pulled over and searched or also arrested
Pure	A lot
Score	Robbery or illegal job about to be carried out
Scran	Food
Skag	Heroin or cocaine
Skunk	Type of marijuana weed
Smack	Heroin
Sneakers	Trainers
Snout	Cigarette
Sound	Good
Spar	Sparring partner as in friend or associate
Speed	Amphetamine
Spliff	Hand-rolled marijuana or cannabis cigarette
Sweet	Nice
Tag	Name used to identify someone without exposing who you really are
Tax	To rob or take something with force
Top	Good
Town	Manchester's city centre

Trippin'	When someone is losing their mind for whatever reason
Trips	LSD
Weed	Marijuana or cannabis
Whizz	Amphetamine

Printed in the United Kingdom
by Lightning Source UK Ltd.
126203UK00001B/58-81/A